COVET THY NEIGHBOR

DENISE CARBO

Editing: N.N. Light Editing Services

❃ Created with Vellum

This book is dedicated to my mother. Thank you for passing down your love of reading.

CHAPTER 1

$\mathcal{A}$ crash echoes across the yard from my neighbor's house. I startle, spilling ice coffee on my hand and shorts. *Crap, that's going to stain.* I place my cup on the patio table and stand, shoving the chair back. Two steps across my deck, I stop, chew on my bottom lip, and shift my weight from side to side.

The last time I set foot on his property he grunted, snatched the plate of welcome to the neighborhood cookies out of my hands, and closed the door in my face. Not an experience I care to repeat.

What if he's hurt? If I do nothing, and he's injured, what kind of person does that make me?

Damn it!

Standing around debating the issue wastes precious time if he's bleeding out or something. On TV, the ambulance always makes it to the hospital at the last possible minute before death or permanent disability occurs, but that's just drama, right?

I jog down my deck steps and across my yard into his. The line of waist high holly bushes separating our properties snag at my clothes and scrape against my skin.

Should I knock on the front door or go to the back? The crash came from his backyard. He's probably fine and simply dropped something, or maybe thrown it in a fit of rage.

Rolling my eyes, I veer towards the back of the gray colonial. Time is of the essence.

I reach the blue stone patio and jerk to a stop. A ladder is on its side and my neighbor is flat on his back.

I gasp and sprint around the low wall edging the patio.

Crap! Is he dead? Did I waste precious minutes debating when I could have saved him?

His eyes are open and staring at the sky. Is he breathing?

I reach for my phone in my back pocket as I step onto the stones. His blond head swivels in my direction and his dark gaze locks on me. I stumble to a stop a few feet away.

"Are you okay?"

"Who the hell are you?"

As charming as ever, I see. I point towards my house. "Your neighbor. I heard a crash."

He springs to his feet in a single flow of movement.

Impressive ab strength to accomplish that feat. My gaze drifts over his tall, rangy build. Yeah, there are serious muscles flexing under those jeans and T-shirt. They all appear to be in fine working order. No damage done. He isn't in need of my assistance. I shove my phone back into my pocket.

"Are you in the habit of barging onto private property?"

He braces his fists on his hips and scowls.

For real? Next time I hear a crash over here, I'll turn on the music and pour a glass or two of wine.

I huff out a breath and scowl right back. "No, like I said, I heard a crash and wanted to make sure no one was hurt."

"As you can see, I'm not in need of a Florence Nightingale."

I glance away. Okay, after our first encounter I tried to give him the benefit of the doubt. Everyone has a bad day, but this guy is a jerk.

Through the open patio door, I spot a gun, some type of rope, and an assortment of knives and sharp objects strewn across a table.

I snap my gaze back to his and swallow hard. "Yup, I can see that." I back up several steps. "I won't bother you again."

Grabbing my phone out of my pocket in case he decides to commit violence against me, I pivot and stride across his lawn as fast as I can, short of breaking into a run. The urge to glance back over my shoulder to see if he is watching me crawls up my neck, but I stare at the solace of my little blue cape.

Once I reach my back deck, I dart inside and lock the door behind me. I grip the doorknob in my fist as I sag against the door.

Okay, not going to panic, I'm sure there are many reasons for him to have an assortment of weapons on his kitchen table.

Just because I can't think of a single reasonable, nonviolent one, doesn't mean I should jump to any conclusions.

Thank God the boys are back at school. I might feel the need to bundle them close, pack up our stuff, and take off for parts unknown.

Imagination in overdrive, Olivia! Dial it back a notch or two.

I wipe the dots of perspiration off my nose with the back of my hand. Not sure if it was from the run, the heat, or the fear, but my clothes are sticking to my skin. One more summer where central air conditioning isn't in the budget. Fans and window units will have to suffice. Besides, it's already September and the heat should give way to cooler temperatures soon.

I push off from the door and walk around the corner to the bathroom and splash cold water on my face and neck and then wipe it off with a towel. I check the time on my phone, ten o'clock. My shift at the bakery starts soon.

Upstairs, I peek out my bedroom window at the gray colonial while slipping into a sleeveless pink sundress. My disagreeable neighbor is nowhere in sight. I walk back into the bathroom and comb my hair back into a ponytail, put on a few swipes of mascara to darken my pale lashes and rub a tinted lip balm onto my lips.

From the bathroom window I can see more of his backyard, but there's no sign of him. He probably went inside. I check the windows of his house. Nothing stirs. What if he's looking out one of his windows at my house like I'm doing to him? I jump back and shuffle backwards out of the room into the hallway.

If I couldn't see into his windows, then he can't possibly see into my windows, can he? Not without a pair of binoculars.

Great, now the image of him staring into a pair of binoculars at my house is stuck in my head. At least it's better than him holding one or more of those weapons.

Or worse, chasing me with those weapons.

CHAPTER 2

"My neighbor is a serial killer."

"Umm...is that fact or supposition?" Lucinda's blonde eyebrows arch halfway up her forehead as she leans against the marble counter nibbling on a piece of muffin.

The aroma of freshly baked chocolate chip and oatmeal raisin cookies wafts across the kitchen after Franny opens the ovens. She puts the trays of cookies on the rolling rack in front of the ovens and props her hands on her hips. "You didn't go back there without me, did you? I told you I would go."

I shake my head and lift myself onto the counter next to the sink. "No—well, not intentionally. I was sitting on my back deck this morning enjoying my second cup of coffee while contemplating my life and what the hell I want to do with it when I heard a crash next door. So, of course, I went over to ensure no one was dying or anything."

"You went over there thinking you lived next door to a serial killer? Why didn't you call the police?" Lucinda drops the rest of her muffin into the garbage and brushes the crumbs off her fingers. "Have you called the police?" She glances at Franny. "She's not serious, is she?"

Franny holds up a finger to her sister. "Hold on, Luce. Olivia, what happened?"

"My neighbor was on his patio, lying on his back, just staring at the sky. There was a ladder on its side near him. To be honest, for a second, I thought he might be dead. Then he jumped up and yelled at me for trespassing. I was ready to give him hell right back, but when I noticed the large assortment of weapons littering his kitchen table, I left."

Franny frowns and glances at her sister. "This guy moved in next door to Olivia and was rude when she welcomed him to the neighborhood. She did a search for him on the internet and came up with nothing. She has her twin boys to worry about, so she's cautious. I told her I would go with her next time because there's plenty of reasons the guy might be unfriendly, but obviously her instincts were right in the first place. There's something fishy going on."

"I know I'm paranoid, but being a mother makes me worry about all sorts of things. So, when someone new moves into the neighborhood or comes into their lives, I do a quick search online and not only the predator lists, but a general hunt to make sure there are no red flags. Luke Hollister has no online presence whatsoever. No social media, nothing. That's weird, right? Now, coupled with his behavior and the weapon stash—I'm not crazy to worry, am I?"

Lucinda shakes her head. "Not at all, I can only imagine what you have to worry over as a parent. And, although there is nothing criminal about being rude or unfriendly, I admit the multitude of weapons is questionable." She raises her hand. "However, he could simply be a collector. Perhaps we shouldn't jump to conclusions just yet."

"Spoken like the lawyer you are." Franny smirks.

"A collector of weapons? I admit I didn't think of that. My mind went straight to murderous intent." I swing my feet and stare at the black and white squares of tile on the floor. All right, my paranoia for my kids' safety might be getting out of control.

"I'm simply throwing out other options. My firm in Connecticut had a private investigator on retainer. Would you like me to call him and ask for a referral for someone here in New Hampshire? Or we could ask our father to check with his former firm and see if they recommend anyone in the area."

"You think Granite Cove is big enough to have a private investigator?" Franny leans on the counter with folded arms. "I'd like to see Mother's face when you ask Dad for the name of a private investigator though."

"Ha ha."

"Thanks guys, but hiring an investigator isn't exactly in my budget." I cross my ankles and sigh. "I guess I'll just have to keep a close eye out and make sure my two devils don't go wandering out of our yard."

"Well, don't go back over there, no matter what you hear."

I nod at Franny. "I have no intention of setting foot on his property again. Maybe it's time I replaced the fence between our properties. There used to be a split rail fence, but it rotted in places so the former owner tore the whole thing out before listing it for sale. I could put in a tall solid fence with barbed wire at the top."

"That would certainly send a message." Franny grins.

The bell on the front door jingles signaling a customer arrived. "Hold that thought." I jump off the counter and walk to the front of the bakery and smile. "Welcome to The Sweet Spot, what can I get for you today?"

The older couple smile and look back down at the glass display cases filled with goodies. I don't recognize them as frequent customers. They're probably vacationers. Not all the summer people have left for the season.

They choose an assortment of pastries. I box them up and cash them out. "Have a wonderful day."

I wave them off and head back into the kitchen, glancing at the clock as I enter. The slow hour between the lunch rush and the pre-closing surge of customers allows us to catch our breaths. The eleven o'clock to five o'clock hours I work for Franny allows me to get the kids on the bus in the morning and be home to cook them dinner every day. I'm thankful for the income, but shouldn't I be striving for more?

I'm twenty-eight years old and the mother of twin ten-year-old boys. I should have a life plan in place—one more ambitious than staying sane while keeping a roof over our heads and my kids healthy.

Lucinda is still leaning against the counter watching Franny flit from one of the ovens along the wall and back to the rolling racks as she puts the trays of sweets on to cool.

Franny glances up. "Everything good?"

"Yup, just a couple buying a box of pastries."

"How about Luce and I come over and spy on your neighbor under the guise of a girl's night?"

"Ooh, I love that idea!" Lucinda claps her hands together. "I could use a girl's night."

Franny chuckles. "Mother driving you crazy?"

"Let's just say I'm so glad you're letting me move into the apartment upstairs once you move in with Mitch."

"You're moving in with Mitch?"

Franny smiles and nods. "I was going to tell you, but then got sidetracked by your neighbor story. I'm over at his house so much anyway, it just makes sense to move in now. Originally, I'd planned on waiting until after the wedding. You know, be traditional and all that." She shrugs. "But it just seems silly to wait."

"That's wonderful!" I walk around the counter and give her a hug. "How are the wedding plans going?"

Lucinda snorts. "Mother is in a tizzy. I'm glad it's taken some of the pressure off me. At least she's stopped her matchmaking efforts for now. Although she can't very well continue since Franny here snatched up Mitch."

"Ha! She accused me and Luce of setting up an elaborate con to trick her when Mitch and I announced our engagement! It took meeting his parents to finally convince her."

"It sounds like you and your mother are getting along better."

"We have a hesitant truce. Planning the wedding keeps her focused and when she gets out of hand, I threaten to elope."

I laugh. "The house must be coming along if you're ready to move in."

Franny's eyes fill with delight. "Oh yes, you have to see it! There's still plenty of construction going on, but Mitch had them focus on certain areas for his parents' visit and now they're concentrating on the kitchen. It'll be done next week! I can't wait. It's my dream kitchen. You should come over when they're done. I'll cook for you in my new kitchen."

"I'd love that. I can't wait to see it." The bell rings again and I turn to the front. "How about tomorrow night for girl's night?"

Lucinda nods, but Franny winces. "Can we make Saturday night instead? Mitch has a hike and picnic dinner planned tomorrow."

"You've agreed to another hike?"

"Yes, well, apparently I'll do just about anything for that man."

"Saturday works great, actually. Ryan has the boys that night. So we'll have the place to ourselves." Chuckling, I walk out front to wait on the customers. More enter while I'm helping the first set. Looks like the afternoon rush is starting early today.

A steady stream of customers keeps me busy the rest of the afternoon until closing.

After helping Franny clean up, we exit together out the back door. Boat motors idle at the dock behind the ski shop next door. A jet ski roars across the mouth of the cove. The wake left in its path sends waves lapping at the rocks edging the property.

"See you tomorrow." Franny heads up the stairs to her apartment.

I wave and walk down the alleyway and up the street to my car parked up the block. Fried food scents the warm air from Billings Creamery. My stomach growls in response.

Franny used to be still working hard in the bakery when I left, but now she often leaves when I do. I guess being in love makes all the difference. She's blossomed since falling in love with Mitch. She glows when he's around or even just when talking about him.

How does it feel to love someone so much? Even when Ryan and I were together, we weren't the bubbly, gushing, lovey dovey couple. I guess getting pregnant right away, dropping out of college, and getting married nixed any chance of us being carefree and in love.

CHAPTER 3

"*B*ackpacks all packed?"

"Yup!" Timmy and Tommy both call out as they race upstairs after breakfast.

I walk over to the bottom of the stairs. "Homework done?"

"No homework this weekend." Timmy peeks from the top of the stairs. He disappears back into their bedroom on the right.

Sighing, I collect discarded shoes and hats and put them on the hooks and shelves by the front door. I glance out the living room window for Ryan. He was due to pick the boys up ten minutes ago.

No sign of him, so I walk into the kitchen. They left their plates on the table. I debate a moment whether to call them back down to put the dishes in the dishwasher, as they're supposed to do, or let it slide this one time.

I'll enforce the rules next time. I didn't sleep well last night, and I'm not up to the hassle. I put the plates and glasses in the dishwasher and putter around the kitchen, wiping down the counters and cleaning out the fire hazard pile of crumbs in the toaster. Burnt bread assails my nose.

Twenty minutes later, there is still no sign of Ryan. I check my phone in case I missed a call or text telling me he would be late. Nope, nothing.

I dial his number only to have it go straight to voicemail. "Hi Ryan. I'm just wondering where you are since you were supposed to pick up the boys a half hour ago. Call me."

It's not the first time he's been late, and I'm sure it won't be the last. He would've called if he had to cancel altogether.

Scrolling through my emails, I stop on one for a local community college. I subscribed a couple years ago, thinking I might take classes. For what subject I have no idea, which is why I probably never followed through.

I should take a class or two. It might get me out of this rut I am sliding into. I pull up the course offerings and scan over them. Business courses are the predominate listings. I wrinkle my nose at the Accounting course. Math wasn't a hardship but sitting around crunching numbers doesn't excite me in the least. Economics isn't drumming up any interest either. Marketing or Management don't sound too bad.

Franny has me participating more in the baking. Would helping with management or marketing be an option down the road? It's not like I have ambitions to start my own business.

I love working at The Sweet Spot and would hate to leave, but I need to think of the future. Part-time income and child support are barely enough to get by. If my mom didn't help out with the childcare, I would be in serious trouble.

Most of the courses are online, which means I can do them on my schedule.

The front door opens and Ryan walks in.

I glance at the time. He's almost an hour late. And he didn't knock...again.

He spots me at the table. "They ready?"

"You're late. And could you please knock?" Next time, I will lock the door so he has no other option.

Ryan shrugs. "What's the big deal? You got plans or something?"

He doesn't wait for an answer but looks up the stairs. "They up there? Tim, Tom, let's go!"

"Yes, as a matter of fact, I do."

"A date?" He frowns and stares at me.

"Yes." He didn't need to know it was with Franny and Lucinda.

"With whom?"

"That's not any of your business, is it?"

"What's got you so uptight today? Is it that time of the month or something?"

I breathe deep and count to ten. The boys come racing down the stairs.

"Hi Dad!"

He ruffles the boys' hair as they shoulder on their backpacks.

"Come say goodbye, boys."

They both walk over and give me a hug on either side. "Bye, Mom."

I kiss them both on the head. "I love you. Be good for your father."

"We will. Love you."

"Love you."

They walk out the door while Ryan holds it open. He looks back. His gaze wanders over me. "Have fun on your date." There's a slight smirk on his face.

I glare at him until he chuckles and leaves.

I know what he's thinking. There's no way I'm going on a date dressed in a T-shirt sporting the logo for a restaurant chain and a pair of spandex shorts.

They're comfortable, damn it.

Why didn't I change?

Because I pulled them on this morning while getting the boys ready. I didn't think he'd be an inconsiderate hour late. I'll change before my shift at the bakery.

Besides, I shouldn't have to dress up for Ryan. At least, not anymore. There was a time when I made an effort to put on makeup and nice clothes, mostly when we had a date night planned.

What does he know? I could be going out on a date after work. After I get all spruced up.

"Ugh." I drop my head onto the table and close my eyes.

Whom am I kidding? I haven't been on a date since…well, let's just say awhile. It's not like I haven't dated at all since the divorce. I have, just nowhere near the amount Ryan has. And that's only the ones I know of.

I have dated. There was Ken. We went on a handful of uneventful dates before he stopped calling, and I never considered calling him because there was no spark. Then there was Paul—dodged a bullet on that one. We went on one date. He never stopped complaining or berating the server until finally she ran off in tears. I left after apologizing to her. My cousin told me he got arrested for assault outside of Finnegan's Pub a few months later. Michael was the last. Again, only one date. I thought we had a fun time. We laughed at the same jokes. But he never called. I considered calling him, but I chickened out which turned out to be a good thing because I ran into him and his ex a month later. Apparently, they had reconciled. Hopefully dating me didn't drive him to it.

That's it, the sum total of three years of single life. Three men.

I bang my head on the table. *I need to get out more.*

There's a knock on the front door. I raise my head. Did the boys forget something? They wouldn't knock. Ryan might to prove a point.

Rolling my eyes, I get up. Great, and now he'll make a comment pointing out how ridiculous it is for him to knock and make me come answer the door when he could have simply opened it and saved us both time.

I swing open the door.

It's not Ryan.

Luke Hollister stands on my doorstep.

I blink several times, hoping he'll disappear. Nope, still there.

"I think this is yours."

He holds out the plate I gave him cookies on—like three months ago.

"Umm…yeah, thanks." I take the plate.

"Listen, about the other day. It was a crappy day and then I fell off the stupid ladder, making it even worse. Then you showed up and I took my frustration out on you. I hope there are no hard feelings."

He holds out his hand. "I'm Luke, by the way, Luke Hollister."

Okay...no need to tell him I know his name because I looked it up when he moved in. "Olivia Banner." I shake his hand once and snatch back my hand, hiding it behind my back just in case he has any plans to grab hold of it again and drag me back to his house and chop me up into a million pieces.

"So, we're good?"

"Uh, yeah, sure." I'll be watching every move you make, buddy. Take one suspicious move towards my boys and I'll be the one chopping you up into a million pieces.

He gives me a half wave before turning and walking away. I shut and lock the door before tiptoeing over to the kitchen window. I stand to the side so I can peek out without him spotting me if he suddenly turns around.

He disappears inside his house. I wander over to the counter and drum my fingers on the top. Perhaps my overactive imagination needs a rest. I should focus on my future. Like those classes. I can swing the cost—barely. Besides, if it doesn't work out, it's not the end of the world. I can try something else the next semester. The deadline is this week.

I whip out my phone and submit the application before I can change my mind.

There, a positive action. I sag against the counter. I'm going back to school.

I tilt my head back and stare at the ceiling. It could be one of the best decisions I've made or the worst, only time will tell, so there's no point in dwelling on it.

My neighbor made the effort to extend an olive branch of sorts. He didn't exactly apologize, but it was something. We're neighbors, after all. I should probably give him the benefit of the doubt. The odds are against him actually being a serial killer. There must be a rational explanation.

Next time I spot him in his yard I'll casually walk over, in full view of witnesses just to be safe, and ask him why he has a stash of weapons. Of course, what's he going to say? I murder people in my spare time?

CHAPTER 4

"We've got wine and sweets, now all we need is the gossip. So dish Olivia, what's going on with your neighbor?" Lucinda pours herself and me a glass of white wine while Franny unscrews the cap of her iced tea.

"I'm so glad we're doing this. We need to make it a regular thing. Next week, it'll be at my and Mitch's house." Franny grins. "Gosh, I love saying that!"

"When do you officially move in?" I take a sip of my wine and sink back against the cushion.

"Monday, when the bakery is closed. I don't have much to move, really. I never got around to decorating the apartment. I can't wait to decorate the house, though."

"Not to worry, I'll be decorating the apartment." Lucinda winks at us.

"You must be looking forward to moving too."

"Most definitely."

"Luce, I appreciate you insisting I have time alone in the apartment. I still feel a tad guilty you stayed at our parents' house instead of moving in with me."

Lucinda waves a hand in front of her. "Don't be silly. You needed time. I wasn't going to be so selfish and hone in on your first apartment. Anyway, I had no desire to be a third wheel for you and Mitch." She sips her wine and smiles. "I am delighted you're moving out so soon, though."

Franny chuckles and blows her sister a kiss. "So, it's settled then? Next week at my house?"

I raise my glass. "I'm in."

"Me too." Lucinda leans forward and clinks her glass against mine, and Franny joins in with her bottle.

"It's official then." Franny clears her throat. "One more thing I'd like to mention before we focus on Olivia's mysterious neighbor." She glances back and forth between Lucinda and I. "Luce, I'd like you to be my maid of honor, or matron of honor, or whatever you call it."

Lucinda squeals and jumps up from her chair. "Oh, I was hoping and hoping you would ask!" She hugs Franny and rocks her back and forth. "I'm so happy for you, Sis, and I can't wait to see you walk down the aisle."

Franny turns to me. "Olivia, would you be one of my bridesmaids?"

My mouth drops open and a surge of delight rockets through me. "Absolutely! One hundred percent yes." I stand and give Franny a hug.

"Oh, I'm so happy!" Lucinda joins in the group hug. "We're going to have so much fun!"

Franny laughs. "I admit I'm starting to get into this whole wedding thing."

Lucinda raises her hand. "I solemnly swear to keep it fun and not drive you crazy."

"Don't worry, I promise not to become a bridezilla on you guys."

I sit back down in my chair. "No worries there. I can't see you ever turning into one of those."

"Mother, on the other hand, will take care of the zilla role. Should we call her Momzilla or MOBzilla?" Lucinda tilts her head to the side and purses her lips.

The yellow cushions on the chair frame Lucinda like a photograph. She looks like a model dressed in a white formfitting dress with cap sleeves. I glance down at my own white shorts and lavender T-shirt. A little more effort in my appearance might be in order.

I dress like a mom. Comfort first. Any sense of style is a distant—distant second.

Franny smirks. "I pick the first. It applies to so much more than just the wedding."

"Did she help you plan your wedding, Lucinda?"

Franny chokes on the iced tea in the middle of taking a drink.

I wince. "Did I say something wrong?" I bite my lip and look at Lucinda. She's going through a divorce and might not be ready to reminisce over her wedding. *Way to go, Olivia.* "I'm sorry."

Lucinda waves her hand. "Don't be silly. My mother planned my entire wedding pretty much single handedly. She hired a wedding planner, but she was only there to do my mother's bidding."

"Didn't you have a say?"

Lucinda sighs. "I have always had the nasty habit of letting my mother do what she wants rather than contradict her. It was easier. I'm trying to stand up to her more, like Franny does."

"That's a newfound courage for me. I usually just avoided her."

Franny tilts her bottle towards me. "What about you? What was your wedding to Ryan like?"

I glance up at the underside of the yellow and white striped umbrella over the table. "It was small and quick. We got married in my parents' backyard with just family there. We were so young in so many ways. I think we were both a bit in shock too from finding out not only was I pregnant, but that we were having twins. It's all a bit of a blur."

Lucinda nods. "I was so worried about everything going smoothly at mine, I never really enjoyed it."

"That's why I want mine small." Franny pulls her feet up onto the chair and hugs her knees to her chest. "I don't want to worry about talking to strangers or if anything will go wrong. I want to celebrate with those we love."

"As your maid of honor, I promise to keep mother in check and make sure it stays the wedding you want, not what she desires."

"On that note..." I lean forward and open the box Franny brought from the bakery. "I think it's time to cut into this gorgeous cake. A celebratory slice or two to mark this joyous occasion."

"Good idea." Franny hands out forks and napkins while I slice into the ivory buttercream with purple and lavender violets. The lemon from the cake wafts up and I inhale deeply.

"A small slice for me." Lucinda tops off her glass of wine. "I've been spending too much time at the bakery lately and each time I do, I nibble on something."

"Tell me about it. I have to exercise extreme will power not to bring something home with me every day." I hand Franny the first slice. "What's your secret Franny? I rarely see you sampling your own wares at the bakery."

"That's because I have to sample little bits here and there all day while I'm baking to make sure the recipe is correct. Believe me, I get plenty of sugar."

Lucinda takes a small bite of the cake after I cut her a slice. "Oh my God! This is so good. I'm going to gain a ton of weight living over the bakery."

Franny and I laugh.

I take a bite of the delicate cake and the tangy lemon and sweet frosting explode over my taste buds. I close my eyes and groan. "This really is spectacular."

"I'm glad I chose this one then. Not everyone likes lemon."

"Then they're crazy." I shovel another piece in my mouth. "I need to add a mile or two to my run in the morning because I know I'm going to end up with another slice of cake before the night is over."

"You run?" Lucinda scrapes the last smear of frosting off her plate and licks the fork clean.

I nod in between bites.

Franny frowns down at her plate. "I wish I had the coordination and discipline to run. Athletics aren't my area of expertise."

I sit back and cross my legs. "For me it's more of a stress relief. I blast my music in my ears and let the rhythm of the run and the music melt away my worries. I get a little cranky if I don't get my morning runs in." I rest my hands on my belly.

"Now that I live right over the bakery, I haven't been walking to and from work every day so I can't even count that exercise. Once I move into the house, it won't be feasible to walk to work either. I need to come up with something else."

"So do I. I used to go to the gym back in Connecticut, but I haven't even checked into one here. Is there one in Granite Cove?"

"Yes, it's in the plaza across the street from the bakery. On the backside. You can't get any more convenient than that, Luce. Once you move in, you can walk across the street."

"I won't have any excuses then, will I?"

Chuckling, I reach for my glass of wine.

"All right Olivia, it's your turn. What's with the neighbor?" Franny jerks her head toward the colonial.

"He stopped by this morning."

Both Franny's bottle and Lucinda's glass hit the table. They pin their gazes on me and when I don't immediately elaborate, they chorus, "And?"

I grin. "What?"

Lucinda scoots her chair in and rests her arms on the table while Franny drums her fingers on the table.

"Nothing really. He returned my plate from when he moved in and I brought him cookies and introduced himself. Said he didn't want to get off on the wrong foot."

"Did you ask him about the weapons stash?"

I glance at Franny and shake my head. "I was so surprised to find him standing on my doorstep, all I wanted to do was get rid of him."

"Good. I don't think blurting out that you saw the weapons is the best idea. At least not alone. Not until you know more details and history." Lucinda sucks in a breath and sits up straight. "I know. I can help you. We'll be our own private investigators."

"Oh boy!" Franny holds a hand over her eyes.

"What?" Lucinda frowns.

Franny peeks through her fingers. "This has disaster written all over it."

CHAPTER 5

"Mom, watch this!"

Tommy pumps his legs on the swing to go higher and higher. The playscape groans and shakes. Timmy sits atop the yellow slide watching his brother.

"Careful. Not so high, honey."

He soars up high and then flings himself backwards. The bottom drops out of my stomach and I jump to my feet.

He completes a backward somersault and lands on his feet.

I grip the deck railing and sink back onto the steps. My legs wobble. It's as if they've become two strands of cooked spaghetti and are no longer capable of supporting my weight.

Tommy swings a fist in front of him. "Yes—nailed it!"

Timmy claps.

Once my organs settle back into place and I find my voice, I say a silent prayer of thankfulness he is okay.

How to warn him never to do that kind of stunt again and not shatter his enthusiasm for his accomplishment at the same time?

He comes running over to stand in front of me. "Did you see?"

I clasp his arms and pull him in for a squeeze. He tolerates it for a few seconds before he squirms for release.

"Tommy, I know you're proud of your accomplishment and that was quite a feat, but it could've gone very badly. You could've gotten hurt—like broken bones and hospital hurt, or even worse. Please don't ever do that again. If you want to do somersaults, I'll sign you up for gymnastics or something where you'll be supervised and there will be mats. Lots of mats."

"Aw Mom, that's no fun."

He turns and runs back to the playscape.

"I mean it." I'm sure my order will fall on deaf ears. That kid will be the death of me. It's a miracle he hasn't broken any bones yet.

Tommy races up the slide and climbs over his brother. Timmy pushes off and slides to the bottom.

Sighing, I hang my hands down between my knees. What am I going to do? Ban him from the playscape? Follow him to school and make sure he doesn't do it on the playground?

A rabbit hops along the edge of the yard and disappears between the holly bushes. Aw, so cute.

I glance up at the house. Luke Hollister is standing in the window.

What is he looking at? I glance over to my sons on the playscape. Is he watching them? It sure looks like he is.

Hell, that's not creepy at all.

"Boys, time to go in!"

"Aw Mom!"

"Come on, it's almost dinnertime anyway and if you hurry up without complaining, we can play Go Fish after dinner."

"War. I want to play War." Tommy comes running with Timmy close behind him.

I wait until they both disappear inside before glancing over to the colonial. He's gone from the window.

Is my mom paranoia getting the best of me?

It doesn't matter. Where my kids are concerned, I would rather be safe than sorry. I need to find out more about my strange neighbor.

~

I SHUFFLE Timmy and Tommy off to school, go for my run, shower, and dress, and then I settle down to dive into my coursework.

I have coursework. A tiny thrill shoots through me. This could be the start of something new and exciting.

Mondays and Tuesdays The Sweet Spot is closed so that should allow me to wade through my studies.

An hour and a half later, I'm ready for a break. I fill a glass of water and wander over to the sink and stare out the window. A bird pecks at the birdfeeder hanging off the corner of the deck. I glance to the other corner where I hung a hummingbird feeder. It needs to be filled.

I take a drink of water. A man strolls across my backyard. I jerk and the water splashes out of the glass. I step back to avoid the water, set down the glass, and wipe the drops from my hand on the back of my shorts.

What the hell?

I recognize the tall blond form. My damn neighbor.

He goes straight to the playscape. What is he doing?

Should I call the police? He is trespassing.

Would they think I'm nuts? Probably.

He has a tool and is doing something to the top of the bar. I lean forward. Is he damaging the playscape? Rigging it to hurt my boys?

I spin away from the counter and run around the corner into the living room and out the back door.

When the door slams behind me, his head swivels in my direction and he frowns.

"What the hell are you doing?"

He raises an eyebrow and turns back to the playscape. "Thought you were at work."

So, he waited until he thought no one was around to trespass and tamper with my kids' equipment? "It's my day off. Answer me. What are you doing?"

I pat my back pocket but it's empty. I left my phone inside like an idiot. I could still scream like a banshee and kick like a mule if he tries anything.

"I noticed yesterday that bolts are loose. That's why it moves so much when they're using it. I'm tightening them up." He swings down from the top of the slide where he'd been squatting and reaches up to grab the top bar and shakes it. "See."

It barely moves.

Well hell, he was fixing the playscape for my sons.

"I thought it moved because they were getting big."

"The bolts need to be periodically tightened."

"Could they come all the way undone?" Had my boys been playing on a death trap?

He walks to the opposite side and tightens the bolts there too. "Not likely, but it's more secure to keep them tightened."

I stuff my fingers in the back pockets of my shorts. "Umm... thanks. I appreciate it. I had no idea."

"Don't mention it. Like I said, I saw it was loose and I have the tool to fix it." He holds up a silver thing.

A wrench? I admit tools aren't my area of expertise. Thankfully, my dad is always happy to help when anything needs fixing.

So I guess he wasn't being creepy yesterday in the window.

Unless this is a diversion.

He finishes tightening the bolts on the other side and gives the structure one last shake. It barely moves at all. An improvement for my little daredevils' safety.

"Listen, this was really nice of you. I..."

"Like I said, don't mention it. It's no big deal. See you."

He strolls back over to his own yard while my mouth remains slightly ajar. I was about to offer to pay him, but I guess he doesn't want anything. Was my strange, rude, antisocial neighbor suddenly turning well—neighborly?

I narrow my eyes. There is a slight hitch to his gait. Not a noticeable limp, but something. Had he hurt himself the other day falling from the ladder?

I walk over to the playscape and give it a good shake. It doesn't budge an inch. I sit on the swing and push off while staring up at the top. Nope, no shaking or groaning. I weigh significantly more than my kids so it should be secure. Planting my feet, the swing comes to a rest. I drop my hands into my lap and stare at the ground. Had I misjudged my neighbor?

If he turns out to be a standup guy and had only been having a dreadful day or in pain those couple of times, I'm going to feel terrible. Thankfully, I only shared my suspicions with Franny and Lucinda. It's not like I had actually called the police and reported him.

I trace circles in the sand with my toes. I ran outside too quickly to think to put on a pair of shoes.

More schoolwork waits inside. Along with the never-ending piles of laundry two active boys manage to produce. They have soccer practice after school today and I'm pretty sure all their soccer socks are still balled up on their floor.

Standing, I look back at the playscape and then over to Luke's. He gained some definite points, but I still need an explanation for those weapons before I cross potential serial killer off the list of possible occupations. He could have gotten that slight limp from a victim.

Hmm...how about an assassin? That is slightly better, right? They tend only to be contracted to kill bad guys by other bad guys. At least in the movies they are. In reality they're probably hired to kill anyone for any petty reason as long as they're paid enough.

I stop at the backdoor and glance over again. He isn't exactly flaunting a rich lifestyle so if he is an assassin, he's being inconspicuous or maybe he is just really bad at it and hasn't made any real money.

Chuckling to myself, I go inside and upstairs to swipe the boys' clothes off the floor around their hamper. Very few items made it inside. I spot a sock under the bed and end up getting down on all fours to inspect underneath both beds and come up with a half dozen other garments that need washing.

After going downstairs to the basement to toss the load of clothes in the washer, I return to the kitchen to finish studying.

Ten minutes later I am googling assassins and uncaptured serial killers.

CHAPTER 6

*T*his is either a spectacularly brave idea or one of the stupidest things I've ever done. Luke is mowing his lawn— again. It's the fourth time this week that I know of. No one does that.

I've been having nightmares all week and I blame him. I need to know once and for all what his deal is.

I march across my yard and sidle between the holly bushes, so they don't scratch my bare legs. I hold the material of my black and white polka dot skirt and white blouse against my body, so it doesn't catch and tear on the branches. My outfit is my attempt to dress slightly less like a mom and more like a single woman. I found the skirt stuffed at the back of my closet during my recent purge of clothes. I have no idea where or when I acquired it, but it's cute.

Ryan should be here with the kids any minute, so I'll have backup and witnesses if Luke tries anything funny. Thankfully, Ryan is rarely late dropping them off. It's only the picking up time he plays fast and loose with.

I slow my pace and wait until Luke comes back around to this side, so we'll be in full view of my house and the road.

He's staring intently at the ground in front of the mower and shows no sign of me standing here in his path. Does he intend to mow me down?

I wave my arms and his head pops up and he frowns. He stops and shuts the mower off. "What?"

Okay, rude Luke is back.

"I don't think it's possible to cut your grass any shorter. You're going to end up with dirt instead of a lawn."

He raises one dirty blond eyebrow and says nothing.

Yup, I'm being a nosy neighbor and he clearly wants me gone, but for the sake of my sanity and the boys' safety, I need to get answers from him.

"Look Luke, I'm not typically the nosy sort—really I'm not, but when it comes to my kids' safety, I've got no boundaries."

"What does mowing my lawn have to do with your kids' safety?"

"It doesn't. You want to mow day and night, go ahead. I can pop on headphones if it bothers me. Although, grass doesn't need to be mowed more than once a week. Heck, I rarely mow my lawn more than once every couple of weeks."

He glances past me to my yard. I know what he sees. My grass is past my ankles and in danger of being too much for my old mower.

"Not the point."

"Could you get to the point then?"

Right. Here goes nothing. I take a deep breath and blurt out, "Why don't you have any online presence and what's with the stash of weapons in your house?"

His brows lower over his dark eyes and he crosses his arms across his chest.

Yeah, I know I'd be pissed too if someone confessed they had done an online search for me and knew what was inside my house and demanded an explanation.

"I know I probably sound like an incredibly nosy b-i-t-c-h right now, but I'm a single mother and I have to be careful. I saw the weapons all over your kitchen table that day you fell off the ladder."

Let him think I did the online search after I spotted the weapons and not when he moved in. I might sound slightly less crazy then. Maybe.

"Did you really just spell bitch?"

"I'm trying to curb my cursing and set an example for my kids, okay?"

"So it's okay if your kids spell the curse word, but not say it?"

"Of course not!" I raise my hands palm up and drop them. "I'm weaning myself off cursing. I don't swear in front of the kids. Well, very rarely have I ever slipped."

Luke sighs and drops his arms. "Come on." He turns and takes several strides toward the back of his house.

He expects me to follow him? Where there are no potential witnesses and after I just confessed to checking into him?

At the corner of his patio, he stops and looks over his shoulder at me still standing where he left me chewing a hole in my bottom lip.

"If you want an explanation, you'll have to look in my house. You can stand on the patio if that makes you feel better." He smirks and continues around the house.

He might as well have added an "I dare you" because that expression said it for him.

If I go, I might get some answers, or I might be his latest victim. If I refuse, then more stress and worry will pile on my full plate.

A car engine rumbles down the road. Ryan's car appears and slows as he approaches my driveway. I wave furtively until the boys spot me from the back and return my wave. There, someone knows where I am.

I march to the back of the house where Luke stands by his slider with his arms crossed.

"Made up your mind?"

"My ex-husband just arrived with my kids, so I need to make this quick." He now knows people know where I am.

"Right." He holds out a hand to the inside of his house through the open slider.

I glance back and forth between him and the inside of the house. Does he actually expect me to go in there?

He rolls his eyes and pushes the slider completely open and then backs away several feet to the other side of the patio.

"Check out the wall."

"Um…okay."

I walk over and peer inside. To the right is a kitchen and to the left is a living area with a large glass display case full of weapons hanging on the wall over the couch. Is he telling me he's a collector?

I do a quick scan of the rest of the house. There's a room off the kitchen, probably a dining room. A door to the basement I'm guessing. A hallway to the front of the house. And another room to the left, but I can't see inside it.

Stepping back, I blink, waiting for my eyes to adjust to the sunlight. Luke's still standing at the edge of the patio with his arms crossed over his chest.

"Are you a collector?"

"Of sorts."

What does that mean? He's not exactly providing the answers I hoped for.

"Can't you just provide an explanation so I stop worrying you're some kind of serial killer or something?"

He snorts and plops down on the low wall edging the patio. "I have no clue why I have no online presence. Probably because I don't do social media. Those are the only weapons I own except for a set of steak knives. Most of them are antiques and useless as a weapon. Satisfied?"

They did appear old, now that I got a closer look at them.

"Where are you from? Why did you move here?"

Luke frowns and looks away. "Pennsylvania and because I have family here. Is this inquisition done?"

I wince. He has family in town? I never see anyone visit him.

He glances back and sighs. "My sister-in-law and nephew live in town with her parents. I get you're a single mother, but I don't owe you a life history."

"No, of course you don't. Thank you for answering my questions. I'm sorry for prying."

He rubs his thigh as he stares out over his backyard.

Was his leg bothering him?

"If the mowing is bothering you, I can find something else."

"Something else?"

"The blades aren't on. It helps me think and keeps my mind off other things."

"Your leg?"

His gaze swings back to mine and narrows.

Oops. Did I go too far?

"I noticed you had a slight limp the other day when you fixed the playscape."

Luke frowns and drops his hand from his leg. "Yeah, it helps."

"Then mow away. In fact, feel free to mow mine."

Ugh, I did not just say that.

"Mom!"

I look over my shoulder. Ryan and the boys are standing there. Ryan has a hand on each of the boys' shoulders and he's staring at Luke.

"Sorry, I was talking to our new neighbor. Boys say hello and thank you to Mr. Hollister. He fixed your playscape for you. It no longer shakes." I walk over to the boys and they step forward to give me a hug and then turn to Luke.

"Thanks."

Luke stands. "You're welcome."

Ryan steps forward to stand next to us and face Luke. "I'm Ryan Banner, their father."

Luke nods in his direction.

"Okay, let's get home and get you two fed." I glance back at Luke. "Thank you."

I herd the boys back towards our property. Ryan falls in beside me.

"Why is your neighbor fixing the boys' playscape?"

"He saw it was loose and took care of it."

"Did you ask him to?"

"No, but I'm thankful he did."

The kids race off into our yard.

"How was the visit this weekend?"

Ryan strolls next to me with his hands in his pockets. "Fine. The boys spent the morning with my parents. Dad took them fishing."

"They must have loved that."

"Yeah, do you think it's a good idea to have a guy you don't know fixing things? Around the boys?"

We reach his car parked in the driveway. I stop and fold my arms across my waist. "First, he's never met the boys until just now. I didn't bring them over, you did. Second, I didn't ask him to fix anything. He saw it needed it and did it. No big deal, as he said."

"Still, what do you know about this guy?"

My back stiffens. How dare he criticize me? I plant my fists on my hips. "Not much, but it hardly matters, does it? He's our neighbor. People aren't required to fill out a questionnaire when they move into the neighborhood. Do you know all the tenants in your condo complex?"

Ryan holds up his hands. "Calm down, I'm only asking out of concern for you and the boys."

Grinding my back teeth together, I count to ten in my head. He knows telling me to calm down has the opposite effect. He once described it as waving a red cape in the face of a bull. Yet, of course, he still does it.

One long slow breath after another. He can't rile me unless I let him.

I can hardly blame him for asking and being concerned, can I? I had a stack of reservations about Luke. Most of which melted away today.

He calls out to the kids, "See you later, boys."

They wave as Ryan climbs into his car and lowers the window. "Be careful."

I force a smile. "You too."

"You know what I mean." He glances over to Luke's house.

"I'm always careful." Well, most of the time.

He backs out of my driveway and I wave as he drives away.

I walk to the deck. "Boys, I'm making dinner. You have a half hour of play time and then you need to come in and wash up." Their back-packs are sitting on the deck. "And bring in your backpacks when you come in."

It's a mac and cheese and chicken nuggets kind of night. I'll deal with the mom guilt of serving them processed food rather than a home cooked nutritious meal later. I've got a whopper of a headache brewing and I'm not up to the vociferous complaints I'll get if I cook a meal with heaven forbid—vegetables. They're going through a stage where they hate pretty much any meal that can be remotely described as healthy.

If I bribe them with their favorite dinner, they might give me a break tonight and let me watch a comedy in peace. I could use a little laughter.

At least I have the lunch date with Franny and Lucinda to look forward to tomorrow. Explaining the latest run-in with my neighbor —not so much.

CHAPTER 7

*T*here are massive black gates blocking the driveway. Franny mentioned nothing about gates. Tall stone walls anchor the gates and run along the property approximately twenty feet in from the road. I spot a small box on top of a pole on the side before the gates and ease my foot of the brake to let my car roll forward.

I brake next to the device. I assume it's an intercom system. I've never been to a house with a gate and intercom before. It suddenly dawns on me Mitch is probably loaded. He's a movie director and former actor, after all. I probably should have realized this a while ago.

I push the button and wait.

"Hey Olivia, come on up." Mitch's voice echoes from the box and the gates swing open.

Was there a camera in there too? How did he know it was me? He hadn't seen me sitting there gawking, had he? I ease my car through the gates and up the driveway. Tall trees line the driveway before opening to a wide yard and an immense house.

Wow! The driveway circles around in front of the house with a large fountain in the center of the circle. Should I park in front or follow the driveway over to what is probably a garage?

The front door opens and Mitch steps out with a smile. He waves his hand towards him, so I assume he means to leave my car here. I park and turn off the engine and take a few breaths.

I'm suddenly intimidated. He's always been friendly and down to earth. I never really thought of him as a celebrity or rich, until now.

Grabbing my purse and the dip and chips I brought, I climb out of the car. He's marrying one of my best friends and he hasn't changed so neither should my perception. "Hi Mitch."

"Hi. Need help?" He jogs down the steps and takes the chips and dip from me. "Mmm, this looks good. I might need to stick around your girls' lunch for a few minutes."

His wide smile and blue eyes have made many women's hearts leap. I never told Franny, but I had one of his posters on my wall briefly when I was a teenager.

Mitch leads me into the house and I nearly trip over my own two feet gawking at the entryway. It's huge and spectacular. "Your house is amazing."

"Thanks, I'd give you a tour but I know Franny wants to do that herself. She and Lucinda are on the back patio."

I follow him down a long hallway into an L-shaped room with a gigantic fireplace. He leads me through a set of French doors to a blue stone patio. Franny and Lucinda are sitting at a long table with a hunter green umbrella. Franny is talking on her cellphone but lifts her hand, waves and smiles. Lucinda stands and comes over to give me a hug and a kiss on the cheek.

Mitch sets the platter I brought down on the table.

Franny ends her call. "Hey stranger."

"Hi. Franny, this place is amazing."

"I know, right? I can't wait to show you around. Luce has already seen it." She stands up and looks at her sister. "Do you want to come along or stay here?"

"You two go ahead." She sits back down at the table. "I'll keep Mitch company."

Mitch smiles. "And I'll keep the dip company."

Franny laughs and shakes her head. "I swear part of the reason he loves me is I can cook."

He walks over and slips an arm around her waist. "That's only a tiny, infinitesimal slice of the reason." He dips her back and kisses her.

I smile and then realize the kiss is not ending. Franny loops her arms around his neck while he deepens the kiss. I look away and meet Lucinda's gaze. She shakes her head and we both stare out at the lake.

The property stretches along the shore with its own private cove. The rumble and whine of engines from the boats farther out on the lake zoom by. A white sail glides into view. I tilt my face back and let the sun warm my skin.

What would it be like to see this view out your window every day? Mitch lives on the outskirts of Granite Cove. His personal cove is probably only a few minutes from the village by water. When I tell people I live in Granite Cove, New Hampshire, they assume I live on the lake. My house is too far away to see the lake, but I take the boys to the public beach in town during the summer to swim.

Franny and Mitch end their kiss.

Lucinda smiles. "I don't know whether to clap or fan myself."

A pink blush spreads over Franny's cheeks and Mitch chuckles. He walks over to the table and points to my platter. "May I?"

"Of course."

"Is that the blue cheese and port dip you were telling me about?"

I nod at Franny while they all crowd around the platter and sample some.

"Oh my God this is good," Lucinda mumbles around the chip in her mouth.

Franny just nods and takes another bite. Mitch sits down and pulls the platter closer to him.

I laugh and take a seat.

Lucinda sits next to me. "Please don't tell me how many calories are in that."

"I actually have no idea."

"Good. I can pretend it's not much."

"Okay, before I eat anymore of this delicious dip, let's go on that tour. Then we can have lunch."

Franny shows me through ornate bathrooms, so many bedrooms I lose count, and ends the tour in the kitchen. "My favorite room in the house." She walks around the giant island wider than my entire kitchen with a wide smile on her face. She leans over and lays her cheek against the white marble. "Is it wrong I want to climb up here and lie down?"

I laugh. "Not at all, I'd probably do the same if it was mine. Your house is mind boggling."

"Come on, we can lie down together." Franny hitches her butt up on the counter, swings her legs up, and lies down on the island face up. She glances over. "Come on." She pats the marble next to her.

Chuckling, I place my palms flat and hoist my body up on the island. Franny has a couple—okay a few—inches of height on me. I lie down next to her and stare up at the bright white coffered ceiling.

"There are days I think I'm living in a fairy tale."

I turn my head to glance at her. "Enjoy it. You deserve it, Franny. The love between you and Mitch is so strong sometimes I think it's a tangible thing you can reach out and touch."

She smiles. "I like that. It's how I feel. I'm so full of love."

"I'm thrilled for you." I take her hand and give it a squeeze.

She squeezes mine back and then sits up. "Okay, it's time for lunch." She swings her legs over the side and slides off the island. "I made finger sandwiches, kind of as a salute to the era of the house. They're also an easy make ahead food to serve."

I sit up and hop off the island while she opens the wide stainless-steel double door fridge and takes out a platter covered with tiny sandwiches. She hands it to me and grabs a pitcher of what looks like iced tea.

"I have dessert for later, of course." She picks up a basket with cups and napkins. "I think that's it."

When we exit out onto the patio from a door in the kitchen, Lucinda and Mitch are chatting at the table.

"Oh good, more food." Mitch stands and walks over to take the pitcher and basket from Franny.

I set the platter down and see the dip has disappeared. Franny leans over my platter and then raises her eyebrows at Mitch.

"Would you believe me if I said Lucinda did it?"

"Hey!" Lucinda scowls.

"Not a chance." Franny hands out the glasses and pours the iced tea while Mitch sets a napkin down for everyone.

I take the cover off the platter and sit.

"I'll just take a few of these with me and get out of the way of your lunch." Mitch puts four of the sandwiches stacked on his napkin, kisses Franny, and waves to us. "See you ladies."

After eating two of the little sandwiches myself, I tilt my head back against the cushion and enjoy the warmth of the sun bathing my face. On the lake there always seems to be a breeze, so it doesn't get too hot. It's the same at the bakery.

"We need a neighbor update."

I lower my head and peer at Franny. She's staring at me while taking a bite of a sandwich. Lucinda is sipping her tea.

"Must I?"

Franny rears her head back. "Most definitely, after that comment. That means there's more to tell."

Lucinda scoots her chair closer to mine. "I've been a little distracted moving into the apartment this week, but I still plan to help you investigate him."

"I don't think that will be necessary."

She frowns. "Why not? I was looking forward to it. Who knows, I might find a new career in private investigation."

"Mother would love that." Franny chuckles and grabs another sandwich.

I tell them my latest Luke encounter ending with, "I felt about this tall by the time I left." I hold up my index and thumb about an inch apart. "I let my imagination and paranoia take over any rationality I have."

"Nonsense. You were justifiably concerned." Lucinda leans back in her chair and crosses her legs. "Besides, you still don't know all that much about him. Did he tell you this sister-in-law's name or her parents'?"

"No, but I didn't ask either."

"I'm for giving him the benefit of the doubt. He's fixed your sons' playscape and given you reasonable explanations." Franny shrugs and takes a drink.

Lucinda raises her finger. "Let's not forget most serial killers turn out to be the unassuming, fade into the background type that no one suspects."

"Luke will never fit that description."

Both their gazes dart to mine. "I just mean he's a good-looking guy. He's not about to be a man people forget seeing."

"How good looking?"

I shrug at Lucinda. "Extremely good looking. Tall, well built, dark blonde hair with a slight curl to it, deep brown eyes—almost black, tan and very fit."

Franny rests her elbows on the table and laces her fingers together to rest her chin on them. "Interesting."

"What's interesting?" I gaze between her and Lucinda. They're both smiling at me.

"What?"

"You're attracted to him."

"Don't be silly. Are you forgetting I thought he was a serial killer?" I squirm in my chair to find a comfortable spot.

Lucinda points her finger at me. "Has it occurred to you that you were dreaming up scenarios to make him unavailable because subconsciously you know you're attracted to him?"

I close my eyes. "You're both crazy."

"Highly possible, but why not? You're single. He's single. You're both attractive adults. I don't see a problem."

I open my eyes and glare at Franny. "Can we please change the subject?"

She stares at me for a few seconds. "Okay, there is something else I want to talk to you two about. You know how I started going to that book club Sally belongs to?"

"Of course, I've heard you and Sally both mention it at work."

"Well you remember you told me you would be interested in going?"

"Sure."

"Good, because it's my turn to host this month and I'm having it here and want both of you to come. I even bought the book I chose for both of you to read. I'll give them to you before you leave." She looks at Lucinda. "Are you in too?"

"Yes, it sounds like fun."

"I picked a historical fantasy romance because who doesn't like to hear about a happily ever after?"

"I could use some of that in my own life." I pick up my iced tea and take a drink. I could use a rather large dose.

"Me too please." Lucinda looks at Franny. "You're already getting yours."

Franny grins. "I know and I want to spread the love. I want you both to get yours too."

We chat for another hour before we say our goodbyes. Franny hands each of us a book before we leave. There's a handsome blond man on the cover brandishing a sword.

Maybe I'll start it tonight.

The drive home is uneventful and blessedly short. I still have work to do around the house, including mowing my lawn before it gets too tall and breaks my lawnmower. I don't need the added expense.

I pull into the driveway and stare at my yard.

My lawn is mowed.

Putting the car in park and shutting off the engine, I rest my arms over the steering wheel and stare at the freshly clipped grass. I can smell the sweet scent through the glass.

He mowed my lawn.

I was joking when I mentioned it before. I didn't think he'd actually do it. Now I need to do something to thank him. He fixed the playscape and mowed the lawn.

Sighing, I get out of the car. Will baked goods suffice? He hadn't said he liked the cookies. It's all I have to offer at the moment. One more thing to add to my to do list.

I peruse the cover of the book in my hands. Could my neighbor be a white knight instead of the monster I painted him to be?

CHAPTER 8

I trudge down my front steps and over to Luke's front door. I made him a pie. It's the right thing to do and guilt is a powerful motivator.

The cement steps in front of his house are cracked and crumbling so I hold the pie high while watching where I place my feet. Standing in front of the door, I nibble on my bottom lip. Which Luke will I encounter this time—the grumpy one or the helpful neighbor one?

"Hey."

I turn my head and spot Luke standing in an open garage door on the left side of his house.

"Umm…hi." I walk back down the steps and over to the garage while he stands wiping his hands on a rag.

"I made you a pie as a thank you for fixing the playscape and mowing my lawn. That was you, right?" Who else could it have been?

"You didn't have to do that."

"You don't like pie."

"Who doesn't like pie?"

"There's always that one person and the way my luck has been going lately, I figured it would probably be you."

The side of his mouth hitches up in the semblance of a smile. "I like pie just fine."

"Good." I hold it out to him. "It's apple." Apple is usually a safe choice. Most people like apple.

Luke tosses the rag on the ground next to a car and takes the pie from me. "Thanks."

The car is cherry red with wide white stripes on the trunk and hood. It's an older car, older than me. My cousin would call it a muscle car and probably be asking a ton of questions and even drooling a bit.

I stuff my hands in my back pockets and give him a quick smile. "You're welcome and thanks again for your help." I back up a step and turn to go home.

"My sister-in-law got quite the laugh when I told her you thought I might be a serial killer. She laughed so hard tears came streaming down her face."

I wince. "Sorry about that. My overactive worry brain goes a little haywire at times."

He shrugs. "It made Barb laugh. She wants to meet you, by the way. It got a little sketchy when Joey, my nephew, overheard though. Ever try explaining to a two-year-old what a serial killer is?"

"Uh no, thankfully. Why does she want to meet me? To see what your crazy neighbor looks like so she knows to avoid me if she spots me in town?"

The corner of his mouth hitches up again and this time spreads almost to the other side in a genuine smile. "No, she liked your hutz-pah, as she called it. I think she'd like to connect with other moms, too. She doesn't know too many other people in town."

"In that case, I'd love to meet her. Tell her to stop by any time." So she must be a recent transplant too. Did he follow her here? They must be close. He didn't mention how they were connected. Married to his brother perhaps? Or had he been married and Barbara is the sister of a former wife?

"I'll do that."

"You want my phone number?"

He just stands holding the pie, staring.

"For your sister-in-law." Great, now he probably thinks I am coming on to him or something.

"Yeah, hold on a sec." Luke turns and walks into the garage and puts the pie down on a workbench against the wall. He pulls his phone out of his front pocket. "Hit me."

I rattle off my number and he enters it into his phone. I half expect him to reciprocate and give me his or his sister-in-law's but he slips his phone back into his pocket.

Okay then. I lift my hand in a wave. "See you."

"Off to work?"

"Yeah, I work eleven to five every day the bakery is open." Why am I over sharing? He didn't ask for my hours or where I work. Will it prompt him to tell me what he does for work?

He gives me a brief nod and turns back to the garage.

Okay, I've been dismissed.

I go back to my house, lock up, and drive to work. The Sweet Spot is slammed with customers so I jump right in.

Two hours later, Franny and I finally get a lull.

"Sheesh, was it like that all morning?"

"Pretty much, Sally and I had our hands full. I've barely been in the kitchen all day."

"Is there some event in town going on that I'm not aware of? Mitch sightings going viral or something?"

Franny chuckles. "I don't think so, but a lot of the summer people are still around because the weather hasn't turned yet."

"Good for business."

"Speaking of which, there's something I've been meaning to talk to you about."

"Oh?" Please be good news. I could sure use some.

"You had mentioned learning more about the baking side and I could use more help in the mornings. Would you be able to and interested in coming in earlier?"

More hours? I can definitely use the money. "How early would you need me? I still have to get the boys on the bus in the mornings. Would this be on the weekends too?"

"If you're available, yes. I know you have to work around their schedule so tell me what works for you. And don't feel obligated either. I can hire on another part-timer if it's too much."

"Oh no, I definitely want it. I'd love to learn more about the bakery. I just need to figure out the logistics."

"Great, you think it over and get back to me."

"I will and thanks Franny."

"Thank you, I need the help and you're the best."

Franny disappears into the kitchen and I clean up the front putting away unused bags and boxes, wiping down the counters, and straightening the displays. The timing would be tight in the morning, but I could get the kids off to school, go for a quick run, and then get ready for work and make it to the bakery by nine. The weekends might be a little tough if Ryan isn't on time.

I stop pulling the muffins to the front of the case and frown. He needs to be on time. In fact, although he's supposed to pick them up at nine, I need to talk to him about picking them up fifteen minutes earlier so I can be to work on time. He has to understand I need the money the extra hours will bring. He only has the boys for part of the weekend. It isn't asking too much.

The extra hours will cut into my studying time, but I can stay up a tad later and get up a little earlier. Who needs sleep anyway?

I walk over and poke my head into the kitchen. Franny is at the marble counter adding flower decorations to a specialty cake. "Hey Franny?"

She glances up and holds the frosting bag away from the cake. "You need me up front?"

I shake my head. "No, I just wanted to let you know I can come in at nine instead of eleven. Would that work for you?"

"That's great. Are you sure? You can have some time to think it over."

"No, I really want to and Saturday is the only day it might be an issue. I need to talk to Ryan to make sure he will pick the boys up on time."

"Okay, but if you need it to be a little later, let me know."

"I will. I'm excited about this."

Franny smiles. "Me too. It will be nice to have you back here working with me."

I head back to the front counter and rest my hip against the edge. Not only will this put extra money in my pocket—or more to bills anyway, but I will get to participate in baking the goods. I can try my hand at helping with the specialty cakes eventually too.

The Sweet Spot does a fair amount of business catering cakes and sweets for events and some of the businesses in town. She could teach me how to do those intricate flower decorations she creates or fondant. The last time I tried to decorate a cake with fondant it looked like a broken-down neglected building instead of a celebration cake. There were cracks and bumps all over the place. It had torn in a few places so I tried to hide it with frosting but it only made it appear lopsided.

Who knows, maybe working with Franny will turn me from a pretty decent home baker into a professional. I could see myself working here alongside Franny for the foreseeable future. Having an actual career would check off a lot of those empty little boxes piling up in my head. All the things I thought I would have accomplished before I turn thirty in a little over a year.

Like having a special someone to share life's ups and downs with.

Not that I'm not doing just fine on my own. I've been a single mother for almost four years and I think I'm doing a fairly decent job at raising my boys and staying moderately sane. I don't think I've emotionally scarred either of them too badly.

However, it would be nice to have someone to snuggle up to when life gets too overwhelming or just to laugh with and have fun. A little fun occasionally would be nice.

I wouldn't mind having an orgasm where I didn't have to do all the work either.

CHAPTER 9

$\mathcal{T}$he cool breeze tickles the hairs on the back of my neck. September is winding down and the hot weather streak broke. Temperatures dropped into the high sixties overnight from the mid-eighties they'd been hovering at for weeks. I moved my studies outside this morning to take advantage of the blue skies and pleasant temperatures.

My extra hours at the bakery started yesterday and even though it was only a couple of extra hours, it packed a punch mentally and physically. Thankfully, I have today and tomorrow to recover. After I get my classwork done, of course.

Ryan was remarkably agreeable when I told him my new hours and I need him to pick the boys up fifteen minutes earlier on Saturdays.

Crunching gravel from a car pulling into Luke's driveway has me craning my neck to see if it's him or a visitor. A minivan, definitely not his car. A dark-haired woman climbs out as the front door opens and Luke steps out with a wave and then jogs down the steps to open the side door. There's a toddler sitting in a car seat waving his arms at Luke. His nephew, Joey? That would make the woman, Barbara, his sister-in-law.

I haven't received a phone call from her yet and I am not about to wander over and introduce myself uninvited. Scooting my chair sideways a bit so I'm not tempted to take any more peeks in their direction, I stare down at my laptop and read. My first test is in less than two weeks. If I do well, it will be proof I'm not wasting my time and money taking classes.

Fifteen minutes later, I take a long drink from my glass of ice water. I read an entire chapter twice and retained nothing. How am I going to pass the test when I can't even get through the chapter?

The trio appear in Luke's backyard. He's carrying the little boy while the woman walks beside them.

And they're headed this way.

I sit up straighter and smooth down the wrinkled T-shirt I yanked from the unfolded pile of clothes sitting in my laundry basket this morning. When they reach the holly bushes separating our yards, I lift a hand to wave and smile.

The woman gives me a wide smile and waves. "I hope we're not intruding."

"Of course not." I stand and walk to the stairs of my deck while they cross over my lawn and stand at the bottom.

Luke nods. "This is my sister-in-law Barbara and my nephew, Joey."

Barbara steps up a step and extends her hand. "Hi."

I step down to meet her in the middle and shake her hand. "Hi, I'm Olivia." I glance over to Joey and smile but he only solemnly stares back. Takes after his uncle, I see. "Would you like anything to drink?" I glance at all of them. "I've got iced tea, water, milk, juice?"

The milk is running low so I hope that's not their first choice. I have to make a grocery list and go to the store tomorrow.

"Joose." Joey purses his lips and draws out the word adorably like only a toddler can.

"Coming right up. Apple, okay?" He nods and wraps his arms tighter around Luke's neck and lays his head on his shoulder. I glance at Barbara and Luke. "Anything for you two?"

"Nothing for me, thank you."

"I'm good." He tilts his head towards the playscape. "Mind if I take Joey on the swing?"

I wave a hand toward the swings. "Be my guest." I look back at Barbara and smile. "Do you want to have a seat? I'll just be a minute getting the juice."

She wanders over to sit at the table while I go inside and grab a juice box from the kitchen. When I come out, she's angled her chair to watch Luke and Joey. Luke stands behind Joey who's clutching the chains and kicking his legs. The swing is twisting more than gliding.

I open the straw and stick it in the juice box while I cross the yard to them. "Here you go, Joey."

He stops kicking and looks up at Luke while he steadies the swing to a stop. Luke takes the juice from me and squats down and hands it to Joey.

"What do you say to Miss Olivia, buddy?"

Joey peeks up with big dark eyes surrounded by a thick fringe of black eyelashes. "Tank oo."

"You're very welcome."

I wink before turning and walking back to the deck to join Barbara. Hovering over my chair, I ask, "Are you sure I can't get you anything?"

She shakes her head. "Thanks for letting us drop in like this. I can see you're busy." She points to my laptop and papers strewn on my end of the table held down by my glass.

"Oh, don't worry about it. I wasn't getting very far anyway. I must have read the same sentence a half dozen times. I'm beginning to wonder if going back to school at this point in my life is a good idea."

"What are you studying?"

"Management and Marketing, at the moment. They were as good a choice as any. I'm still not sure what I want to be when I grow up."

Barbara chuckles. "Plans have a way of changing."

"That they certainly do. I got pregnant my freshman year of college and dropped out. It's taken me ten years to go back."

"I changed my major four times before I settled on nursing."

"You're a nurse? Do you work here in town?"

"Yes, I started last month at Churchill Memorial."

"My twins were born there. Actually, so was I."

She smiles wide. "That's one of the many things I love about Granite Cove. Families have lived here for generations. Who can blame them for not leaving this little slice of paradise?"

"I didn't actually grow up here, but the next town over where my parents still live. But I know what you mean."

"It's very different from Philadelphia."

"Is that where you're from?"

She nods and glances over to check on her son. Luke and Joey have moved from the swing to the slide. Luke stands next to the slide holding onto Joey by the waist as he scoots his little bottom forward and slides down.

"I grew up in a suburb but went to university in Philadelphia and then got a job there after graduation."

"I imagine it's quite a different pace here than what you're used to. What made you move?"

She rubs the tip of her nose and stares at the table. "My parents retired here five years ago. After I lost Wyatt, I had a tough time coping. I came for a visit and never left." She glances up and gives me a small smile.

"I'm sorry for your loss. Was Wyatt your husband?"

"Luke didn't tell you?" She shakes her head. "What am I saying, of course he didn't. Yes, Wyatt was my husband and Luke's brother. He died in a car accident while I was pregnant with Joey."

"Oh my gosh." I reach over and put my hand over hers on the arm of the chair. "I'm so sorry."

Her smile wobbles and she looks away.

I sit back. That must have been devastating to lose her husband while pregnant. Having to go through everything alone?

"It's been over two years, but I still get choked up. Sorry."

"Please don't apologize, it's perfectly understandable."

"Everything okay?" Luke stands by the railing of the deck staring at Barbara. He glances at me and then back to her with a frown.

He's protective of his sister-in-law. Another point in his favor.

"Fine, we're just chatting." She tilts her head back so she can see Joey crawling on all fours across the lawn.

Luke jerks his head in his nephew's direction. "He's pretending to be a puppy."

Barbara grins and turns back to me. Luke stares at me as if to warn me not to upset his sister-in-law again and then walks back to Joey.

She takes a deep breath and huffs, blowing her black bangs up off her forehead. "Anyway, Luke has always been a godsend with Joey since he was born, but I needed the comfort of my parents. They're doting grandparents. Now that Luke has moved here too, hopefully we can all heal and move on."

So Luke followed Barbara and Joey here? They all lived in Philadelphia?

"Family is everything. I don't know what I would do without the help of my parents and barbeques without all my cousins and their offspring would be boring indeed. Even though my brother isn't able to visit often, we talk on the phone all the time. In fact, one of my cousin's engagement parties is next week and the clan will all be there, minus my brother because he's working."

Barbara rests an elbow on the table and props her chin on her curled up fingers. Her braid falls over her shoulder and swings down. The way the sun hits the strands there appears to be a blue sheen to the black tresses. "You have a brother?"

"Yes, twins run in my family."

"He's your twin?"

"Yup, Oliver, Oli for short. I know, not very original, Oliver and Olivia. My sons are Timmy and Tommy. I guess I inherited my mother's lack of originality or corniness." I shrug and give her a half smile. "What about you, any siblings?"

"No, just me. My parents didn't have me until they were in their forties. They tried for years until finally I came along. My mom wanted to call me Hope, but my father wanted me named after his mother so my full name is Barbara Hope Callihan-Hollister."

"There were a few times I wished I was an only child, but truthfully Oli was always my best friend growing up."

"I'm afraid I wallowed in being my parents' only child as a kid. I was their princess." She smirks and a dimple appears in her cheek. "Still am in many ways, but Joey is definitely their little prince."

"How do you feel about books?"

Her black eyebrows almost collide. "Um...I like them?"

I chuckle. "The reason I'm asking is because my friend Franny is hosting her book club at her house next week and asked me to come. Would you like to go with me?"

"Your friend wouldn't mind?"

"Oh no, I'm sure she won't." Just to be sure I'll call and ask her, but I know she won't refuse especially when I tell her Barbara is new to town and needs friends. Franny has a big heart.

"Then yes, I'd love to."

"I can give you my copy once I finish. Honestly, I haven't started it yet. I'll get started on it tonight after I put the boys to bed."

"That's okay, just tell me the book and I'll download it to my tablet."

I rattle off the title and author and she puts it into her phone. "Did Luke give you my number? We can coordinate going together later."

"Yes, he did. Did he give you mine?"

I shake my head and then a few seconds later my phone dings. I glance down at the face lying on the table.

"I just sent you my number."

"Oh, good. I'll call you this week and let you know what time and all the details. I'm afraid I've got mommy brain and can't remember if Franny ever told me or not."

"Please, I never realized that was even a real thing until I had Joey. It's like my brain cells seeped out and into the womb."

"Tell me about it. And I hate to tell you, but it only gets worse. The other day I was talking to Oli on the phone and walking all over the house looking for that same phone."

She bursts out laughing. "I put mine in the fridge once. I borrowed my mom's phone to call mine and find it. I walked into the kitchen to see my dad standing in front of the fridge frowning. He looked at me and said, "Tell me the truth, is the fridge ringing or am I hallucinating?"

I slap a hand over my mouth as laughter shakes my upper body.

Luke walks onto the deck carrying Joey.

"Funny mommy?"

Barbara stands up and plucks Joey from Luke's arms and rubs her nose into his belly until he giggles. "Yes, mommy is funny and so are you."

Smiling, I stand up. "Can I get anyone anything?"

"I think it's time for Joey's nap." Luke rubs his hand on top of his nephew's head.

Joey lays his head on Barbara's shoulder and yawns.

"Thank you, Olivia, this has been fun. I'm so glad I got to meet you and I can't wait for book club next week."

"Me too."

"Book club?" Luke glances at me.

"I invited Barbara to my friend's book club."

"I'll babysit the pipsqueak here while you go."

"Say thank you and goodbye to Miss Olivia, Joey," Barbara whispers.

Joey waves his tiny fingers in my direction and yawns again. My heart melts and I smile and wave back.

Luke puts his hand on Barbara's back as they turn away and walk to the stairs.

Does Luke have more than brotherly feelings for his brother's widow? He's awfully protective of her and following her here to Granite Cove seems a little over the top.

I watch them walk over to his driveway and put Joey in the car then sit back down and power my laptop back up out of sleep mode. It's none of my business what Luke's feelings for Barbara are.

CHAPTER 10

*S*plat! Icy water drenches my face and hair. The sting of a water balloon hitting my cheek freezes me in place. I wipe my hand down over my face to remove some of the water which hasn't already dripped onto my blouse.

The culprits duck behind the hood of a car. Three pairs of widened eyes and an assortment of different colored bangs are all that's visible of the trio of troublemakers.

"Sorry, Aunt Olivia!"

I narrow my eyes and march towards my little second or is it third cousins? I can never remember how that works. They belong to two of my various cousins.

Conner stands and clasps his hands behind his back trying to appear contrite. Perhaps the smartest of the trio and also the oldest.

Danny, the youngest at five, grins.

I round the front of the car. Frank, the same age of my hooligans, squats next to a cardboard box full of multi-colored water balloons. His gaze bounces around, clearly wondering if he should make a run for it.

Snatching up the box, I send my best glare their way and set it on the hood of the car.

Frank stands and backs over to his cousins. "We were told to play with them by the cars."

"I'm sure you were." After all, it was probably assumed everyone had already arrived since the engagement party had started hours ago. No one would have given a thought to late arrivals like me who had to work on Saturdays.

Danny clearly realizes he might be in trouble and shuffles his feet and stares at the ground.

I plant my hands on my hips and step in front of the box. "Run."

Three gazes snap to mine.

I grab a balloon from the box and raise an eyebrow.

Conner sprints away as Frank's mouth drops open and Danny giggles.

I raise my arm and let it fly smacking Conner in the middle of the back.

Frank and Danny take off in different directions and I grab another balloon. Danny goes down in one shot to his shoulder. He rolls on the ground, giggling away, while I grab another balloon. It takes me two tries, but I manage to tag Frank too. This time in the leg.

I make a gun sign with my hand and blow on the tip. "High school softball, boys. You messed with the wrong aunt."

Conner holds up his hands for truce while Frank jogs back to me. "That was so cool. Are Timmy and Tommy coming?"

"Sorry, they're with their dad today."

He frowns but shrugs. Danny runs over gives me a high five as he delves into the box. I wiggle my finger in his direction. "No more throwing them at anyone without consent."

"What's that mean?"

Conner walks over. "It means they have to give permission first."

"Oh."

I rub the top of his head and walk towards all the laughter and conversation at the back of the house. Dozens of people fill the space and I'm related to most of them and I suppose soon to be related to the rest since they're the groom's relatives, not counting the few friends in attendance too.

Aunt Nancy spots me crossing the yard and rushes down the steps. She latches on to my arm. "What happened to you?" She steers me towards the front of her house. "Why don't you go in and clean up? You can use my room. Borrow a top from Violet's room. Yours is all wet."

"Thanks, but it will dry." I glance down and pull the top away from my skin. It's mostly contained to the one spot. The sun is out and besides, my cousin Violet would not appreciate me borrowing her things. She's territorial.

My aunt frowns but drops my arm. "Suit yourself."

We walk side by side to the back deck. "Your flower gardens look lovely."

"I planted purple mums to match Violet's wedding colors."

"They look great."

The smell of smoke and grilled meat taunt me as I walk up the wooden stairs. Empty plates litter the tables. I missed the meal. My stomach growls in protest.

My parents sit on the back deck with some of the other aunts and uncles and my grandparents. Dad is sitting on one side of his parents. Aunt Nancy lowers herself into the empty chair on the other side of them. The family resemblance is strong from the same blue eyes to the slim pointed nose. I walk up and smile. "Hi everyone." I kiss my grandparents on their cheeks.

Mom stares at my damp shirt and wet face and frowns. Her lips purse, but she doesn't ask any questions.

Dad is oblivious. He wraps an arm around my waist and I perch on the arm of his chair. "How was work, honey?"

"Good. Busy."

"Are Ryan and the boys coming? You did invite Ryan?" My mom hands me a napkin.

I wipe off the rest of the water. My hair, I'm sure, is a lost cause at this point. I had even worn it down and curled it this morning. Oh well.

"Yes, I invited them, but Ryan had plans for the boys." Mom frowns and looks away. She's made no secret of her hopes for a reconciliation between Ryan and I, even though we've been divorced for almost two years and separated even longer.

I search the party attendees. "I should go say hello to the guests of honor." Violet and her fiancé are holding court around the firepit in the backyard.

It takes several minutes to reach them because I have to stop and greet people as I go.

"Congratulations Violet." I lean down and give her a hug. She's sitting on the bench of the picnic table while Kyle sits above her on the table. "And Kyle." I smile at her fiancé. Violet probably began planning their wedding from the day they met less than a year ago when she bought a car at one of his families' car dealerships.

"This is Kevin, my best man." Kyle introduces me to a handsome dark-haired man dressed in a white dress shirt opened at the throat and black dress pants sitting on the other side of the picnic table. Not exactly backyard party attire. Perhaps he came straight from work. He looks around my age, he could be a year or two older even.

I smile. "Hi, nice to meet you."

He doesn't smile or say a word, simply nods his head. What is it with the men I meet lately? Am I emitting anti-interest pheromones or something? It's not like I think I'm irresistible or anything, but seriously? Every decent guy I meet lately seems to take an instant dislike to me or total disinterest.

If I wore perfume, I'd be tempted to toss out the bottle. Maybe I should change my body wash, shampoo, and deodorant.

Sighing, I shift back to Violet and the group of women surrounding her. She introduces me to a few of her friends I don't know.

"Saw your dominance in the water balloon fight, champ." Tyler walks up and bumps my shoulder with his.

"Hey cuz. Was it you who directed your son and his cohorts to bomb unsuspecting late arrivals?" Danny is his spitting image. Same brown curls and brown eyes.

He grins and winks. "I seem to recall a few battles when we were kids where you and Oliver planned the sneak attacks."

Absolutely true. I smile back. "I have no recollection of those incidents of which you speak, counselor."

Tyler chuckles. "Don't worry, I'm off the clock."

Aunt Nancy hasn't stopped proudly beaming or bringing it up since he passed the bar last year.

"Where's your better half?" I scan for his wife, Cat.

"She took Heather inside for a bathroom emergency."

"How's the potty training coming?" Every time I run into Tyler or Cat, they ask my advice on their resistant three-year-old. Timmy was my challenge. Tommy began tearing off his own diaper as soon as he started walking. I had to put him in the pullups early and he basically potty trained himself by the time he was two. Timmy was another story. I tried every trick in books, on the internet, and by asking pretty much every parent I came across. He still wore pullups when he was almost five. I worried they wouldn't allow him to enter kindergarten because of it.

"Stubborn like her mother."

"Ha! How dare you call that saint you married stubborn. You forget, I've known you all my life. I vividly remember a certain little boy sitting at the table until he fell asleep because he refused to eat his peas."

"I plead the fifth."

"Olivia, will you take some pictures of us?" Violet hands me her phone.

"Sure."

"I better go check on Cat and Heather." Tyler stuffs his hands in his pockets and wanders towards the house.

I walk around the other side of the firepit to take pictures of the happy couple and their friends.

"Make sure you get a couple with the fire and some closeups of just the two of us."

Violet stands and poses with her arms loosely linked around Kyle's neck. I snap a few pics and she rearranges herself so she's cheek to cheek with him. The different poses go on for several minutes before she holds out a hand for her phone.

Once I hand it over, she scrolls through the pictures, deleting those she doesn't like. She's done that for as long as I can remember, probably since she's owned a phone. Actually, no, even before because she would take any family members phone and do the same if they took pictures. I guess it's a surefire way to make sure no unflattering pictures are left circulating and posted online or put in photo albums.

Violet's a beautiful girl, it's doubtful there would be many unattractive photos of her anyway. She sits back on the bench and crosses her tanned legs. The lavender skirt of her sundress stops about mid thigh. She tosses back her chestnut brown hair over her shoulder and smiles coyly up at Kyle.

"How are the wedding plans going?"

She places a hand on Kyle's leg. "Fabulous! It's going to be so elegant. We're getting married at his parents' country club."

"Oh good, you asked Olivia?" Aunt Nancy arrives with a platter of blondies. "Desserts are out. I thought I'd bring some over." She offers the plate to the group.

"Not yet, Mom." Violet grimaces and receives a commiserative expression from her best friend since grade school.

"Ask me what?"

"Oh." Aunt Nancy frowns. "Well, there's no time like the present, is there?" She nods her head at her daughter.

Okay, what is this about?

Violet gives me a tight smile. "Will you be one of my bridesmaids, Olivia?"

Crap! I didn't see that one coming. Although, I really should have. I must be the required family addition. Why didn't she ask our cousin Iris? Or had she already said no? There's Melanie, she's away at college, but she could still participate.

"I'd be honored." I paste on a smile. My mother would disown me if I said no. At what age do we stop caring about disappointing our parents?

There's none of the excitement I had when Franny asked me to be a bridesmaid because I know Violet is more than capable of becoming the bridezilla we joked about.

59

Aunt Nancy nods sharply. "Good, that's settled. Now why don't you young people come check out the desserts?" She marches back to the house.

I glance around the group as they stand. The one or two that meet my gaze look away. Yup, I'm not imagining it, Violet has likely discussed her reluctance to have me as a forced bridesmaid at length with them. I can't really blame her, I wouldn't want to be told who I had to include either. I'm surprised she agreed.

I follow behind my aunt. I keep a few feet of distance between us so she won't notice me and drag me into a conversation about the wedding or ask me to serve the desserts to Violet's friends. Wrong of me, I know, but I'm tired from working all day and it's clear Violet only asked me because her mother made her.

Damn it! How can I get out of this without pissing off my relatives?

CHAPTER 11

*T*he stars glitter on a blanket of midnight blue in the heavens above. The rough wood of my deck is cool against my back. I can smell the sweet scent of freshly mowed grass. Luke mowed my lawn again. He must have liked my pie.

The engagement party is probably still raging on. I made my excuses and came home to my little sanctuary. The clear night sky beckoned and I found myself lying down on the deck and staring up at the stars like I used to do as a kid. Except back then, it had been on the roof of my parents' house. I wasn't in danger of breaking much if I fell off the single-story ranch house.

"Are you alive?"

The dark rumble comes from the edge of my deck. My heart jumps into my throat and my body tenses ready to spring up and run.

I let out a breath in a whoosh.

It's Luke. I recognize his deep growl of a voice.

"I was. Now I'm not so sure after you scared me to death."

The stairs and boards creak when he walks up and stands next to me. Light from the pair of lights flanking my back door shine on his tall form as he towers over me, staring down at my face. His eyes are black as pitch except for a tiny glint when he tilts his head.

"I saw you from my bedroom window. You looked like a ritual sacrifice with the solar lights casting a glow around you."

I peek over at the solar lights I fastened to the tops of some of the posts edging my deck. I suppose they're bright enough for him to spot me from his house.

He drops down next to me and lies down. "Swap out the lights for candles and your deck for a stone alter and you'd be all set."

"You're starting to sound serial killey again."

"Serial killey?"

"I tend to make up words. Get used to it."

He chuckles.

I turn my head to stare at his profile. His hair brushes his forehead as a breeze blows over us. A tingle of awareness spreads through me.

Nope, not going there.

"You laughed. I wasn't sure you were capable."

He shrugs his shoulder. "Haven't had much to laugh at." He tilts his head back and stares up at the sky. "Are we looking at something in particular? A comet or meteor shower happening?"

"Not that I know of. I just felt like looking at the stars." I turn my gaze back up. "Thanks for mowing my lawn again and coming over to check if I was dead."

"I figured I would return the favor since you came over to check on me that day the ladder fell."

"You mean the day you growled at me?"

"That's up to interpretation."

I snort. "You smiled at your nephew a bunch. He must make you laugh."

Luke sighs. "Wyatt was the fun one. He could find something funny anywhere. He always made jokes and made people laugh."

"Were you close?"

"Yeah, we were. He was my best friend."

"I'm sorry. I can't imagine losing my brother."

He angles his head towards me. "You have a brother?"

I nod. "Twin actually."

"He live around here?"

"No, Boston. He tries to visit as much as he can, but his job requires he travel a lot. He's in sales for an international company."

"Wyatt sold medical supplies. He traveled regionally and occasionally nationally."

"He must have been very personable. Oli is that way. He can talk to anyone about anything."

"Yeah, he could do that too. But he wasn't fake about it, he genuinely was interested in talking to people."

"Barbara said he died in a car accident when she was pregnant with Joey. Was he on a sales trip?"

Silence stretches into minutes. Had I delved too deep? Crossed an invisible barrier?

"No."

Okay. Should I drop it or ask more questions? I have a feeling he's not generally the sharing type so I should let him dictate the pace.

"If I remember correctly, that's Jupiter." I point to the planet.

"Yeah." He points. "That's Mars, Venus, and Saturn."

"You know something about stars?"

"That's pretty much it unless you want to know the Virgo constellation is the second largest one in the sky."

"And how do you know that?"

"Read it once and it stuck. Probably because I'm a Virgo."

I glance over. "Does that mean you just had a birthday?"

"Yup, September 8th."

"Happy belated birthday. How old are you?"

"Thirty-two."

"I turn twenty-nine next week. October 3rd."

"Mm." He's back to grunts and grumbles?

I fold my hands together over my abdomen.

"The car came out of nowhere. A couple of teenagers joyriding with the headlights off. They T-boned us. The doctors said Wyatt died on impact. I know he never woke up all the times I screamed his name until my voice disappeared. My leg was pinned and I couldn't get to him, no matter how hard I tried."

"Oh Luke!" Tears fill my eyes and I reach out to touch his hand.

He jerks his hand away and climbs to a stand, stumbling once until he finds his balance.

"Don't feel sorry for me. It was my fault. I killed my brother."

He stomps off the deck while I climb to my feet.

"Luke!"

He ignores me and disappears into the shadows beyond my yard.

Should I chase after him? He's obviously in pain. Who wouldn't be?

He's likely to bite my head off if I follow behind him—that's if he even opens the door. It's probably better I let him lick his wounds in private.

What did he mean? Why does he blame himself? Is that why he followed Barbara to make amends? Survivor guilt? Or did he actually cause the accident?

CHAPTER 12

"$\mathcal{H}$oly Shit! That's Mitch Atwater!" Barbara slaps my arm and then grabs hold of my bicep like she's applying a tourniquet.

Damn it! I forgot to warn her. In my defense, I don't think about it all that often anymore.

"He's Franny's fiancé."

She slaps a hand over her mouth and looks at me with her eyes popping out of head.

"Sorry, I should have warned you."

She nods and then drops her hand. "I had the biggest crush on him. His pictures were plastered all over my walls and even my notebooks and locker at school."

Wow! Okay then. I really should have given her a heads up.

She releases my arm and pats her chest. Then her eyes go wide again.

"Ladies."

I turn and smile. "Hi Mitch, this is my friend Barbara. She's new to Granite Cove."

"It's nice to meet you, Barbara. I'm relatively new myself. Well, at least this time around."

A high-pitched squeal comes out of her instead of intelligible words.

Grinning, I tilt my head at her. "Umm...she's a fan."

Barbara nods emphatically.

Mitch smiles and takes it in stride. "Always nice to meet a fan."

Franny appears at his side. She takes one look at Barbara and smiles up at Mitch. "Honey, aren't you going to be late?"

He chuckles. "I guess that's my cue to leave." He kisses Franny. "Have fun."

Barbara's gaze tracks him until he disappears into the house. Her breath whooshes out of her. "Oh my God!"

Franny glances at me. "You didn't warn her?"

"I forgot."

Barbara's entire face and chest turn red. "I'm so sorry."

Franny waves a hand. "Don't worry about it. He gets that reaction from time to time. You should have seen Tina when she first met him. All she did was fan herself the entire time."

"Thanks, that makes me feel slightly better to have lost my intelligence and maturity."

We both laugh.

Franny raises her voice to carry to the group. "Why don't we all find seats? I thought we'd start the book club out here on the patio and then if it gets too cool, we can move it inside."

They've added a sectional sofa and two swivel chairs to the patio since my last visit and moved the chairs from the table to the other side of the sofa to accommodate all ten of us. Franny makes the introductions. I, of course, know Sally and Lucinda. I've seen Monica and Aggie plenty of times in the bakery. Rebecca owns the florist shop. Tina was the boys' teacher in the first grade. I don't know Kerry, who teaches at the high school.

Barbara and I sit next to each other on the couch. Sally and Aggie take the two swivel chairs. Franny sits in a dining chair with Lucinda and Monica on each side of her. Rebecca, Tina, and Kerry take up the remainder of the couch.

"Thanks for coming everyone. Who wants to go first?" Franny gazes at all of us.

"I, for one, am not a fan of the whole rescue the damsel in distress plot so I was cheering the heroine on when she bashed the hero over the head with a chamber pot and saved herself." Rebecca lifts her wine glass in a salute.

Most of us nod.

"I don't know, there are days when I'd love for a man to sweep me off my feet and rescue me." Monica shrugs and sips her wine.

I cross my legs and lean against the arm of the couch. "Yes, but the problem with that is then they'll expect you need them to instruct you on every aspect of your life, like you're too dumb to figure anything out for yourself."

"Exactly." Rebecca points her wineglass at me. "I'm with you, Olivia."

Sally folds her arms across her chest. "It doesn't have to be one or the other. Men and women can take turns saving each other. It's called compromise and essential to a healthy relationship."

"True, but my Dennis' idea of compromise is to tell me I can choose between his two favorite restaurants when we go out to dinner. My idea of compromise is only to imagine braining him with my cast iron frying pan instead of actually doing it." Aggie cackles and slaps her knees.

"My soon to be ex thought he was compromising when he suggested we have an open marriage rather than get divorced. That way, he could still have his women on the side and not have to do it in secret."

Several gasps emerge. My mouth drops open and I stare at Lucinda. Is she serious?

Franny reaches over and pats her sister's hand resting in her lap.

"Did you hit him over the head with a frying pan?" Aggie asks.

"I would have run him over with my car." Rebecca leans forward and rests her forearm on her crossed knees.

"What did you do, Lucinda? I cannot imagine what I would do if my Ron suggested that to me." Tina holds a hand to her chest. She was single when the boys were in her class and I was the room parent. She had been still nursing a broken heart over the breakup with her college boyfriend. Ron had come along the same time as my marriage to Ryan was ending. She had been flashing an engagement ring while we were drawing up divorce papers.

They're still in the newlywed and everything is perfect stage of marriage. I never experienced that stage. My first stage of marriage consisted of sleep deprivation and learning how to parent a set of twins.

"The last straw for me was when I discovered he'd been bringing them home and sleeping with them in our bed. One even tried on my clothes. I thought I had been imagining things when I would find my things in different places than I left them. Then one day I found lipstick smudges on the collar of a silk blouse." Lucinda shakes her head. "I think she wanted me to know. It didn't work out for her though because she was only one of many and he had no intention of giving any of them up."

Monica leans forward to glance at Lucinda. "A sound argument for castration."

I choke on my water.

Aggie claps her hands.

Rebecca and Barbara both laugh.

Kerry snorts while Tina gapes at Monica.

"On that note, how about we have dessert?" Franny stands and walks over to the table where there is an assortment of treats.

Barbara leans over and whispers, "I'm so glad you invited me. This is so much better than sitting home watching television."

I chuckle and we both stand and join everyone milling around the table.

"Franny, how is it living with Mitch? Any trouble in paradise yet? Does he have any disgusting habits?" Rebecca takes a bite of a pastry and groans. "You keep feeding me like this and I'm going to gain twenty pounds."

"Actually, it's my habits I worry about. Mitch is a bit of a clean freak where I can be a slob."

"Yes, you can."

Franny sticks her tongue out at her sister.

Tina picks a mini cheesecake from the platter and puts it on her plate. "Ron and I didn't move in together until after we married. We wanted the entire experience to be new."

"I wish I had lived with my husband before the wedding, I might have seen what a scumbag he was." Lucinda glances around and then winces. "Sorry, I guess I'm still a little bitter."

"Don't apologize, you have every reason to be." Kerry pats Lucinda on the shoulder. "I was engaged to this guy once. He made me think I was crazy and paranoid whenever I questioned him. I found naked pictures of his ex-girlfriend on his phone and he convinced me they were old and he forgot they were there. Then I found women's panties under the bed—not mine. He tried to tell me they were a present for me and I spoiled it. He couldn't explain it away however when I walked in and found him screwing her on my kitchen counter, though."

"Men are nothing more than a walking talking set of cock and balls." Rebecca picks up another pastry and eats half of it in one bite.

"Not all guys are like that. We just need to search harder for the good ones. My Wyatt was one of the great ones." Barbara's sad smile prompts me to rub her arm.

I bite back the urge to ask about Luke's declarations. This is not the time or place and she might not know how Luke blames himself or why. If I ask, it could cause all sorts of problems.

"My Herbert was one of the good ones too." Sally walks by and pats Barbara on the shoulder.

"Anyone want to see the latest picture my brother snagged of me?" Monica looks around. "For those of you who are new, my brother and I have this running practical joke we play on each other where we take and post awful photos of one another on social media." She scrolls through her phone. "This time he took a video of me."

She passes her phone to Rebecca who watches it, laughs, and passes it to Tina.

"That's me trying not to do a face plant into the ground after trying to catch a ball and missing."

Tina and Kerry look together and pass it to me.

Monica is awkwardly running with her torso parallel to the ground and her arms spread out like wings ready to take flight.

I chuckle and hand her phone off to Lucinda and Franny. The phone makes the rounds.

"So, anyone have any suggestions on how to pay back my brother?"

"Ever try a water balloon?"

All eyes turn to me.

"One of my little cousins pelted me with a water balloon at a family picnic last week and my cousin Violet posted a picture of me getting smacked in the face with it." I discovered that little treat the day after the party.

"Ouch, did it hurt?" Franny winces.

"It stung for a second or two, but honestly not as much as seeing that picture posted and all the comments under it." I shrug. "It wasn't a flattering picture, but it wasn't as bad as the one she posted of me eight months pregnant with twins, sweating bullets in the summer heat and with my mouth full."

Kerry grimaces. "She doesn't like you much, does she?"

"I'd like to think it's not malicious. She thinks she's being funny."

"It's not funny if it's at another person's expense without their knowledge."

I smile at Barbara.

"How would she feel if a picture of her was posted which was less than flattering?" Rebecca asked.

"That wouldn't happen. She checks anyone's phone if they take a picture and then deletes the photo if she doesn't like it."

"A classic narcissist." Monica wrinkles her nose. "She doesn't see the hurt she causes only cares about her wants and needs."

"She's selfish and spoiled, but I don't think she's hateful. I really hope not since I'm now at her mercy since I agreed to be her bridesmaid."

"Ugh." Rebecca groans. "She's going to make you wear the most hideous dress she can find."

"I hope not."

Monica purses her lips. "I hate to tell you, but I agree with Rebecca."

"Yup."

"Me too."

"You poor thing."

The chorus of agreement has me sighing. Sadly, I agree with them.

CHAPTER 13

"Peace offering." Luke stands at my door holding a pizza box from Joe's Pizzeria. The smell of the magical combination of dough, sauce, cheese, and spices wafts into my house. I stare at the box and then glance up to meet his gaze.

"Can we forget about last week and the things I said?"

"Lucky for you I'm starving." I step back and he walks in. I wave a hand to the kitchen table and close the door behind him. It's Saturday night, I just got home from work and the kids are with Ryan, so I hardly feel like cooking for one.

He glances around my small house. From this vantage point he can see the living room, kitchen, and dining area. Pretty much the sum total of my downstairs minus the bathroom separating the two spaces at the back of the house. Two of my houses could fit into his and there are three of us living here.

It's small, but it's all mine. Well, mine and the bank's.

I walk behind him into the kitchen. "What exactly are we forgetting?"

He stops and glances over his shoulder.

I smirk. "Kidding."

His confession of blame and killing his brother has popped into my head all week, but I can understand how survival guilt might manifest. If he doesn't want to talk about it with me, that's his choice. I can respect that, even while I wonder if he's talking to anyone about it and getting the help he needs to heal.

"Funny."

He puts the box on the table while I walk past and grab a couple of plates from the cabinet and set them on the table.

"What do you want to drink? I've got water, milk, iced tea or I could crack open a bottle of wine."

"Water is fine with me."

I pour two glasses of water and bring them to the table. He's already placed a slice for each of us on the plates. I sit across from him and pick up the pizza. After taking a bite, I close my eyes and savor the flavors exploding in my mouth. When I open my eyes, Luke is staring at me.

"Told you I was starving. I haven't eaten since this morning and I love pizza."

He picks up his slice. "Barb had a great time at your book thing. She chewed my ear off. Went on and on about meeting Mitch Atwater."

"Yeah, I didn't realize she's such a huge fan."

"Fan? I've gained a whole new perspective on teenage girls and celebrity worship."

"Are you telling me you never had a poster on your wall as a teenager?"

He takes a bite and glances up. "I had a poster of Edgar Allan Poe. I don't think that quite compares to the wallpaper of posters Barb showed me a picture of."

"She has pictures?"

"An entire album. There were autographed pictures and magazine cutouts too."

"Wow, no wonder she was speechless when Mitch walked over."

I finish my slice and grab another. "Edgar Allan Poe, huh? No rock bands on your walls or women in bikinis?"

"Nope, Wyatt's side of the room had pictures of cars. Our parents would never have allowed any posters of women or bands. Too distasteful, according to them."

"Were they strict?"

He shrugs. "Not any more than any other kid's parents I knew. We lived in a decent neighborhood in a multifamily house. We lived on the top floor and space was limited, which is why Wyatt and I shared a room. They gave us plenty of freedom as long as we showed them respect."

Luke polishes off his third piece and nods his chin towards my plate. "Are you going to finish that?"

I look down at the crust. "'Fraid not. My stomach is full."

He snags it off my plate and eats it before grabbing another slice. Oli always does the same.

"What about you? Any posters on your walls growing up?"

"A few and I have to admit one of them was Mitch. I don't think I rank as the same caliber of fan as Barbara though."

"I doubt few would."

"So back to Edgar Allan Poe, what's the deal?"

"I liked his work."

"It was always a little too dark for me."

"Rumor has it he was a dark guy."

"Tell the truth, you wore black eyeliner and had crows and dead trees drawn all over your notebooks."

Luke smirks and leans back in the chair balancing it on two legs. He folds his hands together over his flat abdomen. "No eyeliner, but there might have been a few doodles."

"Do your parents still live in Pennsylvania? Philadelphia, right?"

"They moved to Arizona several years ago. My mom has bad asthma and the dry heat down there helps her."

"Oh, do you get a chance to see them? What about Joey?"

"They make an annual trip back to see Joey every year and Barb is real good at keeping in touch. She does video chats with them every week and sends pictures of Joey."

"I like Barbara. She's really a sweet person."

"Yeah, Wyatt lucked out when he got her. She's one in a million."

There's still three pieces of pizza left in the box. "Do you want me to wrap those up for you?"

"Nah, save them for the boys. Unless they're not allowed or allergic or something."

I smile. "God help me if they were. They're pizza fiends like me. I do limit us though, otherwise we'd eat it nightly if my budget allowed. It's a problem."

His lips twitch into a half smile.

"By the way, I owe you for mowing my lawn again. Any requests?"

"You don't owe me anything. I told you it helps me think. But I wouldn't turn down any more baked goods."

"Do you have a favorite?"

"No, I'm not picky. Surprise me."

"Okay." I get up and put the pizza in a plastic container so it will fit in my fridge. "You want to sit outside? It's supposed to be another clear night." I peek out the window. "And the sun is setting."

"Sure." He stands.

"Do you want more water? Or something else?" I open the fridge. The bottle of wine I placed in there this morning sits on the top shelf mocking me. It is my birthday after all.

"I'll take a refill."

My parents called this morning to wish me a happy birthday, but they were the only ones besides Oli who remembered. It's kind of hard for him to forget since we share a birthday. The boys must be forgiven for not remembering because they are only ten. Of course, it would have been nice if their father had bothered to remind them and have them make me a card. I always make sure they do something nice for his birthday.

I fill his glass and then gaze at the wine bottle one more time.

Screw it!

"I hope you don't mind, but I'm going to have a glass of wine."

"Why would I mind? Go ahead."

I pour myself a glass and hold up the bottle. "You sure you don't want one?"

He shakes his head. "I don't drink."

Uh oh, should I not then? Is it a moral or addiction issue? Or maybe he simply doesn't like alcohol. Franny is that way. He said he didn't mind though and I've already poured it. Biting my lip, I carry my glass into the living room and out the back door onto the deck.

The sun lights up the horizon in a fiery ball of orange with pinks and lavender ribbons shooting out from its sides.

I turn my chair to watch before sitting down. Luke glances at his phone and then does the same.

He frowns and then pulls his phone back out. "Didn't you say your birthday was the third?"

"Yup." I raise my glass. "I bought this to celebrate."

Luke glances around. "Am I crashing your birthday celebration?"

"Does it look like I had plans? Other than this glass of wine? You saved me from having to cook and eat alone."

He's still frowning, staring at the table.

"Look, my birthday stopped being an event when I had kids. My parents called me this morning and I got a card from them in the mail. I talked to my brother this morning too and we wished each other a happy birthday."

"I guess mine wasn't much different. My parents sent me a card. Barb and Joey gave me an ice cream cake and a cute drawing Joey made of his handprint." He frowns again. "You should blow out a candle and make a wish at least. According to Barb, it's mandatory."

I laugh. "I'm fresh out of candles. Something else I purged from my life when the kids were little. I was too afraid of fires and burns."

Luke looks around and his gaze lands on the grill. "You got a lighter or something you use to light that?"

"Uh, yes."

"That'll have to do. Where is it?"

"Inside, above the fridge, but really it's not necessary."

He gets up and disappears inside. I take a sip of wine. It's nice not to be celebrating alone and I appreciate his effort. It's been a while since anyone made any kind of fuss.

Luke comes back out carrying the blue long tipped lighter. "Okay, come stand over here."

I join him in the middle of the deck. He holds the lighter up between us and pulls the trigger. A tiny orange flame pops out of the tip.

"Make a wish."

I stare at the flame dancing in the breeze. What should I wish for? My standard is the health of my kids and that's most important, so I lean forward and blow on the flame.

It disappears and I grin up at him. "Thanks Luke, this was a sweet idea."

"Happy birthday."

His head dips and his lips press against mine. I swallow hard and lick my lips. His gaze drills into mine. He kisses me again. A soft brushing of lips once, twice, three times until he lifts his hand and cups my jaw.

I lean forward and capture his soft lips with mine. Pleasure and anticipation build inside me.

Luke's tongue traces along my bottom lip and I open my mouth for him. Our tongues entwine and explore.

I lift my hands and place them on his shoulders with my thumbs caressing his neck.

He pulls away and steps back.

I drop my hands and suck my bottom lip behind my teeth. His gaze tracks the movement then he looks away.

"I better go." Luke jams his hands into his front pockets and walks down the stairs and off into the night.

Well, that was...a heck of a lot more than I was expecting. I walk over to the table and finish my wine in one gulp. "Happy birthday to me."

CHAPTER 14

"While Sally's here to cover the front, I want to talk to you about business stuff." Franny walks to the sink and washes her hands.

The sweet scent of yeast and sugar permeates the kitchen.

Was she unhappy with the work I've been doing? She didn't say anything before. Is she cutting back my hours? That will really suck. I need the extra money. I need new tires on my car.

"Is everything okay?"

She glances at me and frowns as she dries her hands. My worry must be written all over my face. "Everything is great. You've been a tremendous help. Now that you're working here full time, I've been checking into health insurance benefits for you, but before I go any farther I want to know if it's something you want or if you're covered elsewhere."

"Oh...um." That would be awesome. The boys are covered under Ryan's plan, but I only have ridiculously cheap, basic coverage which I avoid using unless absolutely necessary. "If it's not too cost prohibitive. I would hate to put you in a jam."

"I wouldn't offer if I couldn't swing it. It probably won't be the best coverage around, more like middle of the road."

"Anything is probably better than what I have now."

Franny smiles. "Good. One more thing to check off my list. The extra hours you're working are a big help. I plan to focus a little more on the special occasion cakes and the catering to local businesses."

I bite my lip. "You know, one of the things we covered in my marketing course is the importance of an online presence. I know you have the website and Facebook page with hours listed and contact information, but I was thinking you might want to expand on it a little."

"What did you have in mind?"

"Well, for the website you can have separate pages for the catering side, specialty cakes, and desserts, bakery merchandise, etcetera. Add some quality pictures. Start accounts on all the major social media sites and post pictures of the bakery and various goods. You can have specials on certain days. And add testimonials from clients."

Franny taps her finger against her lips. "You've given this a lot of thought."

"Too much?"

"No, not at all, it sounds great. The only problem is I would have to hire someone to not only design all that but maintain it too."

"I could do it. I mean, I can do the social media sites no problem. The website is a little trickier. There's a short class offered at the college where I'm taking courses. One of my teachers mentioned it during class. I know I can figure it out, but I would absolutely tell you if I can't."

"I trust you Olivia. If you want to take this on, that would be amazing. I'll pay for any course you need to take."

"Really? That's great." I grin. "I can't wait to get started."

Franny laughs. "I guess this means a little less baking time for you."

"Why?"

"Because you'll be working on the bakery's online presence, as you called it." She wags her finger. "You'll be doing the work here at the bakery, not taking it home and staying up all hours of the night."

She's right, I would do that. Who needs sleep? I don't want to fail her.

"You can use my laptop at the desk. Unless you prefer your own?"

"Honestly, mine is ancient so if you're okay with it, I'll use yours."

"Okay, it's settled then. Anything else we should discuss?"

I purse my lips and drum my fingers on the counter. "Well, Luke kissed me."

"If this goes well, I might need to hire someone else part-time…" She stares at me and blinks. "What did you say?"

I laugh. "I said Luke kissed me. Not exactly business related, sorry."

"No, no, consider business done. Tell me."

"Nothing more to tell. He kissed me a week and a half ago on my birthday and he's been ghosting me ever since." Technically we've been ghosting each other. I waited until he left and dashed over to deliver the cookies I made for him to thank him for mowing my lawn. He left the empty container on my back porch while I was at work.

Franny squeezes her eyes shut. "I missed your birthday? I'm the worst friend ever!"

"No you're not. Don't worry about it. I don't make a big deal over my birthday—honest."

"I'm making this up to you. We're going to celebrate a little late. What are your plans this weekend?"

"Franny it's not necessary."

She points a finger. "I'm not taking no for an answer. It'll be fun."

I hold up both my hands palm out. "Okay."

She grins. "Should I invite Luce and some of the girls from book club? How about your friend Barbara?"

"I'll leave it up to you."

"I think we should invite Luce at the very least. She needs to get out of the apartment. I swear, she's hibernating or something since she moved in. I have to drag her out of there."

"Then we'll make sure she goes."

"I guess you no longer think he's a serial killer then since you're kissing him. Unless you're into some things I'd rather not know about?"

I snort and clap a hand over my mouth.

She grins.

"No, I'm pretty sure he's not." I can't share the car accident or his brother. That's private and not my secret to tell.

"So you're into him?"

"I...I'm not sure. I mean he's seriously hot, but he's my neighbor. I have the kids to worry about too. If it goes wrong what am I going to do, move?"

"That might be a little extreme, but obviously you've given this some thought."

I squint and scrunch my nose. "Maybe a little."

"I get it. He's handsome and mysterious. I say go for it. You're single. Yes, I get you might have to be more cautious because you have kids, but that doesn't mean you have to stay alone until the kids grow up, do you?"

"God, I hope not."

She laughs and walks over to sling an arm around my shoulders. "I highly recommend finding the courage to follow your heart."

I glance at her sideways. "Who said anything about my heart?"

Chuckling, she drops her arm. "Okay, then whatever body part or parts are attracted to him."

"You did hear me say he's been ghosting me, right?"

"He could be waiting for you to make the next move."

"I don't know, Franny. It may be old fashioned, but I'm more comfortable with the guy making the initial moves."

"I can totally relate, but you can be subtle. Wear something sexy and just happen to run into him or something."

"And what if he's not interested? That would suck. I don't like rejection."

"Well, who does? But I say the proof is in his kiss. He kissed you, therefore he's interested."

Sighing I collapse on the counter on top of my folded arms. "I feel like I'm back in high school."

CHAPTER 15

*T*he peal of the smoke alarm pierces my studying haze. *Damn it! Damn it! Damn it!*

I scramble off my bed, knocking one of my books to the floor, and run downstairs to the kitchen. Gray smoke billows from the oven. The alarm continues to shrill. The timer I set rings beneath it all.

Yanking on the oven dial, I shut it off and open the door. I get a face full of smoke. The stench fills my nose and burns my throat. A coughing fit ensues. My throat is raw. The charred remains of the brownies I made for the boys' class fill the oven. Now I will have to make them all over again.

I wave the smoke out of my face and sprint to the window over the kitchen sink. Standing on my tippy toes I shove it open and grab the dishtowel next to the sink to wave it in the air beneath the alarm. It's futile.

Will it help if I douse the pan of brownies in cold water? I pull an oven mitt out of the drawer and grab the pan out of the oven and carry it to the sink. After turning the water on, I angle the pan under the spray.

The hot pan hits the hole in the thumb part of the mitt. Scalding heat burns my thumb.

"Son of a bitch!"

I drop the pan into the sink. It crashes against the dishes I have yet to put in the dishwasher from this morning. The water sprays everywhere including all over me. I slap at the faucet to turn off the water.

The giggles kick in and I sag against the counter with my good hand over my mouth and the other, still encased in the oven mitt, raised in the air. Leave it to me to laugh when I'm in pain. I also cry when I'm mad. Laughter interspersed with coughs rattle through me.

"Should I ask?"

I whirl around. Luke stands in the archway to my kitchen.

He jerks a thumb over his shoulder. "I knocked on your back door, but you didn't answer."

When I continue to blink silently, he drops his hand. "I saw the smoke." He lifts his chin towards the window. "Heard the alarm." He walks over and stretches to shut off the wail.

Wish I could do that. It would've been my next step, with the assistance of one of the kitchen chairs.

He peers into the sink at the burned brownies. "Those weren't for me, were they?"

The sting of my thumb bursts through my surprise over his arrival. I frown and shake the oven mitt off my hand and onto the floor while turning on the water after angling it away so it won't bounce off the pan. I put my thumb under the cool, steady, stream.

"Did you burn yourself?"

I glare at him over my shoulder. Does that really require an answer?

"You got any aloe?"

I raise my eyebrows and reach with my free hand to shut off the water. "Actually, yes."

He grabs my hand. "Leave the water on and tell me where it is."

"Upstairs. On the windowsill in the bathroom. Top of the stairs."

He nods and walks to the stairs.

I grimace and turn back to stare at my thumb. He's going to witness my less than exemplary cleaning habits. I planned to get around to the bathroom later today. When you have two boys, cleaning the bathrooms becomes a daily chore.

Luke returns with a long green spiky leaf of the plant. I shut off the water and hold out my uninjured hand. "Thanks."

He grabs my other hand and applies the gel like substance to the reddened area.

His bent head is inches from mine. His dark gaze his pinned on my thumb so I take the opportunity to study his features. Dirty blond hair brushes his forehead. It's a little long over his ears and against his neck. Is he overdue for a trim or does he prefer it that way? There's a tiny crescent scar at the corner of his eye. What could cause that?

He glances up. "That should do it. I don't think it's too bad. You don't require a hospital visit."

Of course it doesn't. I've done worse. In the same spot because of the same hole in the mitt which I should have thrown away and replaced a long time ago.

"Do you have medical training?" I still have no idea what he does for a living.

He smirks. "Nope." His gaze scans over me. "Did you decide to take a shower while you were busy burning the..." He leans over to peer into the sink again. "What exactly is that?"

"Brownies. And very funny. The water sprayed all over me and everything else when I burned myself and dropped the pan in the sink."

"Brownies, huh? Sure those weren't for me? I ran out of those cookies you left me days ago." He grabs the dishtowel I tossed on the counter and wipes my cheek.

"They were for the boys' school, but since I have to make more, I suppose you've earned a few."

The side of his mouth quirks up in a smile. "You going to leave them on my front steps when I'm not home?"

"Depends, are you going to leave the empty container on my steps when I'm at work?"

"I was following your lead." The towel brushes my eyelashes as he wipes water from my forehead.

"I wasn't aware I was leading."

"You are. The question is where?" He rests his hands on the counter on either side of me, caging me in. His head is level with mine as he stares into my eyes.

I lick my lips.

His gaze drops. His head dips and he captures my lips in a soft as air kiss.

He leans a few inches back and raises his gaze back to mine.

Why did he stop?

Oh, is he waiting for me to lead?

There's so many questions to answer, but only thing matters right now—his lips back on mine.

I cup his cheeks in my palms and pull his face back to mine. "Gimmee."

He laughs. I kiss him. His full bottom lip pillows mine. I run my tongue along its top edge and scrape my upper teeth against it in a soft nip.

His hands grasp my hips and lift me so I'm resting on the counter. He steps into the V of my legs as his mouth consumes mine.

I wrap my legs around his jean-covered butt. The denim scrapes against my bare calves. The thin material of my capris provides little barrier between us and leaves no doubt of his interest.

My fingers delve into the soft strands of his hair as I cup the back of his head. My heart races as arousal drenches me in sensation.

His hands travel over my back and down to grip my hips.

There's a clatter behind me. I jump and look down. The pan slid all the way into the sink, knocking over a glass. My hip must have bumped into it. Or his hand.

I turn back to Luke. My hands rest loosely on his shoulders. His hands grip my waist with his thumbs lightly caressing my sides.

"How about lunch?"

"Lunch?" I glance at the clock on the stove. Two o'clock. The boys will be home in a couple of hours. I suppose there's time, but for what exactly? Is he asking me to make him lunch?

"Yeah, you know, that time in the middle of the day when people generally eat a meal? I figure you have the kids at dinnertime so I thought a lunch date might work better."

"So you're asking me out on a date?"

He chuckles. "That was the general idea."

I purse my lips and swing my feet dangling against his legs. "In that case, yes."

"You're off tomorrow too, right?"

He knows my work schedule. "Yes, the bakery is closed Mondays and Tuesdays."

"I heard the restaurant on the docks has a good lobster roll. You want to go there?"

"Billings Creamery. You heard correctly. Their lobster roll is excellent."

"Then, tomorrow around noon? I'll pick you up."

"Okay."

Luke lets go of my waist and steps back. He looks around the kitchen. "Do you need help cleaning up? The smoke seems to be gone."

I hop down from my perch on the counter. "No, thanks. I've got to make another batch anyway—more mess."

"Save a few for me?"

I smile and put my hands on the edge of the counter and lean back. "You've earned it."

"How about you set a timer this time?"

I sigh and give him a mock glare. "I did. I didn't hear it go off because I was too busy studying upstairs. Something I will refrain from doing in the future when the stove is on."

He steps forward and gives me a quick kiss on the lips. "See you tomorrow." He ambles around the corner and out of sight. The back door opens and closes and I hear his steps across my deck.

Sighing, I push away from the counter and survey the kitchen. There's still a faint lingering smell of smoke and burned brownies in the air. It's warm enough outside to leave the window open longer.

A smile twitches at my lips. I have a date with Luke tomorrow.

Man, can he kiss.

It's not only the brownies that got singed today. My lips are still tingling.

CHAPTER 16

here's an autumn chill to the air so this emerald green sweater dress should keep me warm enough without having to cart around a jacket. I shift my weight from one foot to the other as I stare in the mirror attached to the back of my bedroom door. Too dressy for a lunch date at Billings.

I swing away from the mirror and pull the dress over my head and toss it onto the growing pile of clothes on my bed. Patches of the baby blue comforter are visible beneath my discarded choices.

Nerves jump in my stomach. How the heck am I going to make it through this date when I can't even decide what to wear?

Standing in front of the open folding double doors of my closet, I scan the racks and shelves. What says casual, but still sexy? Not too sexy though. Understated sexy? Damn it. I want to be attractive, but not like I'm trying too hard. It's our first date and he's never seen me dressed up so I want to make a good impression. The kind that might lead to more of those sizzling kisses.

But not advertise for it either. I drop my face into my hands as I stand there in my bra and panties. Basic white, of course, because I don't want to be tempted to let it go beyond kissing yet. If I wear sexy underclothes, I might think twice about it. It's too soon so I need safeguards in place. I even thought of not shaving this morning so I would have a surefire stop pass burned into my brain, but then I would only be uncomfortable if I did so other measures must be taken.

Three freaking years without sex and my libido is on a constant simmer around my neighbor.

The last time I impulsively had sex, I ended up pregnant and married. Even though I'd been on the pill, I'd still managed to beat the odds. Apparently, antibiotics lower the effectiveness of the contraception. I really wish someone had let me know that little tidbit ahead of time.

So, no impulsively jumping the neighbor's bones.

Jeans—not regular—but white. They say casual, but a step up. I pull them off the shelf and hold them against my waist while I scan the shelf for a sweater. Something fitted and a little flirty. I snag a robin's egg blue one with a V-shaped neck and walk over to stand in front of the mirror once again.

Holding the clothes in front of me, I tilt my head side to side. The combo should look good. I pull on the sweater while clamping the jeans between my legs and then shimmy into the jeans.

I twist side to side and check out how my ass looks. Not too bad.

Okay, clothes selected. Now what the heck am I going to do with my hair? The custom ponytail is out. I should have gotten that haircut I've been meaning to get. Something short and sassy. Sighing, I wander into the bathroom and brush my blonde locks in every direction I can think of to come up with some sort of style.

Nope, my hair is straight as a pin. It hangs down against my cheeks. Well, it will have to do. I don't have time to curl it today, not if I intend to wear makeup.

I put on brown eyeliner and a touch of blush on my cheeks—more than the mascara and lip gloss I usually wear. I check the time and rush downstairs.

Luke strolls up the front walk as I reach the bottom of the stairs. *Damn it.* I thought I would have more time to prepare.

I open the door with a smile. He stops with his foot on the bottom step and scans me from head to toe. "Hey."

"Hey." I smooth the front of my sweater over my abdomen.

He steps back. "You ready?"

"Uh, yes." I reach around the door and grab my purse from one of the hooks on the wall. I follow him to his sedan parked in my driveway. Is it too much to ask for some tiny compliment over my appearance after all the time I spent? Of course, he has no idea just how long I took to get ready and he never will if I have anything to say about it. But, seriously, don't I at least warrant a "you look nice"?

I climb into the passenger side while he walks around to the driver's side. My father would call the car a foreign money pit. He values nothing unless it is American made. I've never seen Luke drive the car he keeps in his garage. Does it not run?

I glance at him out of the corner of my eye while he starts the car and puts it in drive. He's dressed in a navy polo shirt and jeans. A little dressier than I've seen him in the past. I think my choice for attire was sound. I'd be surer if he showed some interest and appreciation though.

"Barb was reading the new book for your book club."

"Oh? I haven't started it yet. Does she like it?"

What was the book pick this month? Damn it. I'll have to ask Franny.

"Seemed to. I think she likes the getting together part the most. Thanks for that again."

"Well, that's really the best part for everyone I think."

We arrive in the village and Luke turns down the road towards the docks. The parking lot in front often fills up during the summer and it is hard to find a spot, but he's able to find one near the restaurant. The summer people have been filtering out over the past several weeks, but the leaf peepers are in full swing.

Billings Creamery perches in the middle of the docks. The white building with red awnings has a wide-open view of the lake from every side. A family waits at the window for ordering ice cream or takeout on the right side of the building. We walk towards the main entrance on the left.

The sign says to seat yourself so I follow Luke over to one of the empty shiny wooden booths with two benches by the front windows. The lake laps against the pier a few feet outside the window.

A server wearing black jeans and a red T-shirt with the restaurant logo on it hurries over with a smile and a couple of menus. "Can I get you something to drink while you look over the menu?"

I take the menu and open it. "Diet cola for me, whichever brand you carry."

"Same, except non-diet."

"I'll bring those right out to you." She turns and strides towards the kitchen. I peruse the restaurant. Only a couple of tables are empty. The place is busy for an October weekday.

Luke closes his menu and leans back against the bench. "I'm having the lobster roll and a side of fries."

I close the menu and stack the two of them at the end of the table. "Me too. The restaurant closes this month so I won't be able to get another one until they open in the spring. Will you share a few fries?"

"Depends. When you say a few, do you actually mean a few or will you devour the whole plate and leave me with nothing?"

"Territorial over your fries, are you? I promise not to take too many. The lobster rolls are huge and filling."

She returns with our sodas and takes out a pad of paper from her short black apron after placing the glasses on the table. "What will you have?"

"We'll both have a lobster roll." Luke glances at me and back to her. "How big is an order of fries?"

She tucks the pad of paper under her arm and holds her hands about a foot apart. "The plate's around this big and it's filled with a mound of fries."

"Then we'll take one of those too."

She writes it down. "Got it. Your order will be ready in a jiffy."

Luke takes a drink of his soda while I unwrap the utensils tucked inside the napkin and set them on my placemat which advertises local businesses. Would it benefit The Sweet Spot to advertise here? Franny may have already checked into it and found it cost prohibitive, but I don't think she'd mind if I asked. She's always been open to any ideas or questions I have concerning the bakery.

I fold my arms over each other on the table and lean forward. "So, what do you do?"

His long fingers fiddle with the straw wrapper. "At the moment, not much."

Oh crap, he's unemployed and I've just nosedived the date into depressing territory. Is it because of his leg? Is he on disability or something? I barely notice the limp most of the time. Could it be worse than it appears?

I take a sip of soda. "I'm taking courses at the community college. I dropped out when I got pregnant and finally got around to enrolling again. Did you go to college?"

"Yeah, I got my bachelor's degree in business. It seemed like the thing to do at the time. What are you taking classes in?"

"Management and Marketing actually. If I need help, can I pick your brain?"

"Not sure how much help I'll be, it was a while ago, but I'll give it a try."

"I've got midterms coming up and I'm nervous. I haven't taken a test in a long time."

"I can help you study if you want."

"Thanks, I might take you up on that."

The server delivers our food. "Anything else I can get for you?"

Luke glances at me and I shake my head. "I'm good, thanks."

She nods and walks over to the table behind me.

He picks up the ketchup bottle on the end of the table. "Okay if I put some on the edge of the plate?"

"You're a dipper then?"

He hesitates with the bottle open and hovering over the plate and cocks his eyebrow up.

"I mean some people like to squirt the ketchup all over the top of the fries and others, like you, make a puddle and dip the fries in."

"Didn't realize there were categories of fry eaters. Which one are you?"

"Oh, I'm a dipper too."

He shakes his head and pours the ketchup while I take a bite of the lobster roll. It's buttery and rich, just the way I like it. There's more lobster than bread so I get a nice mouthful with every bite.

He takes a bite of his roll and I wait until he's finished chewing. "You like it?"

"It's good." He takes another bite.

His roll disappears in a few bites while I'm still working on most of mine. He moves on to the fries. After eating one, he looks out at the lake and then back to me. "I'm a writer, but I haven't written much since the accident."

A writer? I put my roll down and wipe my mouth with my napkin. "It's understandable. You've suffered a significant loss. It's bound to affect you. What kind of writing do you do? Books? Articles? Instruction manuals?"

Luke cocks his head to the side and lifts an eyebrow. "Instruction manuals?"

"That's a thing, isn't it?"

"I suppose someone has to write them. But no, I write books."

"I don't think I've ever met an author before. What kind do you write?"

"Thrillers mostly. That's why I have the collection of weapons. Wyatt gave me my first one when my first book was published. It became a tradition after that."

"That's really sweet. He must have been so proud of you."

He shrugs.

"Thrillers, huh? Do you write under a pen name?" That internet search I did didn't pull up anything about books. Of course, it didn't show anything at all.

"L.H. Morgan. It's my initials and my middle name—also my mother's maiden name."

"Aw, your mom must appreciate that."

"Yeah, she gets a kick out of telling her friends."

"When it's my turn to pick a book for the club, I'll have to pick one of yours."

He smiled and popped a fry into his mouth. "Barb said the same thing."

"Oh, of course, well maybe we can both suggest one."

He nods and nudges the plate of fries closer to me. "Aren't you going to have any?"

"I don't know. Are you sure you want to spare a few?"

"For you, I can make the sacrifice."

"Well now, I feel flattered. You're willing to share fries with me."

A smirk spreads across his face. "I think I've made it rather clear I'm willing to share more than fries."

My cheeks heat and I glance away before meeting his gaze.

"You're blushing. That's cute."

"A curse of my fair skin." And the image of him and I in my kitchen yesterday which popped in my head.

I pick up a fry and drag it through the ketchup.

"What's the deal with the ex? You seem to have an amicable relationship."

The fry lodges in my throat and I grab my soda to guzzle a drink.

"You okay?"

I nod and hold my napkin in front of my mouth while clearing my throat.

"Not so amicable?"

"No, no, we're good. The divorce was final almost two years ago and we were separated for a couple of years before that. We work hard to make it good for the kids' sake."

"Is that typical for it to take so long?"

"Never been married and divorced?"

"Nope, not even close."

"It's probably a little longer, but we were married so young and we wanted to try everything to make it work if we could. My parents pressured us to give it every effort too. We were better off apart, so we moved forward with the divorce."

"Are you going to finish that?" He points to the rest of my roll.

There's a couple inches left. My stomach is full and a fry feels like it's lodged in my throat somewhere. "No, I've had enough."

"You mind?" Luke's hand hovers over my plate.

"Oh, no, go ahead."

He tosses the piece into his mouth. I pick up the plate and place it on the end of the table.

Ryan would never have dreamed of finishing my meal. He wouldn't even let me take a sip of his soda. Of course, his predilection went beyond food, he didn't like to share any of his things. Perhaps it comes from being an only child. Oli and I grew up sharing pretty much everything.

"Your leg seems much better."

He shrugs. "Physical therapy has helped a lot. It usually only bothers me when I over do it."

"Does that mean with time, it should heal completely?"

"Only time will tell, but the odds are in my favor." He looks out the window.

The waves are choppy today. There's a sailboat crossing in front of one of the many islands inhabiting the lake.

A rattle of dishes interrupts the low hum of conversation filling the restaurant as a server clears a nearby table.

"Did you hope moving here away from Pennsylvania would help with your writer's block?"

"It was more like there was nothing left for me in Philadelphia. I wanted to be there for Joey as much as I can. Someone has to."

"That's admirable, not every uncle would step up and be involved like you are."

"He's my family and he's pretty much all I've got. There's nothing more important to me than that kid."

"I feel the same way about my boys. They're always my priority."

Luke nods. "You all set?"

"Yeah."

He signals the server over and asks for the check. I pull out a twenty for my share but he shakes his head.

"Are you sure?" He said he wasn't working. Do writers receive a regular income? I suppose it depends on whether or not his books are successful. I'll have to search his pen name up when I get home and order a few of his books.

"I asked you, remember?"

"That doesn't mean we can't split the bill."

"It does in my book."

"Okay. Thank you for lunch."

He gives the server cash and tells her to keep the change. I stand and sidle out of the booth. He places a warm hand on my shoulder blade as we walk out of the restaurant together. Heat pulses from the area and spreads over my skin.

Is he going to ask me on another date? Should I ask him? I nibble on my lip as we walk to the car. His hand drops from my back. The spot chills from the loss of his touch.

The scenery blurs out the window as I stare at a water spot on the windshield. Will he kiss me on my doorstep? Or drop me off in the driveway? Should I invite him in? Is that too presumptuous, will he think I mean for sex? It's much too soon for that step. I would like more of his kisses though.

Luke turns onto our road. A range of colored leaves fill the trees from rust, maroon, bright red, sunset yellow, and bright green. They'll fall and cover the yard soon. Every year I promise myself I'll get around to raking them up, yet each time I never do.

He pulls into my driveway and parks the car. The engine is still running so he must not intend to get out of the car.

"Thanks for lunch." I smile and grab the door handle.

"See you."

Okay, no mention of another date either. I thought we had a good time, but perhaps it was just me.

CHAPTER 17

*I*s she kidding? The saleswoman holds the dress by the hanger with a polite smile on her face. The dress is super mini, strapless, and deep purple. Is she pranking me? I glance between her and the dress. Her light brown hair with thin blond highlights flows over her shoulders. Tasteful makeup, not overly done, understates her attractive features. If she's playing a practical joke on me, it doesn't show in her polite but distant expression. "This is the bridesmaid dress Violet chose?"

"Yes, it's a special order she picked out when she and her other attendants were in last month."

Last month? Of course, they all came together to pick out the dress. Violet sent me an email last week instructing me to stop by Dress to Impress to get measured for the bridesmaid dress. Since I already had an appointment today with Franny here to look at dresses for her wedding, I came in a little early to handle my cousin's dress choice.

I'll be tugging the bottom to cover my ass while simultaneously yanking on the top so my boobs don't pop out. A tug of war the dress doesn't appear strong enough to endure.

"Ready to try it on?" She carries it over to one of three dressing areas and pulls back the thick, white, velvety, curtain over the opening. At least no one will be able to see me since the curtain stretches from the floor to a foot below the ceiling.

"Sure." I walk over as she hangs the dress on a hook inside the changing space. It's as wide and deep as a small walk-in closet with a floor-length mirror hanging in the corner. At least I won't be bumping into walls while I cram myself into the dress.

"Do you need any undergarments?"

"An industrial sized corset maybe?"

The polite smile cracks and she laughs. "I don't think you'll need that, but you will need a strapless bra. You're a..." She glances at my chest. "34B?"

Dead on. "You're good."

"It is my job. If I wasn't able to estimate women's sizes quickly, my shop would be in trouble."

"This is your shop?"

She nods and holds out her hand. "Kelly Tanner."

I shake her hand. "Olivia Banner. Any chance there's more to this dress somewhere in back that you forgot to attach?"

"Afraid not. It's not a typical wedding attendant dress choice. I had it in the party dress section, but the bride said it was perfect for her colors and theme."

"I wasn't aware my cousin was planning a night club theme for her wedding."

Kelly places her hand on my arm as she laughs. "I didn't ask, but the wedding dress she chose is similarly styled. She had me shorten the design by several inches. She's your cousin?"

"Do you think I would contemplate wearing this for anything less than family obligation?"

"You do seem different from her other attendants."

I raise my eyebrows and give her a sideways glance. "I hope you mean older and wiser?" I am a few years older than my cousin and her friends, but seriously, I would never have worn a dress like this when I was their age. Of course, I already had twin five-year-old boys.

When Franny, Lucinda, and I went out for our girls' night I wore black jeans with a red blouse. Franny dressed similarly while Lucinda did wear a form fitting blue dress, but it ended just above her knees and only showed a hint of her impressive cleavage. Of course, we didn't go to a nightclub, we ended up stopping at the mall and then having dinner at a restaurant. Hanging out with friends and being able to hear our conversation is much more my speed and idea of a good time than loud music and too much alcohol. Maybe I am old.

"I was leaning towards tasteful and approachable."

It's my turn to laugh. "Okay, let's get this over with before I lose my nerve."

"Let me get you that strapless bra."

She disappears and I step into the dressing area and pick up the sides of the dress to inspect it a little closer. There are see through panels in the waist.

Kelly returns and holds out a tiny strapless bra. "As you can see, your choices are limited for undergarments if you want to ensure they don't show."

"You're not kidding." I drop the dress and take the bra. "Well, this explains Violet's comment about signing up for a gym membership." She had ended her email by mentioning the fitness club in town was running a discount special. A less than subtle dig about my mom body?

"You're beautiful. I don't think you have anything to worry about once you get past the exposure elements of the dress."

A snort escapes me. "Very diplomatic."

A chime sounds in the store and Kelly looks towards the front. The dressing area is at the back of the store on the left. A large circle platform in the middle has mirrors strategically placed around the area. For brides to see and show off their dresses? The other side of the platform has a loveseat and two armchairs for viewing. "I'll greet the customers and be right back."

"Take your time." I close the curtain and sigh before removing my clothes and donning the bra and dress. Studying my reflection in the mirror produces another sigh. My budget won't stretch to cover a gym membership, but I can spring for a set of weights or something.

This dress leaves no secrets. My arms could use toning. Sit-ups and crunches might help my abs. At least my legs look fairly decent—even if they're way too exposed for my comfort level.

"How are you doing, Olivia?" Kelly stands just outside the changing area. The tips of her black pumps are visible beneath the curtain.

"Seriously thinking about that gym membership."

She laughs and I hear someone else say, "Olivia?"

I peek my head out while keeping the curtain closed to cover my body. "Hey Franny."

Franny and Lucinda stand by the circle platform together. She tilts her head to the side and half smiles and half frowns. "Did you start without us?"

"I knew I recognized you from somewhere, but it just didn't click. You work for Franny."

I glance up at Kelly standing on the side and nod.

"She's also one of my bridesmaids."

"And I'm one of my cousin's, remember?"

"Oh, are you trying on the dress? Let us see!" Lucinda claps her hands together.

Squeezing my eyes closed and grimacing I drop the curtain and stand in the entryway.

"Holy smokes!"

I open one eye at a time. Franny and Lucinda are both standing there with their mouths agape.

Franny grins. "Wow, you're really hot."

"Not the adjective that came to mind when I saw it, but thanks."

"You look great. That's your bridesmaid dress?" Lucinda scans me from head to toe. Her wrinkled brow and the perplexity etched on her features is surpassed only by the surprise dripping from her voice.

"Uh huh, it sure is." I smooth the material over my hips hoping to stretch it a little. No dice.

"Why don't we get those measurements taken so you can relax and help Franny find her wedding dress?" Kelly glances over her shoulder. "Franny, I've hung several dresses in the bridal dressing area. Why don't you look and see what strikes your fancy while I finish up with Olivia? I'll only be a couple of minutes."

"Okay." Franny smiles and whirls around to search the first changing area which is easily twice the size of the one I'm standing in.

"Don't try anything on until I can see." I duck back into my spot and step back so Kelly can fit.

Kelly closes the curtain. "Don't worry, this will be quick. You won't miss anything."

She's as good as her word and takes the measurements before stepping out and closing the curtain so I can change. "Just leave everything in there."

I scramble back into my own jeans, T-shirt, and canvas shoes. When I step out, Franny and Lucinda are sorting through the dresses hanging up.

"Are you thinking a princess style dress, or something more fitted?" Lucinda holds out the wide skirt with lace and sequins.

Franny fingers the tiny gold cross on her necklace. "I don't know."

"Then you need to try on assorted styles and see how you like them." I walk over to join them.

"Exactly why I put out an assortment for you to look at and try on. Although, if I might make a suggestion?" Kelly lifts a dress off the hook on the opposite side. "With your coloring and shape, I saw this one and immediately thought of you."

The dress is champagne colored rather than white, strapless, and fitted throughout the bodice and hips. The skirt drapes and widens down to an ankle length.

Lucinda wraps her arm around Franny's shoulders. "Oh, you have to try that one on. It's gorgeous."

"It's not white, is it?" Franny steps closer to the dress.

"No, it's not. If you have your heart set on white, I can keep the style, but change the color."

Franny raises her hand runs a finger along the draped material of the bodice. "I don't have my heart set on it, I just never considered anything but white before."

"With your ivory skin and red hair, I think this color is perfect for you." I step closer. "You have to try this one on."

Franny wrinkles her nose. "My hair is orange."

"Even better."

Kelly tilts her head towards Franny. "Do you want to try it on?"

"I really, really do."

We all smile. Kelly helps Franny while Lucinda and I walk over to the sitting area and sit on the loveseat.

"I'm so nervous and excited. I understand the excitement, but why am I so nervous?"

"Because your baby sister is getting married and you want it to be perfect for her?"

She grabs my hand and squeezes. "Yes, exactly that."

The doorbell chimes and Rebecca, Franny's other bridesmaid, sails inside, scanning the store. She spots us in the back and strides towards us. Her brown hair brushes her jaw as she bends over and drops her large tote sized purse on the floor. "Am I late? The flower delivery was late this morning and I had to get my assistant ready before I could leave."

I shake my head and Lucinda pats the arm of the chair next to her. "Franny is trying on the first dress now."

"Excellent." Rebecca sits and crosses her legs.

I glance at Lucinda. "Is your mother coming?"

"Yes." She looks at her watch. "But I told her one o'clock so we would have a little time for Franny to settle into the process before the storm that is our mother descends."

I pat her on the leg. "You're a good maid of honor and sister."

She tosses a smile at me. "I've been slowly taking over the crucial parts of the planning to ensure it is what Franny wants. Mother has graciously allowed me to assist."

Rebecca glances over at the closed dressing area and back to Lucinda. "We need to schedule an appointment to discuss floral arrangements."

"Absolutely. I'll call you later to set something up." Lucinda folds her hands over her knee. "Oh, this is such fun."

The scrape of the curtain sliding open over the rod sounds and we all swivel our heads in that direction. Kelly sidesteps out of the way and stands to the left. Franny steps out.

Lucinda gasps and jumps up.

My mouth drops open. "Oh Franny, you're a vision."

"Nailed it one, you bitch."

We burst out laughing over Rebecca's remark. Kelly guides Franny onto the platform.

Franny looks down at the dress and over to us. "Do you really think so?"

Lucinda stands with her hands clasped to her chest and tears in her eyes. "You're so beautiful."

"You absolutely do, but what's important is how you feel in the dress." Kelly fluffs the skirt and puts her hands on Franny's shoulders to turn her towards a set of mirrors.

Franny's hand trembles over her lips.

The door chimes and we all glance toward the door. Ms. Elaine Dawson glides in wearing a powder blue pant suit with matching heels and purse. Three strands of pearls circle her neck. Her blonde hair is swept up in a fancy do with a pearl comb on the side.

Lucinda bears a strong resemblance to her mother. She has the same cool elegant beauty, but Lucinda has a warm heart. From what I've seen and heard, her mother's is encased in the center of a giant glacier.

She stops dead and stares at Franny on the platform. Her hand flutters up in the air and then she drops it and strides forward. I could swear there's a tear or two in her eyes.

She stops next to the platform and her gaze travels over Franny. I clench my hands together between my knees. Please say something nice for Franny's sake. Don't ruin this for her.

"Mother, isn't she beautiful?" Lucinda walks over to stand next to her mother. She leans forward and grabs Franny's hand.

"Yes, she does. I think you should wear your hair up, perhaps a French twist. A veil at the crown, and a few tiny flowers threaded in your hair." She tugs at the material on Franny's waist and glances over to Kelly. "This will have to be taken in, of course."

Kelly steps forward. "I'll take measurements and tailor it for Franny if this is the dress she chooses."

"Of course this is the dress." Ms. Dawson pulls the bodice up a bit. "Stand up straight, Francine."

Franny's wobbly smile grows. "Yes, mother."

CHAPTER 18

*S*weat pours down my face. I wipe it off my forehead with the back of my hand before it can drip into my eyes and sting. Sia belts out a pop ballad in my ears as my feet pound down the pavement. I swing right onto my road. Less than a mile left of this morning's run.

Gold, orange, and red leaves on the trees wave in the cool morning air. The sky is a clear blue with a few puffy white clouds. A good start to the day.

A car approaches so I hug the side of the road being careful not to slip in the wet brown leaves coating the sides. It slows as it approaches, so I lift my gaze and search the interior. Luke is behind the wheel.

I haven't heard or seen him since our lunch date last week. He mowed my lawn while I was at work on Sunday. I have yet to supply him with baked goods this week as a thank you. The dress fitting took up all of Monday and studying for midterms lasted most of Tuesday.

He lowers the passenger window as he stops next to me. I jog in place and pull an earbud from my ear and lower the volume on my music.

"Hey Legs." His gaze scans me, lingering on my legs before raising back to meet my gaze.

Okay, not feeling quite so self-conscious anymore in my pink tank and black bike shorts.

The rumble of his voice does funny things to my insides. What is it about body chemistry between two people? A look, the sound of his voice and my engine revs.

His lack of calling or dropping by to ask for a second date has had me second guessing his attraction. Maybe he's just not that in to me.

"Hey yourself. Where are you off to?"

"Halloween emergency. Barb bought Joey a costume weeks ago, but he's been wearing it around the house so much it ripped. So, I'm off to the mall to hopefully find an identical match to avert a major meltdown."

"Aw, that's sweet. You're a good uncle and brother-in-law."

He shrugs. "What are your boys doing for Halloween on Saturday? They're still young enough to go trick-or-treating, right?"

"Definitely. Superheroes still rule in my household. What's Joey's costume?"

"Dragon."

"I bet he's adorable. I want to see pics. Are you going trick-or-treating with them?"

"Wouldn't miss it."

"Dressing up?"

He drapes an arm over the steering wheel. "As in a costume? No. You?"

"It's a tradition. I'm going as Wonder Woman this year."

"That I would like to see."

"Then you'll have to drop by on Saturday before we head out."

Luke glances up into his rearview mirror. Another car approaches. "I better get going. Barb is ready to tear her hair out over the costume catastrophe."

He lifts a hand in a wave before driving away. I continue my run.

Did his silence mean he wasn't going to drop by? *Damn it.* Now I'm going to be wondering about it for the next two days.

~

"Olivia, there's a very handsome man out here asking for you." Lucinda wiggles her eyebrows comically. "The sexy neighbor perhaps?" She takes a few steps closer into the bakery kitchen where Franny and I are. "He's got a smile which could melt icebergs. How could you think he was a serial killer?"

"Um…well, he never smiled much before and I really don't think that's a factual measure of whether or not someone is a serial killer." I walk over to wash my hands at the sink. The food dye I was coloring the frosting with dots my fingers. I shake my head as I scrub my hands. I'm a messy baker.

What is Luke doing here? He didn't mention stopping by this morning when I saw him during my run. Is he here to show me a picture of Joey in his costume?

Lucinda has already disappeared back up front by the time I turn around. Franny grins and walks over. "I want to finally meet this neighbor of yours."

I walk through the archway with her hot on my heels.

It's not Luke. "Oli!"

I dash through the opening in the counters and jump into my brother's waiting arms.

He swings me around and gives me a tight squeeze before dropping me back on my feet. Oli got all the height in the womb and left me with the crumbs. He's six foot one to my five foot five.

"I thought I would surprise you."

"You definitely did. Do Mom and Dad know you're in town?"

"Not yet. I stopped here first."

Lucinda clears her throat behind me. I glance over my shoulder. Her and Franny are standing side by side behind the counter with smiles on their faces.

"Oh…" I turn all the way around and hold his arm in my hands. "Oli this is Franny and her sister, Lucinda. You've heard me talk about them a hundred times or more. Girls, this is my brother, Oliver."

They both say, "hi." Franny waves and Lucinda wiggles her fingers in the air.

"Ladies, it's a pleasure." Oli nods and grins. "You never told me how beautiful they were. I would have stopped by much sooner."

I bump his arm with my shoulder. "Behave, Franny is taken."

His gaze settles on Lucinda. "Are you spoken for too?"

Lucinda props a hand on her hip. "Not anymore."

I shake my head and smile and then look up at Oli. "How long are you in town for? Are you staying with me or Mom and Dad?"

"Not sure and I thought I would crash on your couch this time. We need to catch up and I haven't seen my nephews in a while. How am I going to do my uncle duty and corrupt them if I stay at Mom and Dad's?"

I glance at Franny and Lucinda. "He means it too. He thinks it's his sworn right to teach them things like belching the alphabet and potty humor jokes only boys can possibly find funny."

"It's a written rule in the uncle handbook." Oli stuffs his free hand in the pocket of his trousers. "I also need a chance to check out this new neighbor you told me about. One minute you're telling me you think he's a serial killer and the next you're assuring me he's harmless and mowing your lawn every week for you."

I gnaw on my lip and glance at Franny and Lucinda. They've got identical smirks on their faces. Okay, I won't be receiving any help from them.

"About that..." How do I explain I'm kind of dating that neighbor now?

"Why don't you leave early and go spend some time with your brother?"

I glance at Franny. "Are you sure?"

"Of course. It's after three anyway and Luce is here to help. Go."

"Thanks, Franny." I take off my apron and walk behind the counter to grab my purse. I give her a hug and Lucinda grabs hold of me to hug me too.

She whispers in my ear. "Is he single?"

I laugh and nod as I turn to go.

"Ladies, I hope to see you both again."

I push Oli towards the door before he can pursue Lucinda or the other way around. I love them both, but I'm not sure I want to see them together. Lucinda is in the middle of a divorce from her dirtbag husband and Oli is the love them and leave them type. He's never been serious over a woman.

"Bye," Franny and Lucinda chorus as we walk out the door.

"Where did you park?"

He points up the street. I tilt my head in the opposite direction. "I parked in the lot by the docks this morning. Meet you at my house?"

He nods and kisses me on the cheek. "Drive safe."

"You too. Mom will be there in a little while to get the boys off the bus. She's going to be so happy when she sees you."

We walk in different directions. My steps quicken and I clutch my purse strap in my hands. How can I avoid introducing Luke to my brother?

The last man I introduced Oli to was my ex-husband, and he punched Ryan in the mouth before he even said hello.

Granted, I had just confessed I was pregnant and dropping out of college to him the day before. Oli had been away at college and had hopped on a train to come home immediately.

That was an extraordinary circumstance. Oli was being an over-protective big brother. He takes those seven minutes being born before me very seriously.

CHAPTER 19

"*R*yan's here and he brought a friend." Oli's call up the stairs freezes me in place.

What? Ryan wouldn't have brought a woman over without asking. He hasn't even mentioned he's dating anyone. Who the heck would he bring to go trick-or-treating with the boys?

I pull the safety pin from between my lips and climb to my feet. "There, you're all set kiddo. No more tripping over the hem."

"Thanks Mom." Timmy runs over and hops on his bed to put his mask on.

Tommy is still in the bathroom so I knock on the door as I walk by. "You good in there?"

"Yeah, I'll be out in a minute."

"Okay." I turn to go down the stairs but stop dead.

Oli stands in front of the open door. Ryan and Luke are both on the front steps.

I slap a hand on the wall to stop from falling down the stairs.

Shit!

Now what do I do?

Luke has his hands stuffed in the front pocket of his jeans with his gaze glued on me. Ryan is frowning at Oli who has a grin on his face.

He turns and looks up the stairs at me hovering at the top. "You didn't tell me Ryan finally came out of the closet."

What?

Ryan folds his arms over his chest. "Real cute, Oliver. Going into standup comedy now?"

Oli shrugs. "It's always good to have options."

I roll my eyes.

"Oli, behave."

I rush down the stairs and smile at Luke. "Hi. Sorry, it's a bit chaotic at the moment. The boys are getting ready." I glance at Ryan. "Why don't you go up and see if they need any more help."

Ryan brushes between Oli and I and goes up the stairs.

"Luke this is my brother, Oliver. Oli, this is my neighbor, Luke Hollister."

Luke holds out his hand. Oli glances down at it a moment before shaking it with his own.

He folds his arms across his chest and leans against the doorframe watching us.

I give him a tight smile and flick my gaze inside the house. He simply raises an eyebrow and remains leaning on the door.

I never got around to mentioning Luke or our budding relationship since Oli arrived two days ago. It's been a mad dash between work, dinner with our parents, and the kids' excitement over having their uncle to play with.

"Don't you need to get ready?"

Oli glances down at himself and back up. "Nope."

Sighing, I plaster a smile on my face for Luke. "Did you find the replacement costume for Joey?"

"Yeah, but in a different color. He was okay with it though."

"Joey your son?"

Luke glances over at Oli. "Nephew."

"Barbara must have been relieved."

Luke's gaze returns to me and he nods.

A door slams upstairs and Timmy and Tommy come running down the stairs making enough noise for a group five times their size.

Ryan trails behind them.

"Mom, let's go!" Tommy pushes by me.

"Say hello to our neighbor, Mr. Hollister."

He stops on the threshold and tilts his head back. "Hi."

"Hi. I like your costume."

"Thanks." Tommy runs to Ryan's car.

"Appropriate too."

I tilt my head.

The corner of Luke's mouth kicks up. "The speed? He is the Flash, right?"

Laughing, I wrap an arm around Timmy when he stops and leans against me. "Yes."

Luke glances down at Timmy. "And you're his buddy The Arrow. Very cool."

Timmy nods and then glances up. I raise my eyebrow. He knows his manners, but his shyness often gets in the way.

He looks up and then down. "Thanks."

I pat his back. "Okay, kiddo, go wait in the car with your brother."

He shuffles past Luke on the stairs and then jogs over to the car.

Ryan sidesteps me and then Oli. "We going, or what?"

"I left a bowl of a candy out on my front steps if the boys want to swing by."

"Oh, thanks for reminding me." I step back and grab the bowl full of candy from the kitchen table. "I almost forgot."

I step down on the steps and glance back at Oli still lounging in the doorway. "Did you change your mind about trick-or-treating with your nephews?"

"No."

"Well, then, shouldn't you get in the car?"

He stares at me and then Luke before slowly stepping out and closing the door behind him.

As Oli walks down the walk, Luke leans close and whispers in my ear. "Love the costume, Legs."

He turns and walks off in the opposite direction to his house. I set the candy on the stoop and check to make sure I locked the door before hurrying to the car.

My night is going to be an inquisition between stops. While the boys go to the houses, Oli and probably Ryan are going to pepper me with questions about Luke. I just know it.

At least they won't be trading barbs with one another. Oli has never warmed to Ryan.

The passenger seat is empty so I walk around the front of the car. When I slide into the seat, I glance over my shoulder at Oli sandwiched into the backseat with the boys. "You can sit up front, you know. I'll sit with the boys."

He shakes his head. "We're good. Aren't we boys?" He glances at them and they both nod their heads.

Ryan backs out of my driveway and we start the family visits portion of Halloween. It's been the same route every year since the kids were born. We start at Ryan's parents' house because they're the farthest away and then we work our way back stopping at my parents' house and then finish in town.

Oli and the boys are whispering conspiratorially in the back seat. Every once in a while, one or both of the boys giggle. I can only imagine what they're planning back there. I pray, whatever it is, they don't pull it at Ryan's parents'.

Maria and Paul Banner aren't exactly my biggest fans. They never have been. I guess I can understand a little. How many parents are going to welcome the girl who got knocked up by their son and who they blame for ruining their son's life?

It takes two, but I'm the one who didn't know antibiotics lower the effectiveness of the pill. And they know it.

They're never mean, just distantly polite. They tolerate my presence because of the boys. Thankfully, they've never transferred their blame or dislike to Timmy or Tommy. I can endure the few times a year I see them because they love their grandsons without question.

I don't know why they continue to blame me anyway. Ryan never dropped out of college. He finished on time. I was the one who dropped out. Maybe they don't deem me worthy because of it.

When Ryan told them I planned to be a stay-at-home mom, they said it was too much of a financial burden to place on his young shoulders. We were living with my parents rent free. Yes, Ryan got a part-time job to help with expenses for his senior year, but hardly the financial burden they painted it to be.

My parents were the ones who gave us a sizeable deposit for the house once Ryan graduated and got a full-time job. We never would have been able to afford it otherwise. Once the kids were both in school, I got a part-time job. First it was at a bank and then when Franny opened The Sweet Spot I applied there.

We're divorced, I shouldn't be worrying about pleasing my ex-husband's parents anymore.

Ryan pulls into his parents' driveway. The white colonial house with black shutters is awash in shadowy light form the solar lights lining the brick walkway and the porch lights flanking the hunter green front door.

The kids pile out of the door and race up the driveway. Ryan and Oli climb out and amble behind them. I take a deep breath and close my eyes before unbuckling my seatbelt and opening the car door.

The boys ring the doorbell and the front door opens. They both hold up their jack-o'-lantern buckets and sing out, "trick-or-treat."

"Do my eyes deceive me? Are there superheroes at my door?" Ryan's mom bends over and drops a full-size candy bar in each of their buckets. "One for each of you. Now where are my hugs?"

The boys give her hugs and then do the same to their grandfather who arrives behind her. Ryan steps up and kisses his mom on the cheek. "Hi Mom." He nods at his father over Timmy and Tommy's heads. "Dad."

"Hi Mr. and Mrs. Banner. You remember my brother, Oliver, don't you?" I wave my hand towards my brother standing next to me at the bottom of the stairs. They haven't seen him in at least a year, probably more.

They give us both polite smiles. "Of course, we do." She puts her hand on Tommy's back. "Come in, come in."

We all trudge inside. Ryan's dad stands in front of the stairs bisecting the house. He raises his chin when Oli steps in behind me. "Here for a visit, Oliver?"

"Yes sir. Just a few days." He holds out his hand to shake.

They shake hands and Mr. Banner questions him about work. I sidle off down the hallway to the kitchen where I can hear the kids' voices.

Ryan's mom tucks a rolled-up dollar bill in each of the boys' buckets. "Now this is a little extra for later." She glances up at me hovering in the doorway. "You're not too cold in that outfit, Olivia?"

The costume isn't risqué by any means. It covers more than almost any bathing suit I've ever owned has. My maternity swimsuit would probably hide a little more especially now without my belly full of twins. There's a skirt which ends just above my knees. I have on tights and a full cape too.

"No, I'm fine."

She turns back to Ryan rooting through the fridge. "What are you looking for, honey? Didn't you eat dinner?" She shoots me a look over her shoulder.

Not my responsibility to feed your son anymore.

She glances over at the boys. "Did you have anything to eat?"

"Yes, Oli fed them." The boys stayed with Oli today while I was at work. Ryan didn't argue when I asked if they could instead of going with him today like normal. They'll go home with him tonight.

She stares at me a moment before turning back to the fridge. "Go sit. I'll fix you something."

Ryan walks over and sits at the kitchen table while the boys pet the old hound dog lying in his bed by the mudroom.

His mother has a firm opinion on gender roles. She called once during one of the rare times Ryan was handling bath time for the boys and demanded to know why he was giving them baths and not me.

I wander over to the boys while Ryan devours the sandwich she made for him. Oli and Mr. Banner enter the kitchen. Oli joins me while Ryan's dad sits at the table with his wife and son.

"You good?" Oli hovers over my shoulder.

I nod and toss him a smile.

Ryan stands and his mother carries his empty plate to the sink. "We better head out. There' are still a lot of stops to make."

"You're a good father, but you push yourself too hard." His mother hugs him and rubs his back. He kisses her on top of her head.

"Boys, go give your grandparents hugs and say thank you." Tommy and Timmy run to do my bidding while I walk over to the entryway and wave at Ryan's parents. "Nice to see you."

They give me their polite smiles.

Oli and I reach the car first. He gives me a hug. "You're the best mom, Sis."

"Thanks, Oli." I lean on his shoulder and hug him back. Obviously, I didn't do as good as a job as I thought hiding my feelings in there. Never been one of my strengths.

We all pile back into the car after the boys race out followed more slowly by Ryan.

My parents open the door and step out onto the porch as soon as we arrive. Mom was probably watching out the window waiting for us.

She holds her arms out to the boys and they run over to give her hugs. Even though she babysits for an hour every Wednesday thru Friday, she always acts like she hasn't seen them in forever and wraps her arms around them and rocks them back and forth. Dad rubs the tops of their heads and stuffs a hand full of candy in each of their buckets.

"Laura. Mike." Ryan rests his foot on the bottom step and holds the railing.

Mom gives him a hug. "I haven't seen you in forever. How are you?"

Dad shakes his hand and pats him on the shoulder while Oli kisses and hugs Mom before waltzing inside with the boys.

"I'm good. How are you doing?"

"Oh, the same as always." She turns to me when I bend to give her a quick kiss on the cheek and a one-armed hug. "Hi honey, don't you look festive. You always loved Halloween."

Did I? I suppose so. I like all the holidays.

We visit inside for a few minutes while Mom fusses over everyone and offers drinks, food, and the use of the bathroom before we say our goodbyes.

Once again, we're back in the car and headed back to Granite Cove.

Arriving in the village, Halloween banners flutter from the streetlights lining Main Street. Orange, purple, and green lights are strung on the storefronts. Kids and adults wander the sidewalks dressed in costumes carrying their goodies. The village portion of Granite Cove not only decorates for Halloween, but most of the local businesses have people dressed up in costumes handing out candy too.

Ryan finds an empty parking spot in the lot behind the plaza across the street from the bakery. Air filled giant ghosts, Frankenstein, and spiders fill the small medians in the parking lot. A graveyard with plastic headstones sits on one side of the plaza. The boys hit all the stores handing out candy in the plaza before we walk down the sidewalk to Main Street.

Fanny and Mitch dressed in matching Colonial era costumes have drawn a small crowd in front of The Sweet Spot. I wave enthusiastically from across the street to get her attention. She glances up, waves back, and curtseys. I laugh and point up the street and make a U shape in the air to signal our route. She nods and returns her attention to handing out candy.

A zombie and mummy flank the door of the new candy store which opened last month. Spiders on webbing edge their front window. Tommy and Timmy receive candy and coupons for their buckets.

The boys high five friends they come across as we meander up the street. I spot a familiar face carrying a purple dragon across the street ahead of us. Luke, with Joey fast asleep on his shoulder, strides down the sidewalk with Barbara by his side clutching a Halloween tote in her hands. They turn down the road to the docks.

"That his sister?"

I glance up at Oli over my shoulder. He's staring at the back of

Luke and Barbara as they disappear. They must have parked in the parking lot in front of the docks.

"Sister-in-law. Barbara was married to Luke's brother Wyatt."

"Was?"

"He died before Joey was born."

"That's rough."

"Yes, it is." I look to ensure the boys are where they're supposed to be. They're running towards the next store. "Slow down boys, wait for us."

They slow to a fast walk. Oli and I follow behind them. I glance back to see Ryan conversing with a man and woman I don't recognize. They're probably clients.

"He's only been your neighbor a few months, right?"

I glance up at Oli. "Luke? About six."

"His brother lived here?"

"No, Barbara's parents do. She moved here to be closer to them. Luke followed."

"Huh."

"What's that mean?"

"Nothing, just, huh."

I lean against the pole of a streetlight with my arms folded while the boys chat with a group of friends. Oli rests a shoulder on the pole behind me.

"Luke and the sister-in-law must be close."

"Yup." I know what he's inferring. I've thought the same myself. That doesn't mean I want my paranoid suspicions confirmed by my brother.

"Be careful, Sis."

I push away from the pole as the boys head over to the last store before we cross the street and make our way back. Ryan rejoins us.

I haven't told Oli about my date with Luke or mentioned our hot and heavy make out session. There're some things you don't share with a brother.

What clues do I give out? Because he obviously knows I've gotten more than neighborly with Luke.

I sidle over to Oli while Ryan cajoles the boys into sharing some of their candy with him. "We went on one date."

He folds his arms over his chest. "Okay, are you planning to go out again?"

"I don't know. He hasn't asked."

"He will."

I glance up. "What makes you so sure?"

"Because I'm a guy and a guy with no kids doesn't drop by his neighbor's house for Halloween just to say hi. And he couldn't take his eyes off you."

"Oh." A bubble of pleasure rises inside me.

"But I don't know of any guys that would pack up and move to follow their sister-in-law either—unless they had more than brotherly feelings for her."

The bubble pops.

CHAPTER 20

A thin, white, layer of frost covers the ground. The weather changed seemingly overnight as it's prone to do here in New Hampshire. At least we weren't trudging through a foot of snow on Halloween—which has happened before. Barely November, but it's time to drag out the kids' winter coats, boots, gloves, and hats. Hopefully, they'll still fit at least until after Christmas. If I can wait that long, then the stores will start putting the winter gear on sale to make room for spring lines.

"Mom?" Timmy calls from upstairs. "I don't feel good."

Uh oh. I place my mug of coffee on the counter by the kitchen sink and head upstairs. It can't be an overdose of Halloween candy. I've been judiciously handing those out—unless they found the stash.

Timmy huddles in his bed with the covers wrapped around him and a tired pout on his face. I glance over at the twin bed on the opposite side of the room. Tommy is still fast asleep.

I walk over and put the back of my hand against his forehead. He's hot.

"Come on, bud." I free him from the covers and wrap my arm around him to guide him into my room. If I can separate them early enough, maybe Tommy won't get whatever Timmy has. Wishful thinking most likely, but I have to try. "Climb into my bed. I'll get the thermometer and be right back."

He lays down on my pillow and I cover him up, brushing his hair off his forehead. I grab the thermometer out of the bathroom and confirm his fever.

I lie down behind him and wrap my arms around him. "Is it your tummy?"

He nods.

I kiss him on the back of his head. "Be right back." I jog downstairs to get a bowl in case his tummy launches a full-scale rebellion.

Obviously, he can't go to school. Which means I need to decide what to do about work. I can't ask my mom. She works mornings at the bank. Besides, I would hate to expose her and possibly Dad to something contagious. I really wish Oli was still here, but he left on Sunday to go back to Boston.

Which means I have to call Franny—unless Ryan could pitch in? No, I can't do that. I would expose potentially hundreds of customers to whatever Timmy has.

I return with the bowl and settle back in behind him.

"Mom!"

Uh oh, please don't let Tommy be sick too. I scoot off the bed and hurry to his room. He's sitting up holding his stomach. Tears fill his eyes and he turns white.

I run back to my room, grab the bowl, and rush back to his room. He bends over just as I shove the bowl under his face and empties the contents of his stomach into the bowl. Once he's done, I carry it to the bathroom to dispose of it, clean it, and get a wet washcloth for him.

He's lying down. "Where's Timmy?"

"In my bed. He doesn't feel good either."

"Can I go in there too?"

I nod and help him up. There's no point in trying to separate them now.

When he's snuggled into my bed with his sleeping brother, I kiss him on the head. "I have to call Franny and let her know I can't make it to work today. I'll be back in a few minutes. Call if you or your brother need me."

"Can you call from here?"

"Okay, but I still have to get my phone. I left it downstairs." And I want to get two clean bowls just in case. I stop at the threshold of my room and glance over my shoulder. My poor little angels.

Downstairs, I grab two fresh bowls and stuff the other one in the dishwasher. Then I pick up my phone from where I left it on the counter next to my, now, cold coffee. It's early, but I know Franny is already at the bakery so I dial her number as I walk to the stairs.

"Hi Olivia."

"Hi Franny. I'm so sorry, but the boys are both sick. I'm not going to be able to make it in today."

"Oh no, poor kids, poor you. Can I do anything for you?"

"No, thanks, they've got a stomach bug or the flu. They both have a fever and Tommy has already thrown up. I don't think you want me at the bakery even if I can get Ryan to take a sick day to watch them."

"No, that wouldn't be good. Keep me posted and let me know if there's anything I can do to help."

"Thanks, Franny. I'm really sorry to leave you in the lurch like this."

"Don't worry about it. I'll drag Lucinda downstairs to help. You just concentrate on your sons."

"Okay, thanks. I'll let you know about tomorrow."

"Why don't we already call tomorrow a sick day? You let me know about the weekend, okay?"

"That's probably a good idea. I don't know how contagious they are. Bye Franny."

"Bye. Take care and good luck."

I'm going to need it. Leaning against the doorframe to my bedroom I watch my boys. I glance at the clock on my nightstand. Two hours before the doctor's office opens and an hour until I can call the school to let them know the boys will be absent.

Tommy pats the bed next to him and I walk in and put the bowls on the end of the bed within reach and crawl up the bed to lie between them.

Tommy snuggles up to my side.

~

AN ELBOW JAMS me in the throat and drags me out of sleep. I pry my eyes open and gently lift the little arm off me and back over onto Timmy. A peek at them both confirms they're sleeping soundly. The clock reads seven o'clock in the morning. They've made it through the night without getting sick.

I inch my way down the center of my bed, careful not to disturb them. Their fevers broke yesterday afternoon. Two days of holding the bowls for both of them and cleaning up. I ran out of clean bowls last night and forgot to run the dishwasher again so I ended up emptying a bowl of potpourri I had on my dresser and keeping it on my nightstand just in case. I was too tired to go back downstairs and wash a bowl out once I got the boys to sleep last night.

I shuffle down the stairs and turn on the coffee maker. I glance at the overflowing sink full of dirty dishes. Instead of filling the dishwasher, I search the cabinets until I find a clean coffee mug and lean against the counter with my eyes closed waiting for the coffee to brew.

After I fill the cup, I open the fridge to pour a few drops of milk into the cup and then walk over to the table and collapse into a chair.

Ryan will be here in an hour and a half to pick the boys up. Should I have him stay here with them just to make sure they get rest? I sip at the hot coffee careful not to scald my tongue.

I glance down at the T-shirt and pajama bottoms I've been wearing since yesterday afternoon when I changed again after one of the boys' aim was less than exemplary. I need a shower and another gallon of coffee to make it into work today.

Laying my head down on the table, I close my eyes. I just need a few minutes.

My phone rings and I snap my head up staring at the phone and blinking.

Shit!

It's eight thirty. I fell asleep. Ryan will be here soon and I'm not ready for work.

Ryan's name flashes on the screen. He better not be calling to tell me he's going to be late.

I snap up the phone and slide my thumb across the bottom of the screen to answer. "Hi."

"How are the boys?"

"Their fevers both broke yesterday and they haven't thrown up since yesterday afternoon."

"That's good."

"Yeah, but they're both still sleeping and I think they need the rest."

"That's actually what I was calling about."

"What do you mean?" Did he have the same idea to stay with the boys here today?

"Like you said, they need their rest and I can't afford to get sick and miss work. I think it's best they stay with you this weekend. I'll pick them up next weekend."

My mouth drops open and I press two fingers between my eyes—hard. "Ryan, I have to work today and tomorrow."

"You work part time at a bakery, Olivia. I don't mean to be a dick but I think you depend on the checks I give you for alimony and child support more than what you earn there."

Tears fill my eyes. I slant my jaw side to side and resist the urge to bang my phone on the table.

"I work full time now and that's not the point. I've already missed two days. It's not fair to Franny and I need the money."

"Be reasonable. Call your mother if you insist on going in, but I can't take the risk. I think you should stay home with the boys rather than pawn them off on your mother. Tell them I'll call later to check on them."

He disconnects and I stare at the phone for a moment before dropping it on the table and then letting gravity do the same to my head.

The cool wood smooshes my cheek as tears overflow my eyes and run down the length of my nose.

It's not fair.

I don't pawn my kids off on anyone. My job is important. I make approximately the same working for Franny that I get from Ryan for alimony and child support. I need both to survive. Two days without pay was bad enough. Four days will break my budget for the month.

What am I going to do?

I sniffle and raise my head. I'm due at the bakery in fifteen minutes. I must call her.

Wiping the tears from my face with my hands, I scrub my damp hands on my pajama pants and sniffle again.

My mom works Saturday mornings at the bank anyway, I can't ask her. Dad might be home if he didn't have any plans, but is that fair to them?

I dial Franny's number and gnaw on my bottom lip.

"Hey, how are the boys?"

"They're better. They slept through the night. No more fever."

"That's great, but what's wrong? You sound upset."

"I can't make it into work today Franny. I'm really sorry, but Ryan called and he's not taking care of them this weekend. Doesn't want to get sick." My lip quivers and I squeeze my hand into a fist.

"Don't worry about work, Olivia. Lucinda has been helping and if it gets too busy Mitch will pop in and probably cause a riot of customers to storm the bakery."

Tears course down my cheeks once again and I press my lips together to hold back the sobs wanting to shake free.

"Olivia, are you okay? What can I do to help you?"

I let out a choked sigh. "I'm just exhausted."

"Then go back to bed. Don't spend a single minute worrying over the bakery until Wednesday. I'll call and check in later, okay?"

"Thanks, Franny, I appreciate your understanding."

"Don't give it another thought. Bye."

"Bye."

I disconnect and drop my phone face down on the table. Propping my elbow on the table, I hold my forehead in my hand.

The heat pouring off my head registers just as my stomach rolls and my mouth waters.

Perfect.

I run for the bathroom and pray this stomach bug runs its course quick.

CHAPTER 21

The bed dips beside me, but I can't drum up enough energy to open my eyes to see if it's Timmy or Tommy. "What do you need, sweety?"

"I think it's more along the lines of what you need."

My eyes pop open.

Luke sits on the bed next to me staring down at me. I shoot up and immediately sink back down.

"Easy there." He places a hand on my shoulder and nudges me back to my pillow.

"What are you doing here? Where are the boys?" I glance at the clock to see it's eight o'clock on Sunday morning. Yesterday is a bit of a blur, but I managed to feed and wrangle the kids in between bathroom visits. They had been safely tucked into their beds when I peeked in at them when my stomach woke me at three this morning.

"They're downstairs eating cereal. I noticed your car hasn't left the driveway in a few days so I came to check on you. I tried calling, but I got no answer."

"Boys were sick and they gave it to me. You shouldn't be here. You're going to get sick." My phone is probably dead. I forgot to plug it in last night.

I roll on my side and close my eyes. I can only imagine the disaster I look like or the mess my house is in. I don't care. Much.

"I never get sick."

"Neither do I. You can see how that's worked out."

He chuckles and puts his hand on my forehead. "You're warm."

"No, I'm not, I'm freezing." I snuggle farther under the blankets.

He tucks the blankets around my shoulders. "What can I do for you?"

"Forget you ever saw me like this."

Luke laughs. "What? Adorable and pouty?"

I pry open one eye. "You have rather questionable taste."

He grins. "Are you hungry?"

I yank the blanket over my head. "Please don't mention food to me."

"Okay, how about I keep the boys occupied and check on you from time to time? If you need anything, you can just give me a holler."

I lower the blanket. "You're offering to babysit the boys? You heard me say you're going to get sick, right? You could pass it to Barbara and Joey."

"I'll stay away from them for a few days to be safe."

He should go home, but I don't want him to. I want him to stay and entertain the boys so I can sleep. He rolls the sleeves of his royal blue and black plaid shirt up past his elbows like he's preparing for battle.

Ryan will be pissed. We're supposed to discuss bringing anyone into the boys' lives first. Especially anyone we're dating.

I wouldn't be in this situation if he hadn't bailed on me this weekend because he was afraid to get sick.

"You're thinking pretty hard over there. Care to share your concerns so I can help alleviate them?"

"Do you see my phone anywhere?"

Luke glances at my nightstands and then around the room before walking into the hallway and calling down to the boys, "Do you see your mom's phone anywhere?" He sticks his head in the bathroom and then steps inside. He appears a moment later with my phone in his hand. "Never mind," he calls down the stairs.

Huh, I must have brought it in with me during the night and left it there. He walks into my room and I point to the nightstand behind me. "There's a cord there somewhere. Could you plug it in for me please?"

He walks around my bed and I hear him rustling around for the cord. The phone dings so he must have found it and plugged it in.

"Thanks."

"No problem. What else can I do for you?"

"If you're one hundred percent certain you want to stay and you're willing to accept the consequences, then thank you, I appreciate it."

"I'm sure. Anything I should know about watching the boys?"

"They can be demons disguised as angels—especially after they've been cooped up for days. Tread lightly."

He chuckles. "Got it."

"Seriously, they might test the limits with you to see what they can get away with. Tommy is the one you have to watch out for. Don't let them have too much sugar. They will go insane. It's not a myth."

"Understood. I was a ten-year-old boy once, I think I can handle it."

I drum up a tiny smile. "Okay."

"I'm going to bring you up some water and then I want you to try and sleep. The boys and I will be fine."

"Mm hmm."

When he walks down the stairs, I roll over and pick up my phone to text Ryan.

I'm sick. My neighbor, Luke, is here watching the boys. He's not afraid to get sick. Don't call me to argue because I won't answer.

I hit send and drop my phone behind me on the bed.

If Luke survives today, Ryan and I will need to discuss my budding relationship with my neighbor.

CHAPTER 22

$\mathcal{M}$y living room has been turned into a giant tent, or a series of tents. I'm not exactly sure which. Blankets, cushions, and even beach towels drape over every surface linking the entire room together.

Timmy and Tommy's voices are coming from somewhere under the massive creation. I pause on the stairs and listen.

"They're plotting my demise in our next Nerf battle."

Luke stands in the dining area with his arms resting on the banister. The light blue chambray shirt he's wearing looks soft and inviting. "How are you feeling?"

"Like I'm reentering the land of the living." The shower helped immensely—that and the end to my stomach ejecting all its contents constantly. The black yoga pants, T-shirt, and hoodie I'm wearing won't win any fashion awards, but they're comfortable and all I can manage yet.

"Ready to handle some food? Your friend, Franny, stopped by and dropped off a couple casserole dishes and an enormous number of treats. The kids and I have practiced restraint and saved you some."

She did? I must have slept through her visit. Along with most of the past twenty-four hours. "That was sweet of her."

"Got to meet Barb's celebrity crush too."

"Hmm? Oh, Mitch was with her?"

Luke nods as I walk down the rest of the stairs.

"Listen, I can't thank you enough for watching the boys for me. You're a life saver and you not only survived it, but you built them that colossal fort in there."

"Fortress."

"Excuse me?"

"It's a fortress. They're calling it The Banner Fortress."

"Oh, of course they are." I chuckle and shake my head. "Really, thank you."

I put my hand on his arm and lean up to kiss his cheek.

His gaze drops to my lips. "You can thank me later."

"Oh really? I guess I will."

Luke smiles and pulls out one of the chairs. "Sit, I'll get you something to eat."

"Not too much. I better start light."

"How about one of these awesome muffins she brought over?" He tilts the open box from The Sweet Spot towards me. "I'm adding the bakery to my must go to list."

"Yeah, those are good. You have a list?"

"I do now." He brings one over. "How about a cup of tea? Barb said it's better than coffee when you've got stomach issues."

He talked to Barb about my illness. "Okay."

"Hi Mom." Timmy leans against my arm. "Do you feel better?"

I wrap my arm around his shoulders and kiss the side of his head. "I'm feeling much better."

Tommy plops into the chair across from me. "Does that mean Luke's leaving? We were going to have another Nerf war."

The priorities of a ten-year-old boy. "That's up to Luke. He's already been here helping us out. Speaking of which, both of you need to thank him."

They both turn to Luke in the kitchen. "Thank you."

Luke carries over a cup of tea and sets it in front of me. "It's been a blast, boys." He high fives them both. "We'll still have our rematch. How else will I annihilate you again?"

Tommy grins and jumps up. "Come on Timmy, we have to strategize."

The two disappear around the corner. Luke slides into the chair Tommy just vacated. "Strategize? I suppose you taught them that?"

"Of course, you can't have a proper battle without a strategy."

Separating the top of the muffin, I take a hesitant bite and wait to see if my stomach will tolerate the food.

"So, did Franny and Mitch stay long?"

"No, they stood outside. Mitch introduced himself as he handed over the box. Franny stood on the walk and asked where you were and who I was. When I told her you were sick and upstairs sleeping, she came up the steps intending to check on you, but Mitch stopped her and told her to let you rest. The boys popped their heads out then and said hi as they peered into the box and spotted the bakery boxes. Your friend asked them a few veiled questions about what they had been up to and if I was taking care of them and you properly while she told them the treats she'd brought them."

I wince. "She wasn't too hard on you, was she?"

"No, she was just looking out for you. She wants you to call her when you're feeling better."

"Okay."

"Your parents stopped by this morning."

Oh shit!

I halt with the piece of muffin hanging in midair from my frozen fingers. "My parents were here?"

"I'm surprised you didn't wake up when your mother checked on you."

"She checked on me?"

"Yup, after they introduced themselves and asked who I was, she pushed past me and marched up the stairs while she told your father to check on the boys."

Scrunching my face, I squeeze my eyes shut, and then peek one open. "Do I need to apologize? Did she say something rude?"

My mother is the sweetest woman on the planet—until she gets riled. Thankfully, it doesn't happen often.

Luke chuckles and I open both eyes.

"She was fine. They both were. It had to be disconcerting finding a strange man opening their daughter's door. They insisted on taking the boys home with them, but after the boys vociferously announced their displeasure—they relented. We had been ready to have our first battle and they didn't want to miss out. Your parents stayed and watched them for an hour while I went next door to shower and change."

I'm sure I'll be getting an ear full later and will have a laundry list of questions to answer.

"Anyone else stop by?"

"No, those were the only visitors." Luke gets up and plucks a pastry from the box and takes a bite on his way back to the table.

"I feel like I owe you hazard pay or something."

The corner of his mouth quirks into a smirk. "I'll come up with a detailed list along with the various forms of payment expected for each."

I glance over my mug as I take a sip of tea. "Should I be worried?"

"I think the word you're looking for is anticipation."

It's my turn to smirk. "Confident, aren't you?"

The smirk stretches into a grin. "On this I am."

I swear I can see his eyes heat as his gaze meanders over me. A stirring starts low in my stomach which has nothing to do with illness.

"Is it time?"

I glance over my shoulder. Tommy and Timmy are standing outside the kitchen with their Nerf guns.

Luke rises and laces his fingers together and stretches until they crack. "Bring it on."

Tommy races over and hands him a gun.

"What, none for me?"

Luke grins down at me as Timmy disappears into the living room and returns with a gun for me.

I slide the barrel back with a snap. "Let's do this."

CHAPTER 23

Snow coats the ground and my back deck. We must have gotten at least six inches accumulation last night. I need to drag out the snow shovel and clear the walkway and driveway. Good thing I got up early.

There's a knock at the front door. I glance at my watch, it's only a few minutes past eight o'clock—too early for Ryan to pick up the boys. I set my coffee mug down on the counter and walk to the front door.

Stopping along the way to peek out the window in the dining area, I see Ryan. Is he trying to make up for last week by being early? We've barley spoken all week when he's called to talk to the boys.

His gaze scans me when I open the door. "Hi."

"Hi. You're early. The boys are still getting dressed."

"I thought we could talk."

Oh boy, does that mean he wants to talk about Luke being here last week to watch the boys? It's too much to hope he's going to apologize for bailing on me. It's too early in the morning for this.

"Make it quick because I have shoveling to do." I shut the door behind him. "You want a coffee?" I walk towards the kitchen to grab my mug. I need the caffeine.

"I'll do it."

I stop and look over my shoulder. "You want to make yourself a coffee?"

"No, I mean I'll shovel the snow."

He's going to clear the driveway and walk for me? Well hell, he must feel really guilty over last weekend. Maybe he's not going to argue about Luke after all. Could I get him to shovel the snow off the back deck too? If it's not done and it snows again, it'll just get heavier.

"That's nice of you." I hold up my mug. "Coffee?"

He shakes his head. "How about if the boys and I drive you to work this morning so we can pick you up when you're done?"

"Um...why?"

"I thought it would be nice to have family time tonight."

I lean against the counter and sip my coffee.

"We could go bowling or catch a movie. It's been a while. The kids love bowling."

He's right, it has been a while. We used to make sure we scheduled family time at least once a month so the boys know that even though we're divorced, we're still a family.

"Sure, we can do that. It's a good idea."

"Great. I'll go shovel so you won't be late."

Ryan walks over to the door.

"Wait. Aren't we going to talk about last weekend and the fact that Luke watched the boys without us discussing it beforehand?"

I don't want it to fester and worry about the conversation, I'd rather have it out in the open.

Ryan turns back and plants his hands on his hips. "You did what you had to do because I didn't do my part. I'm sorry. I was a dick for leaving you in the lurch like that."

Am I dreaming? If you question whether you're dreaming while dreaming doesn't that mean you're not dreaming? Sort of like people who are crazy don't think they are?

"Thanks, that means a lot."

He nods and then turns and goes outside. I open my mouth to call him back to tell him where the shovel is but stop. He knows where it is. It's the same place it always was. The same place he used to keep it when he lived here.

⁓

THE SMACK of the bowling ball knocking over a pin echoes through the building. Timmy got the spare. He does a victory dance shaking his hips side to side and swinging his arms in front and then behind him.

After jumping up to high five him, I sit back in one of the chairs in the semi-circle behind the score board. Ryan adds the score and it pops up on the overhead projector.

"Last round boys, then we'll grab something to eat and play another game if you're good." He glances over for confirmation and I nod.

I win by a single point and take a bow. The boys grudgingly congratulate me and we gather our things.

We order a pizza which is quickly devoured. The boys race over to the small arcade dividing the restaurant from the bowling lanes while Ryan and I remain in the booth drinking our sodas.

"This was a good idea, I'm glad you suggested it. The boys are having a blast."

"Me too." Ryan rests his arm on the back of the booth. "How's work at the bakery?"

"Good. Real good, actually. I'm taking on more and more responsibilities and I'm designing a new website for the bakery."

"Didn't know you knew how to do that."

"Neither did I." I smile and shrug. "The course I took gave me all the basics and I've been reading a bunch of articles and watching videos about it. It's fun."

"That could lead to a whole new career for you. I imagine there's a high demand for website designers."

"I don't know about that, I'm just concentrating on the bakery." I take a sip of my soda and glance over to check on the boys playing a game. "What about you? How's work?"

"My boss recommended me for a management position in the home office."

"In Boston?"

"Yeah."

"Wow, that's...that's great. Congratulations."

"I haven't gotten yet. I still have to interview for the spot."

"Still, your boss recommended you, that must carry weight."

"It should."

Ryan might move to Boston. Is that why he wanted to have this family time? Get some in before he moves, and then what? How often will he see the boys?

He leans forward and clasps his hands on the table. "If I get this job, it could mean a lot of opportunities open up for me—for us."

"Us?"

"It's more money for sure, but there's a hell of a lot more growth potential at the home office. If you want to take courses on web design, or whatever, there are tons of colleges in Boston to choose from. Or if you don't, and want to be a stay-at-home mom, you could do that too."

"Ryan, what are you saying?"

"I'm saying I want us to give it another try. You, me, and the boys, together as a family."

I drop back against the cushion of the bench, staring. He gazes back with a hopeful expression on his face. He's serious.

I glance over at the boys and back.

"I know it's a lot to take in. I've been thinking about this all week. We're good together. We were so young before. We can make it work this time."

"Geez, Ryan, you need to slow down. Let me wrap my brain around this. First you tell me you might be moving to Boston, and then you say you want to reconcile?"

"Boston is just a possibility, but I still want to give us a chance either way."

"I don't know what to say." My thoughts scramble. I don't even know what to think. Ryan and I back together?

"The kids would be ecstatic."

My head snaps up. "You haven't said anything to them, have you?!?"

"No, of course not."

"Your parents would be happy too."

Mom would throw a party. She interrogated me about Luke for almost an hour. I'm surprised she didn't demand documentation from him when she found him at the house. I didn't even tell her we went on a date. As far as she knows, he's only a friend and neighbor. She wanted to know how Ryan would feel about a strange man in the house taking care of the boys. Did Luke's presence help to prompt Ryan's renewed interest? Is he jealous? Mom has never accepted the divorce. She's told me she prays every night for us to get back together. If she finds out what Ryan is proposing, I'll never hear the end of it. She won't understand my hesitation. His parents will be horrified.

"Yours won't."

"Why do you say that? Of course they would."

I tilt my head to the side and stare. "Give me a break, Ryan. Your parents have never been fans of our relationship and me especially."

"They've done nothing but welcome you."

"Yes, politely and at a firm distance."

He shrugs. "They're not the overly affectionate people your family is."

I shake my head. "It doesn't matter, that's not the point. You haven't said anything to them, have you?"

"No, not yet."

"Don't."

"Why not?"

"Because you've dropped this on me and I can't even think straight. I need time and I don't want to feel pressured. And I definitely don't want the added worry about you telling your parents hanging over my head."

"Okay."

I rub my forehead. "Ryan, I don't get this. Why now?"

"I told you. My life might be changing and it made me think. I don't want it to happen without you and the boys. I want you to be part of it."

"I can't...I can't think about this right now. Promise not to say anything to the boys, or anyone else we know."

"Okay, when can you think about it?"

"I don't know, but it's not going to be an instant decision. Give me a few days, at least."

"I'm meeting a client Monday morning in Granite Cove. Why don't we go to lunch just the two of us?"

"That's only two days away, I said a few."

"We can talk about it, or not. We can just have lunch as friends if you're not ready to discuss it."

"You're being very accommodating."

"I'm trying here. All I'm asking is you to try too."

Lunch is harmless. At least I'd have some time to think about this and figure out how I feel. "Fine, Monday."

"Great, thank you." He glances up. "Here come the boys. We promised them another game."

"Right." I turn and smile as they slide into the booth and sip at their neglected sodas.

"Are we playing another game?"

"We sure are. Let's see if one of us can defeat your mother."

Tommy raises his hands in the air. "It's going to be me."

"We'll see about that. I have to defend my title of reigning champion."

"You only won by one point, Mom. I don't think that makes you champion."

I give Timmy a mock glare. "Of course it does. It doesn't matter how many points you win by."

The boys scramble up and bounce in place.

"Let's go, champ." Ryan stands and holds out a hand to me.

I place my hand in his and let him help me from the red vinyl booth.

What the hell am I going to do?

CHAPTER 24

The wooden stairs leading to Lucinda's apartment thump beneath my running feet like an off-rhythm bass drum. I dropped the boys off for a playdate on the way here and their friend's mom had been in a chatty mood. She regaled me with comments and descriptions about the latest school fundraiser before segueing into a teary-eyed complaint over her sister-in-law's thoughtless question asking her what she did all day as a stay-at-home mom of school-age kids.

After biting back the suggestion to punch her sister-in-law in the face the next time she asks that question, I rubbed Jill's back and instead told her to smile politely and then list all the jobs she performs each and every day for no pay and little or no appreciation. We made our own list which started with chef, maid, nurse, personal assistant, accountant, teacher, and ended it a few dozen titles later with event organizer, financier, and travel agent. By the time I left, we were both laughing, but then she thanked me for commiserating with her even though I was a working mom.

I've been working since the kids started school, but I still thought of myself as a stay-at-home mom because that's what I was for the first five years of their lives. Except for the hour between the time they get home from school and I get home from work, I'm home for them.

I grip the railing on the landing at the top of the stairs to catch my breath and gain my composure after the sprint from my car parked a couple blocks away. The view of the lake is stunning from up here. Most of the cove is visible. The marina is empty of boats and docks. With winter approaching, everything has been pulled from the water before the lake turns to ice. If I lived up here, I would want to extend this landing into a proper deck so I could place a few chairs to sit and enjoy the view.

The door opens behind me and I glance over my shoulder. Lucinda stands in the open doorway dressed in a royal blue cable-knit sweater and jeans. She smiles and then shivers when a blast of icy wind off the lake blows over both of us.

"What are you doing standing out here? You'll turn into an icicle."

She gives me half a hug before steering me inside her apartment.

"I was admiring your view."

"It's great isn't it? I'm trying to figure out how I can fit a chair there for warmer months."

"Maybe you can convince Franny to make an addition?"

"Ooh, I like the way you think."

"Uh oh, that sounds like trouble. Sign me up." Rebecca strolls over and pushes a glass of wine in my hands and clinks her own glass against it in a toast.

"What are you guys conniving over here?" Franny grins as she stops next to Lucinda and bumps her shoulder with her own.

"Olivia has the wonderful idea you should renovate and put a nice big deck so I can entertain outside."

"I don't think I used quite those words or made it sound so expansive."

Lucinda waves a hand in my direction. "Details."

"Actually, I want to put in outdoor seating for the bakery which might mean moving the stairs to the apartment so it's not entirely out of the question."

Lucinda claps her hands together. "Excellent. When can we start planning?"

Franny shakes her head and laughs. "I need to talk to my accountant first. Besides, you won't be able to enjoy it until spring rolls around."

"True." Lucinda pouts and then turns towards the living area where everyone else sits. "Oh well, let's get this party started."

I've never been in the apartment before. Lucinda has only lived here a couple of months, but she's put her stamp on it. Silver walls and comfy white furniture fill the space. That furniture wouldn't last a day in my house with the boys. An area rug with purple, lavender, and varying shades of gray sits under the couch and chairs. A few abstract paintings decorate the walls.

Barbara waves hello and pats the couch next to her, so I smile at everyone as I weave between the extra chairs set up and plop down next to her.

Lucinda sits in one of the chairs and taps on her glass. "Shall we begin, ladies?"

I scoot forward to the end of the couch cushion. "Do you mind if I ask for your opinions on something first? It's not book-related."

Murmurs of assent drift around the room.

I recant the exchange between Jill and I. There are several nods and shaking heads. "Here's the thing, as a former stay-at-home mother I confess to having one or two unkind thoughts of working mothers when they made a comment or flat out asked what I did all day. I interpreted it as judgment against me and basically calling me spoiled and lazy—two things I have never considered myself. Then as I'm mulling over her comment referring to me as a working mother, I find myself thinking she gets to stay at home all day, getting her household in order while I'm at a job and I have to get all my household responsibilities done in the early morning or late at night." I slouch back against the couch and throw up my hands. "What the hell is wrong with me? Am I total bitch?"

Denials fill the room.

"It's human nature." Rebecca crosses her legs. "We want what we don't have. And unfortunately, as women, we have a nasty tendency to compare ourselves to other women and find us lacking in some way. You're not a bitch, Olivia. I, on the other hand, am and I'm proud of it." She raises her glass high amidst the laughter circulating the room.

"As a working mother of a toddler, I feel tremendous guilt whenever I miss out on Joey accomplishing a milestone when I'm not there to witness it." Barbara frowns and glances around the room. "I have to work, but even if I didn't, I don't think I would choose not to. I feel guilty over that too."

"Our mother stayed home, but she didn't volunteer at school or anything." Lucinda takes a drink of her wine. "I think I can speak for both Franny and I and say that it would have been nice if she left for a job and focused on something besides us once in a while."

Franny nods and laughs along with the rest of us.

"I'm not a mother, but I think as women we need to stop competing against one another and start supporting and lifting one another up." Monica lifts her glass. "I propose a toast. Instead of judging others and ourselves, we celebrate the fact that we're all doing our best and we're one hell of a group of kick ass women."

"Here, here!"

"Hallelujah!"

"Damn straight!"

Lucinda claps her hands. "Okay, what did you all think of the book?"

She chose a compilation of couples' first meetings as the book of the month. The stories ranged from sweet to awful, and some were hilarious. We chat about the book and the individual stories as we sample the treats from the bakery Lucinda has spread out on her glass coffee table.

"All right, we've discussed the book. I want to hear all of your first dates." Lucinda sits back and crosses her legs. "I'll even go first."

I place my wine glass down and lean forward with my arms folded over my legs.

"I met my soon to be ex-husband in college at a sorority party. He asked me for my number and because he was charming and handsome, I gave it to him. Obviously, a mistake on my part. Oh, what I wouldn't give to go back and tell him no or skip the party all together."

Lucinda turns to Franny on her left. "Your turn, although I already know the answer."

Franny sighs. "Mitch and I met on the beach when we were kids. We were inseparable every summer when his parents returned to Granite Cove."

After a round of "aw" circles the room, Franny looks at Rebecca.

"I'm single. So…" Rebecca looks over to Sally on my right. "Next."

"You may be single now, but what about a first meeting for your most recent relationship?"

Rebecca glances at Lucinda and frowns. A blush steals over her cheeks.

"Now we really want to know." Monica laughs and grabs a cookie from the platter.

After the laughter dies down, Rebecca taps her high heeled shoe against the bottom of her foot as it dangles in the air and stares at the floor. "It was a one-night stand involving too much alcohol and poor decision-making skills. I'm not proud of the lapse in judgment and prefer to forget it ever happened."

"Moving on to me then." Sally closes her eyes and smiles. "I met my Herbert on a blind date. My cousin set us up. He brought me flowers and took me to dinner. We talked for hours. He called the very next day and we were married within a year."

I reach over and pat her hand when her eyes get misty. "I'm afraid mine isn't very interesting. My ex-husband and I met in a Philosophy class my freshman year of college." I glance to Barbara. "Your turn."

She giggles. "I met Wyatt on a date with his brother, Luke."

Say what now?

Barbara glances at me and winces. "Luke and I were at a restaurant having dinner. Wyatt walked up to our table and ended up joining us. We couldn't take our eyes off of one another. That was it, love at first sight."

Poor Luke. That must have been awful having his brother steal his girl. A painful hitch catches in my chest. The likelihood of Luke carrying a torch for Barbara just jumped into the most likely category. He'd dated her so obviously he'd been attracted to her. He followed her here. Was he hoping to get another chance with her?

Was he killing time with me while he waited for her to get over Wyatt?

Monica and Tina both talk about their firsts, but I don't hear them.

Oli warned me something was going on with Luke and Barbara. My own instincts had nudged me. Here was undeniable proof. Why didn't I listen?

At least I found out before my heart got involved. One date and a make out session aren't enough to fall in love over. We were just having fun. So what if he took care of me when I was sick? He's a caregiver type of guy.

I stand and walk over to the window facing the lake. The room and my face reflect back. I look past both to the darkness of the lake.

A tightness pulls at my skin.

I may not have fallen head over heels, but I had passed the deep like stage and hurdled right into the raging attraction stage.

Damn it!

What was wrong with me that guys always chose to love someone else?

Tears fill my eyes. I swallow hard and press my tongue against the edge of my teeth.

One of the many reasons Ryan's mother never deemed me good enough for him was because she adored his high school girlfriend and hoped they would reconcile. She even called her his soul mate in front of me while we were married.

I thought they might get back together after we separated. I know he's still in touch with her because their families are close. Had he tried, but she'd already moved on? Was he asking me to give us another chance because he hadn't found anyone else?

Should I do the same?

"Hey, everything okay?"

Franny appears at my shoulder.

"Yeah, it's just been a long week—month—year."

"That doesn't sound good, it's only Monday. What's up?"

I force a chuckle and rub my forehead. Glancing over, I see everyone else occupied in conversation. "Ryan dropped the bombshell he wants to give our relationship another chance."

"Wow!"

"Yeah, I told him I'd think about it."

"Really?"

I turn and prop my shoulder against the wall. "What does that mean?"

"It means you didn't say no outright so there's a possibility. I thought you said you were better as friends?"

"I didn't know what to say. He shocked the hell out of me."

"I bet."

"It's not like it's a crazy idea. I mean he is the father of my children."

"So, you're thinking about it for the kids' sake?"

I shrug a shoulder. "Maybe—I don't know. We were supposed to have lunch and discuss it, but he had to go to Boston for a meeting instead."

"What about your neighbor? Aren't you dating him?"

"You mean Luke, who dated Barbara and never said a word? The man who followed her to another state when she moved? Who probably is just waiting for his chance at her again?"

Franny opens her mouth and then closes it. "I was surprised when she said she dated him."

"Me too."

"It doesn't mean he's been pining for her all these years though. I'm the queen of jumping to conclusions. Trust me on this. Ask him."

"What? Just come out and ask him if he's in love with her?"

Franny lifts her shoulders. "What's the worst that can happen?"

I snort and roll my eyes. "Oh, I'm sure plenty of terrible things can happen. I don't think we're at the point of asking questions like that."

"When is the right time to ask if he's in love with someone else? When you're already in love with him?"

I wince.

"You're not, are you?"

I shake my head and look back towards the window.

Franny leans closer to me. "Olivia?"

Glancing back, I wrap my arms around my waist. "I have feelings for him. I really didn't enjoy hearing they dated."

"Then you need to talk to him before it goes any further. As for Ryan, I suggest you take it slow. You just said you have feelings for Luke. Don't make any hasty decisions."

"What are you two whispering about?" Sally approaches us with a frown.

Franny smiles. "Are you leaving already, Sally?"

"Yes, I can't stay up late anymore. Those days are behind me."

"I'll walk you out."

Franny glances over. "You're leaving?"

"Yeah, I'm tired. Will you give my goodbyes?"

"Sure."

Lucinda walks over as Sally and I turn to the door. "Wait! We have to decide who's hosting next month and what book we need to read."

Barbara holds up her hand. "If no one objects, I'd like to volunteer."

Lucinda glances around the room and when no one else chimes in she grins. "I think it's all yours. Have you decided on a book?"

"I sure have. *Dark Demons* by L.H. Morgan. He happens to be my brother-in-law." She stares at me.

I smile and look away right into Franny's wide-eyed stare. Yup, all sorts of complications cropping up.

Was Barbara wondering if I knew Luke is a writer? Or maybe she's warning me away and making it clear he's hers.

"Good night everyone." I open the door for Sally and follow her out on to the landing. My head pounds. Franny is right. I need to think things through and not make any decisions yet.

CHAPTER 25

"*H*ey, need help?"

The back of my head hits the ceiling of my car and I wince. Luckily, it's covered in a soft material so I'm not likely to do any damage. I push the green tote of groceries onto the back seat and reverse myself out of the car with as much dignity as I can muster, which probably resembles a lurching goat rather than the graceful move I intended.

Luke stands next to the grocery cart holding the last of my bags.

"Thanks." I snatch it from him and practically toss it in the car. It falls on its side and a box of tampons tumbles onto the floor. *Of course.* I grimace and slam the door shut.

No solutions have miraculously popped into my brain since book club last night. I tossed and turned most of the night. Luke and Barbara are only one of many problems swimming around in my head.

It's not like we're even a couple, let alone an exclusive relationship. I haven't talked to him in a week.

"Getting ready for Thanksgiving?" He nods towards the groceries in the back of my car.

"Um, yeah, kind of. I'm making a couple of pies, blueberry and apple. My mom hosts the dinner. How about you?"

"Barb invited me over to her parents' house."

Of course she did, it makes perfect sense. They are family. It doesn't mean either one is necessarily pining away for the other.

"That's good." I lean against the side of my car and fold my arms across my waist. "Are you grocery shopping?"

He glances over his shoulder at the store. The large glass front of the entrance has a Thanksgiving scene painted on it complete with turkeys and pilgrims. All the cashiers and deli workers are wearing turkey hats to work too. "Just wanted to grab a few things. I need to stock up on mac and cheese and juice boxes for Joey. I'm watching him while Barb works later."

I smile. "I'm sure he's looking forward to hanging out with his uncle."

He shrugs. "He's a great kid."

"Barbara is lucky to have such a helpful brother-in-law."

Luke looks around the parking lot. "I didn't think the store would be so busy in the middle of the day."

Okay, he's not going to respond to that conversation topic, apparently. "It's not usually, but it's the holiday season and the weather report called for snow, so everyone panics and stocks up on the essentials."

He glances up at the sky and I follow his gaze. It's gray and overcast. There is a chill to the air. We'll probably get a few inches by morning.

"I might get a chance to use the new snowblower I bought."

"Is it going to replace your love for your lawnmower for the season? Have you been having withdrawal?"

He smirks and drags his gaze back down to mine. "I have been itching to test it out. Barb's dad has someone plow his driveway for him and doesn't understand why I don't do the same. Of course, he hires a landscape service to take care of his lawn too. He doesn't get the draw of a good machine."

"We had book club last night. Barbara is hosting next month and chose one of your books. I'm looking forward to reading it."

"Yeah, she told me she was going to do that." He stuffs his hands in the front pockets of his jeans.

"She also mentioned you and she dated before her and Wyatt."

He stares a moment before looking away. A truck pulls into an empty spot two spaces down from my car. "It was one date and she left with Wyatt."

"That must have been awkward."

He lifts one shoulder. "It is what it is."

What does that mean?

Here goes nothing. "Are you in love with her?"

His eyes narrow. "Are you seriously asking me if I'm pining after my brother's wife?"

"Yes, I suppose I am. It might be none of my business, but we have been heavily flirting with each other and I would like to know if your heart already belongs to someone else. I'm not looking to be someone's stand in or second choice."

"Barb is my brother's wife, that's it."

"Widow."

"Excuse me?"

"You keep referring to her as his wife, but she's his widow. Are you calling her that because you're trying to remind yourself she's off limits?"

"This is ridiculous." He put his hands on the handle of the cart.

"Is it? Why? Would you still say it's ridiculous if Barbara was interested in you romantically?"

Luke rears his head back and then scans the parking lot. "Did she say something to you?"

Wow! Was that hope? Why else would he be wondering if she said something to indicate interest?

"I guess that's my answer, isn't it?"

"What the hell does that mean?"

"It means you do have feelings for her and I'm wasting my time." I push off my car and walk around the back and over to the driver's side door. "Look, I have no idea what Barbara's feelings are. I would suggest you be honest with her concerning yours though."

"You have no clue what you're talking about."

"Maybe not. Maybe I'm paranoid. Maybe I have an overactive imagination. Or maybe, you're the one not being honest about your feelings. Something you should think on."

I open the door and rest my arm along the top. "You didn't deny anything, Luke. Denial would have been your first reaction if there wasn't any truth behind my suspicions."

The cart rattles and shakes as he spins it around to face me.

"Ask yourself why you're so angry right now."

He slices his gaze over to mine. "You know, you're acting awfully self-righteous about my feelings and motives for someone who has spending a heck of a lot of time with her ex lately. What about your feelings for him? You don't see me demanding an explanation."

"Maybe you should. If you had asked, I would have answered honestly. Ryan wants to reconcile. I told him I would consider the possibility."

"So that's what this is really about. You want excuses to take him back. Don't dump shit on me to manufacture reasons. I'm not standing in your way at all. Don't use our nonexistent relationship as an excuse."

He pushes the cart out from between my car and the next.

"No, that's not what this is about, but you go ahead and avoid the tough questions. Run away."

He doesn't stop. I climb into the car and slam the door. My hands shake as I grab the keys and stuff them into the ignition.

He wouldn't have been angry if he didn't have feelings for her, right? He wouldn't have attacked me over Ryan if he wasn't trying to deflect attention to my feelings, not his. And if he really gave a damn about me possibly getting back together with Ryan, he would have said something, wouldn't he?

I drop my head to the steering wheel. Nonexistent relationship?

The answers are staring me in the face. Luke has feelings for Barbara even if he's not ready to admit them and he's right, our nonexistent relationship has no bearing on my decision to give Ryan another chance.

I start the car and back out of the parking space. I should have followed my initial instincts and stayed the hell away from my neighbor.

The light turns red at the parking lot exit. I ease to a top and prop an elbow against the window and lean my head on my fist. If we're not in a relationship, why does my chest ache and why do I feel like bawling?

A horn beeps behind me. The light turned green. I wave a hand to apologize as I pull out onto the street.

Obviously, my feelings were a lot more invested than his. How did I let that happen? I thought I was being smart and cautious.

Oli warned me. Heck, I saw the signs and ignored them.

Lesson learned. Follow your instincts. And stay the hell away from your neighbor—too many complications.

A tear slides down my cheek and I swipe it away. There's nothing to cry over. It's best I found out now rather than after I lost my head and slept with him or something. I'd have a hard time blissfully living next to him if we had slept together.

I sniffle and reach over to open the glove box and grab a napkin to blow my nose with.

Damn it! Tears course down my face and my nose drips like a leaky faucet.

I turn onto my street and glance at the clock on the dashboard. I should have just enough time to unload and put away the groceries and clean myself up before the kids get home from school.

Maybe a few minutes to wallow in misery first. I park, shut off the car, and wrap my arms around the steering wheel. It's better to get all the tears out now rather than being caught by surprise later trying to bottle them up.

CHAPTER 26

"This is the best Thanksgiving we've had in a long time. Ryan, I'm so glad you joined us."

Mom smiles at Ryan and I swear there are tears in her eyes. She invites him every year, but this is the first time since the separation he accepted. Timmy and Tommy both cheered when Ryan announced it over the weekend. I wish he had talked to me about it first.

"Me too. Holidays are meant to be spent with family." He looks at me and smiles.

I smile in return and glance up the table to my beaming mother. Dad is busy filling his plate with more turkey. The boys are shoveling the mound of mashed potatoes on their plates into their mouths. At the opposite end of the table, Oli leans back in his chair with his hands folded over his abdomen staring at me. One blonde eyebrow lifts as if to say wtf.

I haven't told him about Ryan or Luke. He arrived late last night at my parents' house. We've only talked briefly on the phone lately and it never seemed to be the right time. He's been relatively silent since Ryan, the boys, and I arrived together. I'm sure he'll give me an earful when he gets me alone.

One reason to be thankful we must leave early to go to Ryan's parent's house. Two Thanksgiving meals in one day. I'll be in a food coma by nightfall.

"Can I have another biscuit?" Tommy reaches across my plate for the basket of biscuits on the other side of me.

"May I and you don't reach across someone's plate." I squeeze his hand and place it down next to his own plate. "Now, how do you ask?"

He heaves a sigh. "May I have another biscuit?"

"Please."

The next sigh gets louder. "Please."

I hand him the basket. He grabs a biscuit.

"You shouldn't let him fill up on bread." Mom frowns and points to the green bean casserole with her fork. "Have some vegetables."

Tommy wrinkles his nose and peeks up at me. I can't blame him. There are no green beans on my plate either. I can hardly be hypocritical and insist he eat them. "How about some salad?"

"There's no ranch dressing."

"I'll get some from the fridge." I stand and push my chair back.

"There should be a bottle in the cabinet if there isn't one in the refrigerator." Mom waves her fork in the direction of the kitchen behind her.

"I'll find it."

I walk around the table to the open doorway into the kitchen. My parents have lived in this ranch house since before Oli and I were born. I asked them if they ever considered moving. Mom said there were too many memories. Dad had shrugged and asked why would he do that?

There isn't an open bottle in the fridge, so I search the lazy susan next to the stove. Mom hasn't rearranged the cabinets ever as far as I know. Everything is located in the same place as when I was a kid.

"Need help?"

I glance over my shoulder as I bend over and open the cabinet. Oli stands behind me with his arms folded over his chest.

"I think I can handle it." I turn back and spot a bottle of ranch dressing and pick it up. He's still standing there when I close the cabinet and turn around. "What?"

"You know what."

I glance behind him to everyone in the dining room. Yes, I know what, but I won't have this conversation with everyone in ear shot. "Not now." I step around him.

Oli puts his hand on my arm. "Just tell me you know what you're doing."

"Not a clue." I walk into the dining room and place the dressing next to Tommy. Ryan helps him open the bottle while I sit.

I can sense Oli's gaze on me after he takes his own seat, but I stare at my plate and move the now cold food around with my fork. Conversations continue without me as everyone finishes eating.

What does he expect me to say? I couldn't very well tell Ryan not to come when he announced it in front of the kids. If I had ever told my mother not to invite him, she would have been appalled and lectured me on manners and family. It's not like I mind him coming. I just don't want the kids to get the wrong idea. Now I have to talk to Ryan about not getting the kids' hopes up. If there's any chance of a reconciliation, we need to figure it out in private before involving the kids. If he can't do that, then there's no chance I'll even consider it.

Having that conversation over Thanksgiving dinner though is not an option.

"What do you think, Olivia?"

Mom stares expectantly across the table.

Crap! What did I miss? "I'm sorry, what?"

"Ryan said you need to leave soon to go to his parents' house. Should we have dessert right away?"

Normally, the men go watch the football game while mom and I clean up the kitchen and then we have dessert. "I think we're going to skip dessert this year. We need to get going. I'll help you clean up first, though. Boys, bring the dishes into the kitchen."

Mom frowns but stands and picks up her dish. Timmy and Tommy both shove their chairs back and grab their plates. I stand and pick up my plate and reach for Oli's. He grabs the edge and holds on.

He's glaring at me. "You're going to his parents' house?"

I glance over. Ryan carries his plate into the kitchen. Dad is gone.

I'm sure he's already lowering himself into his recliner in the living room. The boys are standing at the sink with my mom. "Yes."

"What is going on?"

"Not now, Oli."

"Then, when?"

"Later. We'll talk later."

Oli lets go of his plate and I carry the dishes into the kitchen. He follows behind me with the turkey platter and a bowl of mashed potatoes. The boys bring in the remainder of the food while I pack up the leftovers and Mom washes the dishes. Oli and Ryan walk towards the living room when Mom waves them away with a dish towel.

I've given up arguing why Oli gets to go relax instead of helping clean up. Women cook and clean while the men eat and unwind in my mother's house. Not in mine. If I cook, then the men can clean up. Ryan would always grumble a bit, but he helped with the dinner dishes. Unless his mother or my mother came for dinner, they would shoo him away. So, of course, that meant I would have to clean up with them while the men disappeared to watch TV.

"Now that's a picture."

Mom leans forward to peer into the living room. Timmy and Tommy are on either side of Ryan sitting on the couch. Two blond bookends flanking his brown head. I've seen the same picture many times over the years, it always fills me with love. For my boys, of course, but Ryan too. We've been through a lot together.

I dry the plate she hands me. She's never been subtle about wanting Ryan and I to get back together. Kids should have both parents together, no matter what. If Ryan and I don't reconcile, she will blame me.

Ryan leans against the opening into the kitchen. "We should get going."

"Go, I can finish these."

"Thanks, Mom." I kiss her cheek. "And thanks for dinner. It was wonderful, as always."

She smiles. Ryan walks over to kiss her cheek. "I second that."

I dry my hands and go into the living room. "Boys, say your goodbyes, we have to go." They scramble up and give out hugs before racing over to the door and putting on their coats. I hug my dad and Oli. "Happy Thanksgiving."

"See you tomorrow." Oli follows me to the front door.

I nod while donning my coat. It's his less than subtle way of telling me we'll be having a long talk tomorrow. I still have to work. Oli is watching the boys tomorrow. Does he plan to grill me over dinner? No, not in front of the boys. He'll wait until we're alone. I just have to worry about what to tell him. He won't like hearing any of it, and he certainly won't like that I'm even considering a reconciliation.

The boys chatter with Ryan and each other on the way to their other grandparents' house while I lean my head against the window and watch the scenery blur by.

I made double the number of pies this year. One set I left at my parents' house and the other is in the back of the car for Ryan's parents'. When we were married, we suggested alternating Thanksgiving dinner. One year we would have it at my parents' house and dessert at theirs, and the next year the opposite. Neither of our families went for it. So we ended up having two dinners every year. When we moved into the house, I hosted dinner one year, but it was a disaster. Not only did anyone barely speak, but I burned the turkey on the outside while the inside was raw. The bottom of the biscuits were charred black. The mashed potatoes were a lumpy mess. I decided enduring two dinners was the better option. Then when we divorced, the boys alternated. I always miss having them with me when they're with Ryan. I wouldn't have to endure holidays without them if I say yes.

We pull into their driveway and Ryan turns to me. "Ready?"

"Yup." I climb out of the car and walk to the back to grab the pies. Ryan takes them from me while the boys run to the front door. They disappear inside when his mother opens the door.

"I've held dinner as long as I can. We need to sit now."

I pull my phone out of my pocket to check the time. We're not late.

She ushers us into the dining room after we hang our coats in the entry closet.

"Boys, go wash your hands. Ryan, pour the wine. Paul, carve the turkey."

Everyone jumps to do her bidding. "What can I do to help?"

She gives me a tight smile. "Just take a seat."

What has Ryan told her? When he suggested we do the two dinners again this year, he said his mother had lamented over not seeing the boys for Thanksgiving Day this year and couldn't we go back to tradition and make her happy. I, of course, gave in. Perhaps what she had wanted was for the boys to come alone and for me to stay at my parents' house.

I could be reading too much into the tight smile, though. There's a lot of baggage between us. Ryan always said I worried too much and attributed bad feelings when none existed whenever I broached the subject of his parents, and his mother especially, not liking me.

The meal begins with grace and then pleasantries over what the kids have been up to and what they want for Christmas.

"Surely you're going to eat more than that?" She gazes at my plate and then the boys'. "Timothy, Thomas, try the sweet potato casserole and take some more stuffing."

"I'm not very hungry." Tommy peels apart a roll over his plate. Timmy takes a scoop of the casserole and puts it on his plate.

She frowns and smooths the napkin in her lap.

"Alice is home visiting her parents for the holiday. I invited them all over for dessert later."

I glance between Ryan and his mother. She's smiling at him while he's pouring gravy over his mashed potatoes. Alice, as in his girlfriend before me? The girlfriend his mother has referred to as his soul mate more than once in my presence?

This should be fun—not.

The last I heard, she was engaged, much to his mother's disappointment. That was a few years ago. Ryan's parents are still good friends with hers and socialize on a regular basis. They've never come over for Thanksgiving as far as I know, though.

"She's single now. Joyce hinted Alice might move back to New Hampshire permanently."

I sip my wine and resist the urge to guzzle it down. Her match-making efforts between Ryan and Alice are less than subtle. Why doesn't she simply tell him to ask her out on a date, or skip the dating part altogether and propose?

"You should spend some time together this weekend."

Ryan's eyebrows dip down over his eyes. He glances over to his mother. "I'm busy this weekend."

"Doing what?"

"The boys and I have plans. We're checking out the new indoor go-cart track in Manchester."

"Then the next day."

"Nope, have plans then too. Olivia and I are taking the boys to pick out a Christmas tree. It's tradition."

I blink. It *was* tradition—when we were married. The boys and I have picked out our own tree the past couple of years. I can feel the weight of her stare.

"I want a fat one this year." I glance at Tommy and back to Ryan.

We need to have another conversation about ground rules and soon.

"You can pick out the fattest tree on the lot, buddy." Ryan grins and cuts another piece of turkey.

"We have to make sure it's not too tall. Last year we couldn't put the star on top because the tree was too tall. The top bent over and mom clipped it. It looked weird and there was nowhere to put the star."

I wince as Ryan laughs and smiles at Timmy. "Don't worry, we'll find the perfect tree."

Should I point out there is no such thing as perfection? No, there's no point dampening the mood. It looks like we'll be shopping for a tree together this year unless I want to be the bad guy and tell Ryan he can't go with us.

Once we finish dinner, I clear the table with the help of the boys while Ryan and his dad disappear into the den. His mother tells the boys to go play.

I walk over to the dishwasher.

"I'll do that. I like it done a certain way."

I hold up hands and step back. "Would you like me to package up the leftovers?"

"There are plastic containers in that drawer there. I'll put them away in the refrigerator when you're done."

"Okay."

Silence reigns throughout the kitchen while she puts the dishes in the dishwasher and I handle the leftovers. I should make more of an effort at conversation, but nothing comes to mind. I suppose I could bring up the boys' holiday recital at school. I'm sure Ryan has forgotten to mention it.

"You can put the dessert plates on the table along with the pies I made."

She points to the counter where a stack of plates and two pie containers rest. I glance around the kitchen until I spot the pies I made on the counter by the back door. She'll probably toss them in the garbage in the cabinet underneath that counter. I should save her the trouble and do it myself. What would she do then? She'd probably do nothing but turn away. I've never seen her lose her temper. It might be easier if she would explode and yell instead of the frosty indifference she projects around me.

Ruin one Thanksgiving dinner and you're labeled for life. It doesn't matter I work for a phenomenal bakery and can bake scrumptious pies.

Sighing, I carry the plates into the dining room and come back for her pies.

What dire emergency can I come up with as an excuse to leave before her guests arrive? I pick up one container and set it down.

"You're never going to accept me, are you?"

Her back straightens and her hands freeze in place holding a plate over the sink. She doesn't turn around. "I don't know what you're talking about."

"Yes, you do."

"This is not the time for your theatrics."

"What theatrics? I asked a simple question." Okay, perhaps it's not so simple, but one question is not theatrics. My hand trembles. I sag against the counter.

She raises her head and turns around. Her gaze travels over me and she lifts her chin. I stand up straight and grip the edge of the counter behind my back.

She clasps her hands in front of her.

"Nothing is ever enough for you. I have done nothing but welcome you into my home and still you complain...on Thanksgiving no less. Ryan married you. Got a job to support you. Moved into your parents' house for you. Worked a full-time job and had to come home and care for the kids. None of it was ever enough. You always demand more. Then you divorce him and you still make demands on him."

My fingers press underneath the edge of the counter. A tremor rattles my body. I take a deep breath and slowly release it and open my mouth to defend myself.

A smile teases my lips. I close my mouth and the smile turns into a grin as laughter bubbles up from the pit of my stomach.

"What is so amusing?"

I choke back the chuckles and clear my throat. "Thank you for your honesty." I walk over and give her a hug. She stiffens. It's a bit like embracing a telephone pole. I drop my arms and walk over to pick up the pie and bring it into the dining room.

Nothing I say or do will ever change her mind. I've wasted so much time over the years trying to please her and make her like me— always questioning myself. Am I good enough?

No more. I'm done trying to make her accept me. And I'm done always questioning if I'm a good person. Because I am, damn it.

CHAPTER 27

"*T*he kids are occupied for at least an hour. Start talking."

I dry my hands on the dishtowel and lean with my back against the sink. "Yes, let's talk about the kids and how you spoil them."

Oli shrugs and straddles the chair resting his arms along the back. "It's an uncle's prerogative."

"Remember that when you have kids and I buy them a video game system without discussing it with you first."

"First, it was a Black Friday deal too good to pass up and I can't wait until Christmas to give it to them. Second, you know I have no intention of having kids so I don't have to worry about future retribution from you."

"You never could wait to give out presents when you bought them."

"Part of the reason I usually wait until the last minute to do my shopping, but there we were minding our own business at the mall when we saw the sign advertising the incredible deal. What could we do?"

"Tell them to put it on their Christmas list and let Santa decide."

"Uh huh, you didn't see their faces."

Shaking my head, I walk over and sit at the table. Oli stands up and turns the chair around to face me and sits down again.

"You know you say you don't want kids now, but life has a way of surprising you. Look at me."

"Which is why I don't get near a woman without protection even when she insists she has it covered."

"Ouch."

"You know I didn't mean it that way. It wasn't your fault, Sis. I just mean, I'm not taking any chances."

"I may not have planned them, but my boys are my life. I wouldn't trade them for anything."

"I know, but that's not what I want to talk about."

I cross my legs and fold my arms over my waist. "You want to know why Ryan was at Thanksgiving."

"To begin with, and why Mom is under the impression you're back together."

I roll my eyes. "You know Mom, she's been trying to get us back together from the start."

"So there's no truth to it?"

I close my eyes.

"You've got to be kidding me."

My eyes pop open as Oli stands up and rubs his hands over his face.

"It's not what you think."

"Then explain it to me because the boys were chattering on about family bowling, going tree shopping together, and Ryan mentioned spending Christmas morning together while we were watching the game yesterday."

My mouth opens and closes. Damn it. I really need to talk to Ryan before he does irreparable damage with his loose lips.

"Ryan has asked for us to give it another try, but I haven't decided yet. I told him I would consider it, that's all."

"Why didn't you say no right off the bat? What's there to think about?"

"It's not that simple. There're the boys to consider."

"Please tell me you're not going to say something asinine like you're thinking about getting back together for the kids' sakes."

"People do it all the time."

"Seriously, that's your argument?"

"Keep your voice down."

He heaves a sigh and holds out his arms. "Do you love him?"

"Of course I do, he's the father of my boys."

"That's not what I mean. Would you love him if you didn't have the boys?"

"That's an impossible question to answer. I don't know."

"It's not impossible and your answer should tell you something. What about the neighbor?" He tilts his head to the side.

"What about him?"

"I thought you had something going with him?"

"Yeah well, I think you were right about him and his sister-in-law. Turns out they dated before she met the brother."

"Sorry Sis."

I shrug.

Oli straddles the chair again. "You can't get back together with Ryan just because you think it will make the kids happy."

"I didn't say I was. I only promised to think about it. He shocked the hell out of me, okay?"

"How was dinner at his parents' house yesterday?"

I frown and roll my eyes. "His mother invited his newly single ex-girlfriend and her parents over. She told Ryan point blank to spend time with Alice."

"Jesus, and what did Ryan say?"

"He gave excuses including the one about going Christmas tree shopping together which was news to me."

"How did the ex act? She interested in Ryan?"

I rub my forehead with my palms. "I don't know. She wasn't blatant about it if she is, but her parents and Ryan's couldn't stop reminiscing over the two of them and how inseparable they were."

"What's she look like?"

"What does that have to do with anything?"

"Is she hot?"

"Again, your point?"

"That's a yes."

"Fine, yes, she's beautiful. Her mahogany brown hair was expertly styled with not a single stray hair out of place. Her skin looked like a porcelain doll's. She wore charcoal gray wool slacks with a white sweater cardigan. She looked like she stepped off the pages of a fashion magazine."

"Stuck up?"

I rest my head on the back of my chair. "No, she got down on the floor and played with the boys and the dog. She was nice." She even chatted with me about working at the bakery and her job as a marketing consultant. When the conversation turned to reminiscing, she tried to include me.

"Jealous?"

"Only of the way Ryan's parents fawned over her. Nothing I ever did made them like me."

"You want to marry back into that? You think they'll treat you any differently?"

I angle my head to meet his gaze.

"His mother would probably hire a hitman to take me out."

Oli chuckles. "She's a fierce woman, but I don't think she would take it that far."

"Probably not, but I have no delusions of her welcoming me with open arms." There's no point telling him what she said to me about nothing ever being enough for me. It would make him mad and I wouldn't put it past him to confront her over it and give her an earful of what he thinks of her precious son. I don't need any more bad feelings between us.

"Why do you think Ryan suddenly wants to reconcile?"

"He's up for a promotion. It would mean moving to Boston. He wants us to go as a family."

"What about your life here? Your job at the bakery, friends, kids' friends, family, this house? He just expects you to pick up and go?"

"At least I'd be closer to you."

"As much as I'd like that, I don't want you to up heave your life or settle for less than what you deserve."

"What do you mean?"

"Do you think Ryan is madly in love with you?"

"Geez, thanks a lot, Oli. Is it so hard to imagine someone being madly in love with me?"

"No, that's my point. You deserve someone who is and someone who you're madly in love with."

"So I need to find a guy to fall in love with me and a guy I can fall in love with? A threesome?"

"Ha ha, very funny, smartass."

"Who's to say that even exists out there? Have you ever been madly in love?"

"No, but I have no intention of ever marrying unless I do and you shouldn't either."

Franny and Mitch appear madly in love. I'd like to have someone stare at me the way Mitch looks at Franny. Or get all giddy over someone like Franny does when she talks about Mitch.

Ryan and I never had a chance to feel that way. We got pregnant and found out we were having twins. The shock of that superseded everything else. Would we have fallen madly in love if I hadn't gotten pregnant?

"How about if I promise you that if I don't believe Ryan truly loves me or I'm not in love with him, I'll end any chance of reconciliation?"

"Okay, and how are you going to decide?"

"I'm not sure yet. He just sprang this on me a little over a week ago and with the holiday and my finals coming up along with my life in general, I haven't had time to really consider the situation. You're right though, I won't say yes just for the kids' sake. It has to be because we're in love with one another too."

I don't want to feel second best for the rest of my life. I want to be loved for me. I want to be someone's first choice. Their only choice.

CHAPTER 28

*L*uke's house is dark again. It's been that way every night this
week. It's not like I'm spying on him or anything, but I've
noticed when I've come home from work and while I'm in the
kitchen or in my room.

Should I check on him? Just because we're no longer dating
doesn't mean we can't eventually be friends. He's still my neighbor.
What if something happened to him?

He could have gone on vacation.

I get out of my car and go inside. It's not any of my business. The
kids are at a sleepover. I have the house to myself. I even bought a bottle
of wine and brought home a cupcake from the bakery to treat myself.

What if he's sick or dying?

The last time I thought something was wrong and went to check
on him he bit my head off. Now he's already mad with me. I'd have to
be a glutton for punishment to go over there.

After putting the wine in the fridge and the bakery box on the
counter, I walk over and stare out the window at his house. I'll call. If
he answers I'll explain I'm being neighborly and checking in on him.

I dial his number and listen to it ring. An automated voice comes on stating he isn't available and to leave a message. Should I hang up? He'll see I called anyway.

The same voice announces the mailbox is full.

Crap!

Is he hurt and not answering his phone so his voicemail is full?

I grab my coat off the peg by the front door and stuff my arms into the sleeves. I'll never be able to relax until I check. I slip my phone into my pants' pocket and walk out the front door.

There's over a foot of snow on the ground so I have to walk down to the street and up his driveway. My toes are already freezing in the flats I wore to work by the time I raise my hand and ring his doorbell. I didn't dress for a traipse down the road in the cold. My pants are thin and the wind blasts against my legs. I wrap my coat tighter around me and press the bell again and listen to it ring inside the house. Odds are he's not home, not inside hurt.

There's snow in front of the garage. He hasn't used his new snow-blower to clear it for at least a few days. Only my steps mark the path to his door and the snow coating my shoes and feet attest to the fact no one has been here or shoveled the steps or path.

My feet are turning numb.

I'll call Barbara and ask her. It doesn't rank high on my list of fun things to do tonight, but I'll rest easier knowing he's not in there dying. I turn to walk down the steps. Glass shattering comes from inside.

I swing back to face the door. Should I dial nine-one-one?

I ring the doorbell again and pound on the door. "Luke?"

Damn it, if he doesn't answer I'm calling the police. I pull out my phone and press the button to turn it on and bring up the keyboard.

I dial nine and then one. The door swings open. Luke stands there glowering. His hair is plastered to his forehead. His wrinkled clothes look like he slept in them—for a week. The smell hits me then. Alcohol.

Luke has been drinking. He told me he doesn't drink.

Without a word, he wanders down the hallway and disappears

around the corner. He left the door open. I guess I should be thankful he didn't shut it in my face. Am I supposed to follow him?

I glance around at the darkened snow-covered landscape behind me. It's freezing and I need to warm up my feet before I lose a toe or two to frostbite. The heat from inside the house drifts out to taunt me. I step inside and close the door behind me.

There's a jumble of shoes inside the door including work boots, sneakers, and a pair of slippers. Pay dirt. They're going on my feet. I slip off my flats and brush the remaining snow off my frozen ankles. Thick plaid material lines the tan slippers. I slip my feet inside and pad down the hallway to find Luke.

He's slouching on a brown couch below the wall of weapons I once wondered if he used in his role as a serial killer. His eyes are closed and his head rests on the back of the couch. There's an open bottle of vodka on the rustic wooden coffee table in front of him. It's empty. Broken pieces of glass litter the floor next to the table.

I glance behind me into the kitchen. Dishes fill the sink. Rows of empty beer bottles sit on the gray and black speckled granite counter next to a pizza box. Stale food and alcohol linger in the air. If it wasn't so cold out, I'd crack open a window.

There's a magazine on the table. I grab it and carefully pluck the broken glass off the floor and use the magazine to carry it into the kitchen. I open the white cabinet under the sink hoping to find a garbage can. A trio of trash cans reside in the cabinet. He recycles. I toss in the broken glass and then grab the empty beer bottles and add them too.

Luke doesn't make a sound or move even when I retrieve the vodka bottle from in front of him. I open the pizza box. A few pieces of stale pizza remain. I throw them in the garbage and fold the box to fit into one of the cans.

"That's still good." He frowns. "Possibly. What day is it anyway?"

"Friday."

"Oh, well then probably not."

I open the dishwasher and load the dishes.

"You don't have to do that."

170

"Yes, I do."

The sting from my feet thawing makes me wince. I spot a coffee maker on the counter and open cabinets until I locate the coffee and clean mugs. While it brews, I finish loading the dishes, put detergent in, and turn it on.

A peek in the fridge doesn't produce any milk or cream so we're both having our coffee black. I only want it for the warmth anyway.

I stand in front of him holding out the coffee until he slits open his eyes, sits up, and takes the mug from me. I sit in the corner of the couch and pull up my feet with the mug cradled in my hands. Luke stares at the slippers next to him. He glances over to me.

"Yes, they're yours. My feet are freezing. I'm not taking them off. Deal with it."

He pulls the slippers off and drags my feet onto his lap with one hand. He lifts his black sweatshirt and places my feet against the warmth of his abdomen.

"Holy shit! They're like icicles." The coffee sloshes over the rim of his mug onto his hand. He holds the mug up in the air and swears an impressive length of expletives while holding my feet against him with his other hand.

I bite my lip and then blow over the top of my coffee. I wiggle my toes against his stomach. His skin is toasty. He winces and sips his coffee.

"Did you come here barefoot or something?"

"No, I was wearing the flats I wore at work. There's snow covering your driveway and walk."

He grunts and rests his head back against the couch. "What are you doing here?"

"Your lights have been off for days. You didn't answer the phone. Your voicemail is full. My conscious got the best of me and I wanted to make sure you were alive. I was dialing nine-one-one when you finally opened the door."

We sit in silence while my body warms from the coffee and his body heat. He finishes his drink and leans forward to place it on the table.

"How was your Thanksgiving?"

He shrugs. "Fine. Yours?"

"Fine."

"Glad we got that out of the way."

I chuckle. "You want to tell me what's going on?"

Luke puts my feet off his lap and stands. He walks over to a chest against the wall and pulls out a red cable knit blanket. After covering me with it, he sits and lifts my feet back on to his lap.

"It was the anniversary of Wyatt's death two days ago."

"I'm sorry."

I put my empty mug on the table and put my hands under the blanket. "You've been here drinking for two days?"

"Three actually. I started the day before."

"Is this typically how you spend the anniversary of his death?"

He swivels his head on the coach to look at me. "I haven't had a drink since the day he died."

"Why now?"

"I don't know. I flew down to see my parents on the day after Thanksgiving. I spent the weekend with them. They're still grieving hard for him. I went so far as to list his car for sale online thinking it might help. I took it down a few minutes later."

"The car in the garage?"

"Yeah, it's the car he was driving that night. Wyatt loved that car. It wasn't much more than a hunk of junk when he bought it. We worked on it together for over a year before it was restored and street ready. After the crash, I bought it from the salvage yard and fixed it up. I thought I would save it for Joey to have someday. It's stupid, why would he want the car his father died in?"

"Hard to answer that one. It could go either way. He might have a sentimental attachment to the car like you obviously do if he knows how much the car meant to Wyatt or he might resent it. How does Barbara feel about it? My guess is Joey's reaction will depend on yours and hers."

"She doesn't know I have it."

"Oh."

"I was drunk. He wouldn't have been there if I hadn't called him to come get me so I wouldn't drive."

"Is that why you blame yourself?"

"It's my fault."

"No, it's not. You weren't driving the car that smashed into you both. You had no idea what would happen. I'm sure no one blames you."

"No one says it out loud."

"Luke..."

"I should have called a taxi or service to pick me up. Instead I dragged him away from his pregnant wife to come get me in the middle of the night."

"Did you make it a habit of drinking and calling him to come get you?"

"No, that was the first. I had signed a new book deal and was celebrating. I wanted him to celebrate with me, but he said he couldn't. So, I got drunk and then made him come out anyway."

"If the situation was reversed and he called you to drive him home, would you have gone?"

"What does that matter?"

"It matters because that's what family does. If Oli called me, I would go get him. Would it be his fault if something happened to me while I was doing it? Would it be Wyatt's fault if you were the one picking him up?"

Luke pinches the bridge of his nose and closes his eyes.

"Barbara doesn't blame you. Do you really think she'd let Joey spend so much time with you if she did?"

"I miss him. Every damn day."

Tears fill my eyes and I lean forward to rest my hand on his shoulder. He turns his head to meet my gaze. His eyes are wet. He slides over and rests his head in my lap. I wrap my arm around his shoulders as tears leak down my cheeks.

CHAPTER 29

y mouth is as dry as cotton. My body aches from sleeping in the same position too long. I drag open an eyelid to see bright sunlight. I promptly slam my eyes shut, only to pop them back open. I'm still on Luke's couch with him asleep in my lap.

I peer up behind me at the sunlight streaming in his sliders. Crap, what time is it? I search around under the blanket and my twisted clothes to find my phone and check the time. I lurch up.

Luke sniffs and raises his head.

"I have to go. I'm supposed to be at work in less than an hour."

He sits up while I wrestle out from under him, the blanket, and my coat which has somehow twisted around my body like a straitjacket.

"You want me to make coffee?"

"No time. I have to get home, shower, and dress."

The slippers are on the floor under the table. Putting my flats back on and walking through the snow on his walk will seriously suck.

"I'm borrowing the black boots by your front door. I'll give them back."

"Um, okay…"

I jog over to the hallway and then stop and turn back to him. "You okay?"

He nods. "Yeah, go, I'll talk to you later."

I race down to the door and hop on one foot while putting on a boot and then do the same with the other foot. I stuff my flats in the crook of my arm and trudge out the door and down the walk.

By the time I get in my house and pull off the boots and my coat, I have less than a half hour to shower and dress. I turn on the shower to heat while I grab clean clothes and a towel. The lukewarm shower does little to brighten my day. Goosebumps cover my skin as I stand shivering outside the shower drying off.

I trip over the trail of discarded clothes I left on my way to the shower and land on my knees. Pain soars through me and I struggle to a stand.

There's no time for makeup after I dress and brush my teeth. I run a comb over my hair and shove it into a ponytail. I need a haircut. It's still on my never-ending to do list.

I make it to the bakery with one minute to spare. When I walk in the front door, Sally looks me over after finishing with a customer.

"Whose bed did you just roll out of?"

She cackles when my face heats.

"That bad, huh?" I frown as I walk behind the counter.

"I'm just playing with you."

"Thanks." I walk into the kitchen. Franny and Lucinda huddle together by the back door. Franny looks upset.

"What's wrong?"

Lucinda looks over and tilts her head. "Wedding dilemmas."

"Uh oh, what happened?"

"Mother keeps adding people to the wedding list. I wanted to keep it small, no more than fifty tops. Now, the list is over a hundred and growing by the day. Mother insists every invitee is essential and will be offended if they're not invited."

Lucinda puts her arm around Franny. "Who did you make your official wedding planner?"

Franny gives her a sideways glance. "You."

"Exactly, so it's my job to manage Mother and the list. You and Mitch have already made your list and we're sticking to it. It's your wedding and you get to decide who to invite or not to invite. I'll handle Mother. No more worrying."

"Well that sounds settled. Is that the only wedding worry?"

Franny nods. "Lucinda has taken over all the planning. She gives me the options and I point and say which one I want and she arranges everything. It's great."

Lucinda nods. "It's a lot of fun. Mother did most of the planning for mine. I'm having a blast with all the wedding details."

I smile. "Maybe you've found your new calling."

She flips her leg up behind her and twists to the side. "Perhaps."

"Franny, do you have a few minutes to see the new website design?"

"Absolutely! It's all done?"

"Yes, well, mostly. I'm sure there'll be a few things you want to change." I've been tweaking everything for the past two weeks trying to make it as perfect as I can before unveiling it to her. The instructor for the introduction to website design class I took was an immense help and suggested I enroll in the semester long course next semester.

"Ooh, let's see." Lucinda rubs her hands together as I set up the laptop.

I type in the domain name and then step back so they can see the website.

"Oh wow, look at that. Olivia, it's so professional. You did this all yourself?"

I nod.

"I love how you used my logo and the colors. The pictures are gorgeous."

"I wanted to keep the bakery's theme consistent across the website, store, and social media. The pink, black, and white colors and the logo all match."

Lucinda points to the screen. "What a great photo of you Franny."

Franny grimaces. "I didn't know you were putting a picture of me on here."

"I know, but it's not a close up and people like to have a face of the business to connect to. I can take it down if you really hate it, but I think it looks terrific." I chew my lip as Franny stares at the photo of herself standing outside her bakery.

"No, it's not a close up, like you said, and I don't hate it."

"Oh good."

"You should definitely keep it up there. I love it." Lucinda reaches over to pat me on the shoulder. "Fantastic job."

"It really is, Olivia. I'm so impressed. I never imagined it would be so detailed."

I grin at Franny. "I'm so glad you like it. I've been a nervous wreck waiting to show it to you."

We finish looking over the website and Lucinda goes up front to help Sally while I stay in the kitchen to help Franny prepare more baked goods.

"Have you decided what you want to do for the holiday decorations?" I pull out the ingredients to make a couple of trays of mini cheesecakes.

Franny sets the bowls and pans on the counter and frowns. "Not really. Would it be awful if I just put up the lights and window clings from last year?"

"Of course not, they're cute."

"But...?"

"I had this idea for a snow scene. There's a window spray for the snow. I looked online and there're stencils for a sleigh, trees, all sorts of winter themes. Then I thought we could decorate mini Christmas trees on the patio with white lights. We could hang white lights in the front too."

"Sounds good. You are officially in charge of decorations."

"Really?"

"Yup, I'm happy to put it in your hands. Buy what you need, just don't bankrupt me."

"I promise."

Franny drops the blocks of cream cheese in the giant bowl of the mixer. I measure out the sugar and flour.

"You're happy with how the wedding is going, right? You didn't just say that for Lucinda's benefit?"

"Oh no, she really has been doing everything. I've never been one of those women who planned their future weddings in their head before they even had the groom. All the details make my head spin. If I had to plan it all, I'd end up with an ulcer. Lucinda is in her element."

"Good."

"How's your cousin's wedding going?"

"I wouldn't know."

"Aren't you still a bridesmaid?"

"Technically yes, but she doesn't include me in anything. I find out what she and her other attendants have decided or done after the fact. I've been wondering how awful it would be to ask her if I can back out. She doesn't want me in it anyway. She only asked as a family obligation."

"If you're sure that's what it is, then talk to her. What's the worst that can happen?"

"My mother might disown me."

Franny laughs and then stops while she gazes at my face. "You're not serious?"

I wince and glance up at the ceiling. "I'd say there might be a fifty-fifty chance. If she finds out Ryan wants to reconcile and I decide not to, then she's most assuredly going to disown me."

"You decided then?"

"No, not yet. All the time Ryan and I have spent together lately is with the kids. We need to go on a date with just the two of us and see how that goes. I won't get back together just for the kids. I need to know it's because we both want to be a couple, not just parents. Does that make sense?"

"Yes. You need to know he loves you for you, not just the mother of his children."

"Exactly. I promised Oli I wouldn't consider it otherwise."

"Why would you? You deserve to be loved."

"It's hard when you consider the family pressure of my mother."

"I think your mother wants your happiness. If that's not Ryan, then she'll understand."

"I hope so."

"When are you going out on a date? Do you need me to babysit?"

I laugh. "Actually, I might take you up on that. Otherwise, I'd have to ask my parents and I don't want them to know."

"Name the day."

"I have to talk to Ryan, but how about Monday?"

"We've got the book club."

"Oh, right, I forgot."

How could I forget that? I read his book—all of them, in fact. I totally forgot he was the author while I was reading, I was just engrossed in the stories. He's so talented, I hope he starts writing again. Once he stops grieving so hard for Wyatt, he might get over his writer's block.

"You don't want to go, do you?"

I scrunch up my face. "Is it that obvious? It feels weird to go to her house and socialize. Am I horrible person?"

"No, of course not, I wouldn't want to go either." Franny purses her lips. "You know what, we'll both cancel. You have to get this settled with Ryan and I need to support my friend."

"You don't need to do that. I can schedule it for another night you're available."

"Are you going to book club?"

"I don't think so."

"Then I'm not either. It's the holiday season, everyone will understand. We all miss a meeting here and there for one reason or another."

"Are you sure?"

"One hundred percent. Let me know if anything changes."

"Thanks Franny."

Lucinda pops her head in the kitchen. "Franny there's someone here who wants to order a cake."

"On my way." Franny washes her hands and walks out front.

I add the rest of the ingredients to the mixer and turn it on. Should I call and check on Luke?

I hate to think of him sitting alone drinking for days while mourning his brother. No one should go through that alone. I hope he can stop blaming himself and start the healing process. I can't even fathom how I would feel if I lost Oli. If I blamed myself for his death, how would I live with that?

I wash my hands and then dial my phone. He answers on the second ring.

"Hey."

"Hi. I just wanted to check in and see how you're doing?"

"You don't have to do that. I'm okay. But thanks, and thanks for last night too."

"Anytime. I mean it. If you ever need to talk, or even just someone to sit with...call me okay?"

"Thanks."

Should I offer to stop by, maybe bring him something from the bakery? Or would that be too pushy? He shouldn't be alone when he's feeling so low.

"Do you want me to bring you something from the bakery? I could drop it off on my way home. Ryan is picking the boys up from their sleepover this morning."

"Thanks, but I'm good. I'm going to get some groceries and then head over to Barb's to see Joey."

"Okay, that's good. I'll talk to you later."

"Bye."

I shut off my phone and slip it back into my pocket. It's good he's going to see her. I need to study for finals and concentrate on Ryan.

CHAPTER 30

"What do you think?"

My reflection in the beauty parlor mirror stares back. There's a cool breeze on the back of my neck. My bare neck. I've never worn my hair so short before. It's shaved on the bottom of my neck. The top is longer and brushes my ears.

I said I wanted something stylish and easy to care for. She delivered. I turn my head side to side.

"I love it."

"This style compliments your features rather than detracting from them. If you added dark eye makeup, it would make your eyes totally pop. Sexy."

"You think so?"

"I know so. If you have a few more minutes, I can show you."

I stare at her reflection over my shoulder. "Go for it."

Slightly more than a half hour later, and she's not only added eye shadow, liner, and mascara, but she's done my whole face with concealer, contouring, foundation, blush, and powder. It's like watching an artist paint a canvas. She dabs on lip gloss and stands back to inspect her work—my face.

I doubt I'll be able to recreate this look on my own, but I can watch a few videos online and hopefully figure it out. If I ever have time or the inclination to actually follow through.

"I hope you have somewhere to go today because you are seriously hot."

Laughter bubbles up from the bit of my stomach as a grin stretches across my face. "I do look pretty good, right?"

"Oh yeah, so you got somewhere to go?"

"Actually, I do have a date tonight."

"Excellent. Knock 'em dead, honey." She spins my chair around so I face the shop.

"Thanks, Tammy. You've exceeded all my expectations."

After paying her with a generous tip added on, I speed walk to my car. The boys have a half day today and I need to beat the bus home.

The manger scene sits in front of the church on the corner of Main Street. Double wreaths hang on the front doors. I glance up to the top of the steeple. At night it will be lit with Christmas lights. Farther up the street the giant menorah decorates the synagogue. The boys and I love taking car rides in the evenings to check out the holiday decorations.

Garland strung with lights loops around the light posts lining Main street. Red and green banners wishing everyone happy holidays flap in the wind. The garden club has been busy setting up mini decorated Christmas trees on the town medians. The store fronts have decorated with various themes, everything from snowmen to reindeer and a sleigh in front of Petopia. I better get The Sweet Spot decorated. It's looking pretty bare in comparison.

While waiting for a light to change, I glance in the rearview mirror. A stranger stares back at me—one ready to embark on a new journey. A new look for a fresh start.

I have finals this week and I feel prepared for them. Franny loves the new website I designed and my final projects are both centered on The Sweet Spot. I developed a marketing strategy with the website and social media as the key ingredients and I drafted a mission statement with goals and a plan how to attain them. Once my professors grade them and provide feedback, I'm going to present them to Franny and see what she thinks.

There's the date with Ryan tonight, which will hopefully help us decide if a reconciliation is even a possibility. We must have chemistry to make it as a couple. It can't be because of the kids. It won't be all that long before they'll be grown and off living their own lives. Then what?

I rub the pang in my chest over the images popping into my head of Timmy and Tommy going to high school, graduating, going to college, and beyond. God, I'll probably be a grandma someday.

If my mother is to be believed, then I'm right on schedule to be a grandmother. When I told her I was getting a haircut today, she said it was time. A middle-aged woman shouldn't have long hair. Middle age? When I reminded her I'm not even thirty yet, she said thirty was middle age. I stopped myself from replying if thirty is middle age wouldn't that mean sixty is dead? She turned sixty-two this year. I doubt she would have appreciated my interpretation.

I arrive home with only ten minutes to spare before the bus will drop the boys off. I prepare a couple of snacks for them to eat because I know it will be one of the first things they ask for. They must be going through another growth spurt because they're always hungry lately. As soon as they finish one meal, they're asking what's for the next.

The rumble of the bus engine brings me to the front door. The familiar yellow appears down the road when I step out onto the front steps. I wrap my arms around myself to contain some heat. I should have grabbed my coat. The kids jump off the bottom stairs of the bus and I wave to the bus driver as the boys run to the house.

"What's for lunch?" Timmy cranes his neck up to peer at me from the bottom of the stairs.

"Didn't you have lunch at school?"

"Yeah, but we're still hungry." Tommy scoots past me into the house.

"Good thing I made some snacks for you. Hang up your coats and backpacks, take off your shoes, and go wash your hands. Food is on the table when you're done."

They both scramble to follow instructions.

"How was school?"

"Fine."

"Good."

"Anything interesting happen? Do anything fun? Learn something new?" Tommy's coat falls to the floor from the peg he tossed it at. I pick it up and pull the sleeves out so it's ready for him to put on the next time and hang it up.

"I don't know." Tommy finishes washing his hands first and sits at the table and stuffs an apple slice into his mouth.

Timmy shrugs as he walks out of the bathroom. "Not really."

Trying to get any specifics of their day at school is an exercise in futility. You would think I'd have given up by now.

"Can we play outside when we're done?" Tommy looks up as I walk into the kitchen. A drop of peanut butter dots his chin.

I lean over and hand him his napkin. "Do you have homework?"

"Nope."

I glance at Timmy and he shakes his head.

"Then yes. Make sure you dress warmly, which means boots, coats, gloves, and hats. Don't forget Franny is watching you two tonight."

"Yes!" Tommy punches a fist into the air. "We're going to her house, right?"

"Yes, and you better be on your best behavior."

"We will." Timmy carries his plate to the sink.

I kiss him on the top of his head. "I know you will, baby." I put both hands on Tommy's shoulders and kiss his bent head. "I love you two monkeys."

"Love you." Timmy sits on the stairs to put on his boots while Tommy puts his plate in the sink. "Love you."

Once they're bundled up and playing in the backyard, I go upstairs to search through my closet for something to wear which will complement my fresh look. Hopefully, Ryan will be more observant than his sons and notice my new haircut and makeup.

A sapphire blue cashmere sweater lies on my bed with an assortment of choices for my lower half below and next to it. Pants or skirt? I don't want to freeze, but I need something date like not business or funeral like.

One of the boys yell outside and I cross to the window. Tommy waves at someone. I lean farther forward. Luke's walking toward my backyard.

By the time I get downstairs, put on my coat and shoes, stuff my phone in my pocket, and open the back door the boys are standing at the edge of our property chattering away to Luke standing on the other side of the bushes. He raises a hand to wave when I walk across the deck.

"Hi." I wave and then stuff my hands under my arms. I should have grabbed my gloves too.

Tommy runs over to the deck. "Can we have a snowball fight with Luke?"

I glance over to Luke. Timmy stands next to him waiting for my answer.

"What does Luke say about this?"

"It was his idea."

"Oh really?"

Luke laughs. "Technically, I asked if they were building a fort over there for a snowball fight." He jerks his chin over by the playscape.

There's a pile of snow where the boys must have dug out an area and made a wall of sorts.

"We were making an igloo, but a fort and snowball fight is more fun."

"An igloo, huh?" Luke studies the falling down mound and glances over to me. "What do you think? Can the boys and I play in the snow?"

Chuckling, I gaze at the three earnest faces. "Sure, you three boys can play in the snow."

Timmy and Tommy grin and run towards their structure. Luke strolls over to the deck and gazes up at me.

"I don't think either one of them is cut out for architect school, but they get points for imagination."

"Everyone has to start somewhere."

A weight bumps against my leg and I glance down. My phone clunks against my foot and rests on the deck.

"Where did that come from?"

"My coat pocket. I keep forgetting there's a hole in it." Actually, there's one in both pockets now. I've sewn them both more than once, but my tendency to stuff my keys in the pockets keeps opening up the seams.

"You should zip up." He nods at my coat as he pulls a pair of gloves from his pocket.

I would, but the zipper is broken. I wrap it tighter around me instead.

"Nice haircut." He walks over to the boys and hunkers down to inspect their creation.

Smiling, I turn and walk back inside.

CHAPTER 31

"*Y*ou look beautiful." Ryan stands and kisses me on the lips. He lingers for a second and pulls back and smiles.

"Thank you." I sit in the chair he pulls out. Being on time has never been one of Ryan's strengths, yet he was already waiting at the table when I arrived at the restaurant. He's making an effort I can't help but appreciate. "I haven't eaten here in a while." I glance around the room. There's a fireplace on the other side with a crackling fire inside. Hurricane lamps with a wreath of evergreens circling the bottom flicker in the middle of the white tablecloths.

"The last time I ate here was with you. Remember when I got the job? Your parents watched the boys so we could celebrate."

"Of course, I do." Ryan had gotten hired right after college. We thought we were so grown up having dinner at the White Birch Inn and celebrating his new job. "It seems like so long ago, doesn't it?"

"In some ways, in others it seems like it was just yesterday." He takes my hand across the table. "We were planning to go house hunting, remember?"

"Yes, we debated where to search. You wanted something in an up-and-coming neighborhood. I don't think we succeeded with that one."

"I don't know, property values have gone up, haven't they?"

"Maybe a bit, but not enough to make me rich or even enough to warrant selling."

"You've considered selling?"

The server arrives and Ryan orders wine for both of us.

"Not seriously. The thought has crossed my mind. The boys are getting older and it's only a two-bedroom house."

"We could get a bigger house in the Boston suburbs. I can commute to work on the T."

"You're moving too fast, Ryan. We haven't even started dating again."

He closes the menu and leans forward. "Then what is this, if not a date?"

I scan the menu. I'm feeling carnivorous tonight. Steak sounds good. Closing the menu, I put it on the end of the table. "It's a date to determine if we're compatible as a couple to start dating."

"We were married. I think that proves we're compatible."

I tilt my head and raise my eyebrows. "We're divorced, remember?"

"So you're not willing to give us another chance?"

"No, that's not what I'm saying. I want to make sure if we try again, it's for the right reasons. We can't just get back together for the boys' sake. They're ten. It won't be long before they're grown and it will just be the two of us. We've never had that. It's always been the four of us."

The server returns with our wine. I order the New York strip with mashed potatoes and a salad while Ryan orders the prime rib and baked potato. When the server leaves, Ryan picks up his glass and swirls the wine. I take a sip of mine while he studies the glass.

"We had a fun time hunting for the perfect tree the weekend after Thanksgiving, didn't we? The boys will live at home for a minimum of another eight years, probably longer. These days kids live with their parents well into their twenties. I don't see what's so wrong with wanting to provide them with a stable family."

"There's nothing wrong with it, but it can't be the only reason. Why do you want to get back together? Would you even consider it if we didn't have the boys?"

Ryan stares at me over his glass. "How can I possibly answer that question? We do have the boys."

"Do you love me Ryan?"

"Of course I do."

"I mean, are you in love with me? Not just as the mother of your children."

He gazes around the room and back to me. "What's the difference? Love is love."

I look out the window at the puffy snowflakes drifting down to the ground. How do I explain there are different types of love and I want the chance to have the happily ever after type of love? The kind where simply thinking about me makes him happy. I want to be loved like that and love someone that way in return.

"Tell me how you felt about Alice."

"Alice? What does she have to do with anything?"

"Did you love her?"

"This feels like a trap."

I shake my head. "It's not, I promise."

"I guess so, sure."

"You guess so? You dated throughout high school. Your mother calls her your soul mate."

"Is that what this is about? My mother inviting Alice and her parents over for Thanksgiving? My parents and hers are friends. They go on vacations together."

"No, that's not what I'm referring to. I want to know how you felt when you were with her. Did she make you happy?"

Ryan shakes his head. "I don't see what any of this has to do with us."

The server places salads in front of us and a cutting board with bread and butter.

"Were you attracted to her? Did your breath catch when she walked in the room? Did you count the minutes until you were with her again? Did you smile for no reason when you thought about her?"

He glares while he takes a bite of his salad and butters a slice of bread.

I pick up my fork and poke at the lettuce on my plate before staring at him. "Do you feel that way about me? Have you ever?"

He pauses with his fork halfway to his mouth and then looks away.

"I didn't think so." I place my fork onto my plate and stare out the window. Ice and snow coat the lake. As winter progresses and the ice gets thicker, fishing shacks will appear on the lake and snowmobile tracks will crisscross the lake.

Clasping my hands in my lap, I gaze at his familiar face. His brown hair is neatly clipped. Light brown eyes, always so serious, stare back. "I love you Ryan. You're a good father. I care about you. I want you to be happy. I'm not *in* love with you. And I want that for both of us, don't you?"

Ryan drops his fork onto his plate with a clang. He swallows a gulp of wine and puts his glass down. "So, you are saying no."

"I guess I am."

He wipes his mouth with his napkin. "So you're not coming with me to Boston?"

"Have they made a decision? You got the position?"

"Not yet, but it looks good."

"Is that what this is about? You're afraid you won't see the kids if you take the job?"

"It's a couple hours away if traffic isn't a nightmare. It's Boston, traffic is always a nightmare."

"We'll make it work."

"Does the neighbor have anything to do with your decision? Are you in love with him?"

"Luke? No, this isn't about him. We're not dating anymore, just friends." Ryan doesn't need to know Luke stirs some of those feelings in me. It doesn't matter anyway. Luke feels that way for his sister-in-law—not me.

Ryan nods and takes a bite of bread and picks up his fork. "Any chance you'll change your mind?"

I smile and pick up my fork. "No."

The server arrives with our meals after I take one bite of my salad.

"Besides, can you imagine your mother's reaction if you told her we were getting back together?"

He winces as he cuts into his steak.

"I saw that. Admit it, your mother hates me and always will."

"She doesn't hate you."

I glance up as I cut my steak. "Come on, Ryan."

He sighs and takes a bite of his steak. "Hate is a strong word. She might never be your biggest fan though."

I dip the steak into a dab of steak sauce before taking a bite. Ryan shakes his head. He could never understand how I can ruin a good piece of steak with sauce. The tangy sauce touches the tip of my tongue and I smile.

"She gave me quite the earful after Thanksgiving. Wanted to know why you were there and why I went to your parents' house." He glances up from his plate. "Tried to get me to ask Alice out on a date."

I nod. "I bet. What did you tell her?" I lower my fork. "Please tell me you didn't mention the possibility of a reconcile. She doesn't want it to happen, but she'll blame me even more if she finds out I turned down her precious son."

He smirks while adding sour cream to his baked potato.

"Ryan, you didn't, did you?"

He glances up at me and slowly cuts the baked potato into sections.

"Ryan!"

"Relax, I didn't."

I lean back into my chair and glare. "She's never going to forgive me for trapping her baby with a baby."

"You didn't trap me."

"Tell her that."

"My mom is a bit old fashioned."

"A bit?"

"I never blamed you."

"Didn't you?"

He puts down his knife and fork. "I've never said the pregnancy was your fault."

"No, but you resented me for not knowing antibiotics lowered the effectiveness of the pill. You resented having to work while in college to help support me and the boys and moving out of the dorm and into my parents' house. You resented having to marry me."

"I may have resented the situation, but I didn't blame you. We were in it together. I always thought you resented me because you had to drop out of college while I stayed."

"No." I wince. "Well, maybe a tiny bit if I'm being completely honest."

He smiles and picks up his knife and fork.

"I'm signing up for more classes next semester. It'll take me a while, but I'm going to get a degree."

"That's great. What do you plan to do with it?"

"Do with it? Hang it on a wall?"

Ryan laughs. "I mean for work."

"Oh." I shrug and eat my mashed potatoes. What do I plan to do? Start my own business? Get a job as a manager?

"I'm not sure. I haven't thought that far ahead. Right now, I'm using my new knowledge on the bakery. It's fun."

"You think it could lead somewhere? A partnership?"

"I don't know if that's an option Franny would be interested in." Would she?

He shrugs. "It's something to consider. You could also move to Boston and get a job there. Finish school quicker. More opportunities."

"Ryan, I told you we'll make it work with the boys. You could check out places halfway between here and Boston to live. Could you work remotely part of the week?"

"It's a possibility once I'm established, not for the first few months."

The server clears our plates and asks us if we want to order dessert.

"None for me."

"Are you sure? We can split something."

"I'm sure, but you go ahead."

"Just the check," Ryan says to the server.

I reach over and squeeze Ryan's hand. "Just because we're not getting back together doesn't mean we can't still have outings as a family."

He smiles and clasps my hand in his. "How does a family weekend in Boston sound? I'll show you all the sites, the museums, colleges..."

"I don't remember you being this tenacious."

"I followed Alice around for weeks before she agreed to go out with me."

I point my finger. "See, you loved her. A bit stalkery too, but you were a teenager. Why don't you ask her out? Doesn't she live in Boston? I'm sure someone mentioned that at Thanksgiving."

He laughs. "Yeah, she does and maybe I will. We'll see what happens with the job."

"You'll make your mother very happy."

After he pays the check, we stand. Ryan puts his hand at the base of my back as we walk through the restaurant. As we near the entrance Luke walks in with an incredibly attractive brunette wearing a fire engine red power suit.

I stumble and Ryan clasps my waist. "Okay?"

I nod and peek back at Luke and his companion. He whispers something in her ear.

Who is she? The muscles in my stomach clutch as we close the distance. I force a smile to my lips.

Our gazes meet and he nods in my direction and walks right past me.

Ryan retrieves our coats. "Wasn't that your neighbor?"

"Yup."

"Who's the woman?"

"No idea."

CHAPTER 32

The driveway and path to my front door is clear of snow.
Had Ryan done it before he left with the boys this morning? I dreaded coming home from work to shovel the snow which fell
last night. I need to thank him. I could have him over for dinner
during the week. Ever since our date on Monday and our honest
conversation, we've settled into a new camaraderie. There's no
tension.

My grades came in for my final exams and projects. I aced them
both. The professors were so complementary and encouraging. One
even said I had an aptitude for business. I enrolled in two more classes
for next semester, an accounting course because it's a necessary evil
and another marketing course. This one specializes in social media
and websites as well as advertising.

I hang up my coat on a peg and slip off my shoes and wiggle my
toes. I should have picked up something special for dinner to celebrate. Oh well, there's always tomorrow.

There's a knock on the door which stops me halfway up the stairs.
Who could that be? I turn and trudge back down the stairs and open
the door.

Luke stands there holding a plant.

"Hey."

"Hi."

"It occurred to me I never did anything to thank you for being there for me after Wyatt's anniversary." He lifts the plant. "I was going to buy you flowers, but they just die so I went with a plant. It's called a Christmas cactus. I don't exactly know what that means, but anyway...thanks."

He holds the plant out so I take it. "Um, thanks, but you didn't have to do anything. We're friends that's what friends do." I step back. "Do you want to come in? It's freezing outside."

"Yeah, sure." He steps in and closes the door while I back up and then turn and carry the plant into the kitchen and put it on the kitchen table.

I'm not much of a plant person. My mother insisted the couple she brought over are impossible to kill. I need to research how to care for it. The last thing I want to do is kill someone's gift. He's right, flowers die, but at least then I don't get blamed for it when they do.

"The boys with their father?"

I nod. "Can I get you anything?"

He shakes his head. "How's that going?"

"How's what going?"

"You and their father."

"Oh, it's not." I shrug. "We decided it wasn't a good idea."

"When did this happen? You looked pretty chummy at the inn."

So did you and the brunette. I walk over and lean against the sink. "We are chummy. We're friends, but we both agreed it's best we stay just friends."

He puts his hands in the front pockets of his jeans. "Kids okay with that?"

"We never started dating or even mentioned the possibility of it happening so as far as they know, everything is the same."

He stares at the plant on the table.

"Who was the woman you were with?"

He frowns and glances over to me. "What woman?"

"At the inn."

"Oh, my agent."

"Your agent travels to see you? Or does she live in New Hampshire?"

"She lives in New York, but as she put it, she wanted to make sure I was alive since I hadn't returned her calls."

"That's dedication."

He shrugs. "We've been friends a long time."

What kind of friends? Friends with benefits?

"Why hadn't you returned her calls?"

"I had nothing to say." He walks over and leans against the oven perpendicular to me. "I have nothing new to submit to her."

"You could have told her that and saved her a trip."

"If I'd known she was going to get on a plane and come here, I would have."

"You sure that was her only reason for visiting you?"

"I said we're friends."

"Friends as in friends who have dated?"

Luke folds his arms over his chest. "Friends as in we both pretty much started out together. I was one of her first clients and she took a chance on me."

"Does she know about Wyatt?"

"She knows it was the anniversary of his death recently which is why she was concerned. I should have responded to her calls."

"You weren't in a good place. I'm sure she understood. You explained, right?"

He rolls his eyes. "Yes Mom, I apologized and explained."

I stick my tongue out and wrinkle my nose. His gaze locks on to my mouth.

Heat pools in my core.

I bite my lip and glance away.

"I aced my finals. You're looking at an A student."

"Congratulations. We should celebrate."

I look back.

He stares at me. "We could get dinner. Are you hungry?" His gaze drops to my mouth again.

I swallow and prop my hands on the counter behind me. "Not particularly."

He moves in front of me and puts his hands over mine on the counter. "Thirsty?"

My fingers tingle beneath the warmth of his. My breath quickens and my mouth waters. I shake my head.

"How about something sweet?" His breath flutters my bangs against my forehead.

I tilt my head back and stare into his dark eyes. The temperature outside is below freezing, but I'm beginning to perspire.

He bends his head drags his lips across mine. His tongue traces the seam of my lips. "Definitely sweet."

My eyes drift close and my lips part with a stuttered breath. He kisses me deeply. His hands cup my jaw and angle my head up. I loop my arms behind his neck and arch into his body. He presses me back against the counter.

My knees grow weak.

He nips at my bottom lip before devouring my mouth.

I delve my fingers into the hair at his nape and clutch his head to mine.

His leg pushes my legs apart as his hands grip my butt and pull me against him.

I gasp for air and turn my head slightly. His lips graze my cheek and his tongue traces the vein in my neck.

My chest heaves. I clutch his shoulders and ride his thigh.

"Upstairs? Or right here?" His raspy voice whispers in my ear.

Heat spirals through me. I bite my lip hard. "Upstairs, but hurry."

He lifts me in his arms and I wrap my legs and arms tight around him.

Each step he takes up the stairs creates a delicious friction. By the time he reaches the top step, we're both moaning.

He props me against the wall of the upstairs hallway and kisses me senseless. The next thing I know the soft cushion of my bed is beneath me and he's removing my shirt and bra.

His tongue and hands worship my breasts while I squirm and clasp his head to my chest. His fingers unfasten my pants and slip down into my panties. I open my legs and press against his fingers. "Please." I can't stop the plea from leaving my lips.

He lifts his head. His tongue wraps around my nipple. "Please what?"

I arch my back and then reach forward to pull his shirt up and over his head. He pauses for a second to pull it the rest of the way off and tosses it behind him. He lowers himself back over me and kisses me while his fingers return to drive me crazy.

My hips move of their own volition. My eyes close and my head digs into the bed. My mouth opens in a soundless moan.

The orgasm washes over me.

I gasp and pant as Luke wrings every last drop of pleasure from my body.

He removes my pants and panties and then stands next to the bed to remove his own. He takes a condom from his wallet and opens it.

I bite my lip as he eases it over his erection. My mouth waters and I reach for him.

His lips capture mine as he settles between my legs and nudges inside.

He groans low and long. His hand squeezes my hip.

Our breaths mingle as our bodies find a rhythm.

Desire spikes and climbs ever higher. I press my forehead against his shoulder as I begin to pant once again. His mouth drags over my neck and burrows into the space where my neck and shoulder meet.

His heartbeat pounds beneath my fingers as his breaths come faster and shorter. My breath catches as a lightning bolt of pleasure zings through my body.

Luke clutches me to him as he finds completion.

My mind drifts and my body relaxes beneath the warm weight of his. He kisses my shoulder, my cheek, and then my lips.

I open my eyes and stare into his hovering above me. I smile. "That was most definitely something sweet."

CHAPTER 33

"All right, you've been glowing since you walked in here. What's going on?"

Franny leans a hip against the marble counter I'm practicing my buttercream roses on.

I smile and peek behind me towards the front of the bakery to make sure no one is within eavesdropping distance. "I slept with Luke."

Her mouth drops open. "What? When? I thought that was over?"

"So did I, but apparently not. It's complicated."

"Complicated how?"

"As in I can't keep my hands off him and don't really want to. He came over Saturday night and didn't leave until Sunday afternoon when the boys were due to come home." I glance over to her. "I saw him Monday and Tuesday while the boys were at school too."

Her eyes are as round as quarters. "That's quite the change. Barbara was a misunderstanding then?"

"We haven't discussed her since that day at the grocery store." I concentrate on the bag of frosting in my hand.

"Is that wise?"

I put the bag down and sigh. "Probably not, but if I've got my eyes wide open and know the score then it's my choice, right? Is it so wrong to take a little pleasure even if I know it's not going anywhere?"

"Of course not, you're both healthy, single, consenting adults." She leans down and nudges my arm with hers. "I don't want to see you hurt."

"I don't want to see me hurt either. I know there's an expiration date on this side of our relationship. For once I want to do something that makes me happy without exploring and analyzing all the ramifications of a single decision."

"Okay then, enjoy." She walks over to the ovens to check the cakes. "And share regularly. I want to know everything. Well, you can leave out a few details."

"I'll smile slyly like you do when anyone asks you for details about Mitch."

She smiles.

"Yup, that's the one." I point to her face.

"There are some things too private to share, but our imaginations can fill in the blanks."

I laugh and turn to lean on the counter. "True. It's been so long since I've had any of those details happening to me, I was beginning to worry I was going to forget how."

"I'm sure Luke was happy to remind you."

I suck on my bottom lip. "He really was."

She shakes her head and fans herself. "I'll have to go home for a lunch date with Mitch if we don't change the subject."

Laughing, I rub a spot of dry frosting off the edge of the counter. "Actually, there's something I want to discuss with you at some point. About the bakery."

She closes the oven and faces me. "Shoot."

"Now?"

She looks around. "Why not? Sally has the front covered and there's nothing pressing back here."

"Okay, well, you know how I took those classes?"

"Oh yeah, how did your finals go? Did you get the results?"

"Yes, I did really well. I've signed up for more classes."

"That's great!"

"Thanks."

"You're not trying to tell me you're quitting, are you?" Franny puts a hand on the counter. "I mean, of course, I would never hold you back, but please don't quit on me."

I laugh and shake my head. "I'm not quitting. As part of my final project, I had to draw up a business plan and a marketing strategy. I used The Sweet Spot for the business."

"Cool, can I see them?"

"Yes." I go over to my tote bag and pull out the folders I made to show her and hand them to her. "I've already told you about most of the marketing one with the website and social media. The business plan includes a proposal for increasing the catering part of the business, opening seven days a week, hiring more part-time and seasonal workers, expanding the outdoor seating, offering online ordering and delivery."

Franny flips through the pages and then wanders over to the desk area to sit. She thumbs through the proposals slower. "This is so detailed and ambitious."

"I know. We wouldn't have to do everything at once, or you could pick and choose which ones you like. It's just a class project."

"No, it's not." Franny closes the folder and turns to stare at me. "You worked hard on this."

I bite my lip and nod.

"This is too much for me to take on."

My shoulders slump and I nod. "I understand."

"But, with the right partner I could do it." She stands. "Someone with vision, determination, a strong work ethic. Someone who I could get along with, that didn't drive me crazy." She walks over and stops in front of me. "Know anyone who fits that description?"

"Are you saying what I really hope you're saying?"

Franny grins. "Will you be my partner in The Sweet Spot?"

"Yes!" I launch myself at her and give her a hug.

She laughs and rocks me back and forth. "I've been meaning to talk to you about it. You've already done so much with the new website and everything. This proposal cinches the deal. We need to talk numbers and contracts at some point with a lawyer."

Money, a partnership means money. Not a resource I have an abundance of, or any of.

"Your face just fell. What's wrong? Is it the lawyer?"

"No, I'm just trying to think where I'm going to come up with money. I could check into a home equity loan, but I doubt that is going to come close to covering it."

I could ask my parents for a loan, but I dread asking. They've done more than enough for me.

"Don't be silly, we can set up a payment plan and deduct it from your weekly paycheck. As a partner, you'll be sharing in the profits, so you'll have a salary increase to cover it. We'll make an appointment with the accountant and lawyer together to go over everything."

"Wow!" I slip down to sit on the floor. "Are you sure?"

Franny laughs. "Yes, I'm sure. I told you I've been thinking about it. You know I want to expand the specialty cake business. With you as a partner, I can do that. I'm also sure we need to get some more chairs or stools in here."

I shake my head and smile. "My legs feel like jelly."

We definitely need a couple more chairs in here. Maybe a couple of stools on one side of the marble counter in the middle of the room when we're working on detailed work like cake decorating. We'll leave the other side open so we don't trip over the stools every time we have to cross the ovens, sink, or refrigerators.

The desk area could use a set of shelves and another file cabinet. I chuckle.

"What?"

"Everywhere I look, I see possibilities." I describe the stools and desk area.

She studies the kitchen. "I like both those ideas. I never cared about the desk because I avoid the business side as much as I can, but you need more of a work area with all the wonderful ideas and plans popping out of your brain. We need to talk to a contractor. I want to expand the allergy free section of the kitchen too. I'm getting more requests for different options."

She drops down next to me. "This is going to be fun."

CHAPTER 34

*T*here's a patch of blond hairs in the center of his chest. A darker trail leads down over his abdomen. I trace the line with my fingertips.

"I must say I heartily approve of the way you decided to celebrate your partnership in the bakery."

I tilt my head up on his shoulder. There's a slight smirk on his face as he smiles down at me.

"Pizza, sexy as hell new lingerie, finishing off the evening in bed, I feel like it's my birthday or something."

I chuckle and glance over my shoulder. "Where did my lingerie end up?" The emerald green matching set wasn't cheap and blew my clothing budget for the foreseeable future. It was worth it though the way his gaze lit on fire when I did my little slow reveal after dinner.

"Think they're on the floor somewhere." He lifts his head to look. "Wait, your bra's at the end of the bed."

"Mmm…okay." I caress his leg with mine.

His fingers trail up the length of my spine and back down. "What did your family say about the partnership?"

"I haven't told them yet. We've had the meetings with the lawyer and accountant, but until everything is official, I'm a little leery of announcing it to the world. It should be finalized by the beginning of January. The holidays delay everything. Besides, Franny wants to throw a celebration at the bakery to announce it."

"Are you worried something will mess it up?"

"No, not really, but you never know. I want the contracts in hand, I guess. It still feels surreal I will be part owner in the bakery. Franny will own the majority, of course, but twenty-five percent will be mine. I can't wait to implement my ideas."

"An ambitious entrepreneur."

I chuckle and burrow closer to his warmth.

"Are the boys excited for Christmas?"

"They're ten."

"So, that's a yes?"

"Yes. They made their lists around Halloween when the toy catalogs arrived. One thing I love about the holiday season is I get to remind them Santa is watching so they better be on their best behavior."

"Does it work?"

"For the most part, once they stop believing, I don't know what I'll do. The thought of some of the magic disappearing from their eyes makes me sad. I want to hold on to it as long as I can."

"What are your plans for Christmas?"

"The boys go with Ryan for Christmas Eve to his parents'. They host a party every year. I get them Christmas Day. We open presents here in the morning and then go to my parents' house for brunch and spend the day there. What about you?"

"Barb invited me to her parents' house. This is the first year Joey understands there's a holiday where he gets presents. He's excited. He's sent a letter and an email to Santa just in case something happened to one of them."

"Aw, that's adorable. What's on his list?"

"The better question would be what isn't on it?"

"The boys have been asking for a dog."

"You going to get them one?"

"They're old enough to take care of one and I would hate to deny them the joy of owning a pet. I checked the area shelters and organizations. I prefer to adopt one which needs a home. There's a lot of paperwork and cost involved though. You're required to fill out extensive applications to prove you're a worthy pet owner. It's like applying for a job or mortgage. What if they turn me down?"

Luke chuckles. "I'm sure you're a good candidate."

"We'll see. I don't know how I'm going to explain it to the boys if I'm not."

He stretches over to my nightstand to check his phone.

"Everything okay?"

"Yeah, I just have to go soon. I have a ton of things to do before my parents come on Tuesday."

I lift my head. "They're coming for a visit?"

He nods and puts his arm underneath his head. "Yeah, they're staying for a week, until after Christmas."

"With you?"

"Mmm hmm. I bought a bedroom set for the guest bedroom when they told me they were coming. Barb had me buy bedding, curtains, towels, and a whole slew of other stuff."

"That's great."

I roll over onto my own pillow and pull the sheet and blanket over me.

He went shopping with Barbara for his parents' visit. I shouldn't be surprised. I know the score.

"She even made me a grocery list to stock up for their visit. It took me over an hour in the grocery store today finding everything."

Something a girlfriend would do, not a sister-in-law.

"What do you have planned for their visit? Are you going anywhere special? Sightseeing?"

"We're all taking Joey to the Christmas Village and Mom wants to go shopping up here rather than have to worry about shipping everything, so it looks like we'll be going to the mall. They're excited to see Joey and spend the holiday with him."

Taking the boys to the Christmas Village amusement park used to be an annual excursion, but we haven't gone the past couple of years. The boys used to love going. Would they want to schedule a visit this year, or are they already getting too old for waiting in line at Santa's workshop to tell him what they want for Christmas? The reindeer sleigh ride used to be their favorite. I have many photos of the two of them laughing as they soared through the air in bright red sleighs.

"I have fond memories of the Christmas Village with the boys. You'll have a blast watching the wonder in Joey's face."

"Yeah, I'm looking forward to it."

"Your parents must be looking forward to seeing you and your new house too."

"I guess."

No mention of meeting his parents. I'm not his girlfriend, but what am I? His neighbor he has sex with?

Do I even want to meet them? It's not like we're in a committed relationship. Why should he want me to meet them?

Why does it bother me so much Barbara is helping him plan for their visit and will spend the majority with them and Luke? She's their daughter-in-law, the mother of their only grandchild.

"I should get going." Luke sits up and flings the sheet off himself.

I sit up and wrap my arms around my knees.

He pulls on his clothes and grabs his phone, then leans onto the bed and kisses me on the cheek. "You stay in bed. I'll let myself out."

"Good luck. Have fun."

The stairs creak beneath his weight. The front door opens and closes.

No mention of when I'll see him again. Probably after Christmas when his parents leave. I should have given him the present I bought for him. Will it make him feel awkward because he didn't intend to get one for me? I'll wait. I don't want him to feel obligated to get me something in return. I'll give it to him after his parents leave. I can't leave it at his door. With my luck, his mother or father would open the door and want to know who the strange woman leaving presents for his son was.

Maybe I shouldn't give it to him at all.

I lie down and curl on my side.

I guess I'm not the type of woman who can have a sexual relationship with a man and not let my feelings get involved. Now what am I going to do? End it before I do something really stupid and fall in love with him?

CHAPTER 35

"**H**ang all your stuff up."

The boys shove their boots into a pile and hang up their coats. They both have one foot on the bottom stair.

"Say goodbye to your father."

They turn back and hug a chuckling Ryan. "Bye Dad."

"Love you. Be good for your mother."

They run up the stairs and I turn back to Ryan and tilt my chin towards the door signaling him I want to talk outside. I know my boys. They have super hearing, especially around the holidays and their birthday.

Ryan opens the door and steps out on to the steps. I grab my coat, pull it on, and follow him out in my slippers.

"What's up?"

"You know how the boys have been asking for a dog?"

"You're getting them a dog?" His head rears back and he looks at me like I've lost my mind—which I probably have.

"Shh, keep your voice down." I peek over my shoulder and listen a moment to make sure the boys didn't hear him. "Yes, well, I have an appointment on Tuesday to check one out. I've researched the best family breeds and I've found a local rescue dog nonprofit which has a one-year-old golden retriever lab mix for adoption. If all goes well, I'll be bringing him home."

"You want money for it?"

"No, I just wanted you to know."

"Okay, better you than me. Pets are a lot of work. You sure you don't want to start off with a fish or something?"

"They're responsible enough to help and they don't want a fish, they want a dog. Doesn't every kid deserve to have a dog? You did."

"Yeah, and that's how I know they're a lot of work, but it's on you, so if you say you're ready, I'm fine with it."

I wrap my opened coat around me and fold my arms. I chose lingerie over a new coat. Probably not the best choice considering the situation. Hindsight is twenty twenty.

"Okay."

Ryan jerks his head towards the door. "Go inside before you freeze to death. We'll talk later."

"Drive careful." I turn and open the door as he lifts a hand in a wave while he walks down the path to his car.

I shut the door behind me and hang up my coat. Hot coffee, I need something to warm me up. Shuffling into the kitchen, I rub my arms. I've made a list of all the necessary dog paraphernalia I need to buy before Tuesday.

I couldn't sleep last night so I researched and made lists. Lots of lists.

A list for the dog. A list for Christmas. A list for the bakery. Actually, I made a few of those. And a list of pros and cons of ending my sexual relationship with Luke.

The coffee maker brews while I grab a mug from the clean dishwasher.

The pros far surpassed the cons, logically I should end it.

There's a double thud on the front door. What did Ryan forget? And why does it sound like he's kicking the door instead of knocking or ringing the bell? I walk over and pull open the door.

It's not Ryan. Luke stands there holding a bunch of presents.

"Hey, is it okay to bring by the boys' presents?" I stare at him speechless. "I guess I should have called first."

"Oh, no, sorry, you just surprised me. Come in." I back up and hold the door wide for him.

He carries the presents into the living room and sets them down in front of the tree.

"You didn't have to buy them anything, but it's really nice you did."

He smiles and shrugs. "It's Christmas."

"Should I call the boys down or do you want them to wait until Christmas?"

"Up to you, but they can open them now."

I lean my head up the stairwell. "Boys come downstairs. Luke is here."

They come rushing down the stairs. Their gazes immediately land on Luke and the pile of presents at his feet. Their eyes grow wide.

"Are those for us?"

"Can we open them now?"

Luke holds his hands out. "Have at them."

They race over and drop down on the ground in front of the stack. Luke hands each of them a present and they tear the paper off.

Identical Nerf guns.

"Oh, wow!"

"Cool! Can we have a battle?"

"Sure, but don't you want to see the rest?" He hands them each another and places another in front of each of them.

There's a kit for making different shapes in the snow, including blocks for an igloo or fort. A racetrack set, extra darts, and a couple of building block sets are in the remaining packages.

The boys launch themselves at Luke and he falls over laughing beneath their exuberant hugs.

Just like that, my heart bursts open.

The lights get extra bright, but my vision narrows. An ache squeezes my chest and my stomach flips.

The boys are chattering away with him and I can't understand a word they're saying. There's a roaring in my ears. My heart thuds.

I'm madly in love with Luke.

How did I not see it before? Denial? Naivety? Blatant stupidity?

I plop down on the couch before my weakened legs give out and I fall.

What am I going to do? Does this negate my list entirely or validate it further? How could I fall in love with a man I'm sure is in love with someone else?

"Falling asleep over there?"

I blink several times and stare at Luke's smiling face. The boys have opened every package and are busy loading the guns.

"What?"

He chuckles. "You look like you're in a daze."

"Oh, I was just thinking." I glance down at the boys. "You really went overboard."

"I couldn't resist." He reaches over and picks up the one remaining present. "This one is for you."

"Me?" I take the box from him with one hand, but then grab it with both when I almost drop it. I put it in my lap and peek up. "Yours is under the tree. The one closest to the fireplace. In the red paper with wreaths all over it."

He laughs and looks behind him.

"I'll get it." Timmy scrambles up and gets the present to hand to Luke.

"Thanks." Luke turns the box right and left and gives it a shake. He jerks his chin toward me. "Open yours."

I glance down and bite my lip as I find a seam and rip the paper. After removing the paper, I crumble it into a ball and throw it at the boys who giggle and start crumbling the rest of the paper littering the floor into balls and throwing them at each other.

The top of the box separates and I lift it off. Neatly folded inside white tissue paper decorated with red Santa hats is a beautiful pink wool coat.

"This way your keys won't fall through the hole in the pocket anymore and I noticed the zipper was broken on yours. If you don't like it, you can exchange it."

I run my hand across the soft material. "I love it." I look up and smile. "Thank you, it's perfect." He noticed my zipper was broken.

"There's something underneath too."

I peek under the corner of the coat. Brown leather. I lift the coat out of the box.

"It's a briefcase slash tote or something. I forgot what the saleslady called it. I figured you could use it for school or..." He glances down at the boys busy playing. "Work."

I wrinkle my nose as my eyes well with tears. "It's perfect. Is gift giving your superpower?"

He laughs. "It might be."

"Open yours." I bite my lip. I didn't spend anywhere near what he must have.

Luke rips off the paper with a grin on his face. I hold my breath.

He glances up at me and back down to the box in his hands.

"They're not first editions or anything, but I thought you might like them."

He lifts the case of Edgar Allan Poe books up and looks at me. "Looks like you share the same superpower."

"Really? I saved the receipt. You won't hurt my feelings if you want to return them if you already have them, or whatever."

"I love them."

Luke stands, walks over, and takes my hand to pull me up. Once I'm standing, he pulls me in for a hug. I lean my head against his shoulder and hug him back.

"Merry Christmas," he whispers and kisses the top of my head.

"Merry Christmas."

He releases me and turns to the boys playing on the floor. "All right, are you ready to lose to the master?"

The boys scramble to a stand and grab their new guns.

"I'll go get you a gun." Tommy runs up the stairs and stops halfway. "Are you playing, Mom?"

"Not this time, honey."

He continues up the stairs while Luke and Timmy admire the new gun. I collect the discarded wrapping paper balls and carry them into the kitchen and throw them in the trash can under the sink. Tommy thuds back down the stairs and the three of them discuss rules of their battle.

I lean against the sink and stare out the window. The sun makes the blanket of snow sparkle like diamonds. The sky is clear and bright blue. A perfect winter day.

I hate ultimatums—giving and receiving, but what else can I do? If there's no hope of him ever returning my feelings, then I need to know and end our relationship. I can't go blissfully along falling deeper in love and letting the boys fall in love with him too if there's no future for us. It's not just my heart at risk, but my kids' too.

He cares for us, I know he does, but is it more than that? Or is he really holding out for Barbara?

The last time I broached the subject, we fought. He didn't give me a definitive answer, but his silence and avoidance were telling. This time I need to know where I stand and what his feelings for her truly are.

But when and how? I certainly can't have this conversation with the boys running around. Luke's parents arrive on Tuesday, which leaves tomorrow while the boys are in school. I can't wait until after Christmas when his parents leave. I'll stew over it the entire time.

"Everything okay?"

I spin around. He's standing in the doorway.

"Yeah, I'm just lost in thought. Did you lose the battle already?"

"They annihilated me. We're taking a break and building the sets I got them."

"What are your plans tomorrow?"

"My parents are coming on Tuesday so I'm cleaning up the house to make it presentable, why?"

"How about I bring over breakfast and help after the boys go to school?"

"Uh, sure, if you really want to."

Not the most encouraging answer. He always comes here. I don't think he's ever actually invited me over to his house. Intentional? Is there a hidden meaning there? Does he not want me in his house around his personal things?

Am I crazy?

"If you don't want me to, you can just say so."

"No, it's not that. I do have to clean though."

"I know. Like I said I want to help."

"Okay, thanks." He glances over his shoulder. "I promised the boys I'd help."

"You're great with them, thank you."

"They're great kids." He disappears into the living room.

I wrap my arms over my stomach and stare up at the ceiling.

My stomach churns. What if he admits flat out he's in love with Barbara? Am I strong enough to walk away to protect mine and the boys' hearts? Or should I fight for him? He must care for me, it's not just sex. Is it?

CHAPTER 36

"I'm in love with you."

Luke gets a deer caught in the headlights expression as he stares at me over his kitchen table. Perhaps not the best way to broach the subject. I could have waited until we were done eating instead of blurting it out as soon as we sat down, but I've tried so many scenarios in my head that my head is killing me. I took a handful of pain relievers before I brought the French toast casserole I made over.

"Say something please." My heart pounds so hard I'm afraid it's going to explode out of my chest like a sci-fi horror film.

"I...don't know what to say." He gazes down at the table and back up several times.

Okay, that's rather telling. My face burns.

"Is it Barbara?"

His gaze shoots up to mine.

"I just need to know straight out. Are you in love with her?"

He leans back in his chair and shakes his head. "We already talked about this."

"Yes, but you didn't answer me. You evaded."

"I didn't evade anything. There's nothing to evade."

"Then are you, yes or no?"

"No."

I frown. "No, you're not in love with her or no you won't answer?"

He squeezes his eyes shut and rubs his forehead hard like he's trying to erase something. This conversation?

"No, I'm not in love with Barb." He sends the chair sliding across the floor when he stands up and paces the length of the table and back.

"You haven't been carrying a torch for her since she chose Wyatt over you?"

He stops and stares with his hands planted on his hips. "Jesus, no. Barb and I went on one date. We had, like, one conversation before Wyatt showed up and they became totally engrossed with one another. I was never in love with her. She's a nice-looking woman I asked out on a date once. End of story."

"You moved here to follow her."

"I moved here to be near my nephew and help the widow of my dead brother because I was the reason he's not here to take care of them himself. And..." He paces again.

"And what?"

He stops and stares at me before plopping back into the chair. "Wyatt was planning on leaving her. He told me the night he died."

The air gets trapped in my lungs.

"He said he wasn't ready to be a father."

I let out a whoosh of breath and rub my damp palms on my pants. "Does she know?"

"Hell no! She has Wyatt on a pedestal."

True, she does. "So you're what, trying to make up for the possible abandonment your brother was planning before he died?"

He shrugs.

I sigh and lean my chest against the edge of the table with my arms folded on top. "You know expectant parents can panic when they realize they're about to be responsible for a helpless being. Are you sure he wasn't sending out a cry for help? Maybe for you to talk him out of it and tell him it was going to be okay and reassure him he would be a great father?"

"I told him that. He seemed pretty adamant he wanted out." Luke looks out the back slider. "He said there was someone else. Some woman at work."

Poor Barbara. The jerk was cheating on his pregnant wife and planning to abandon her and Joey?

"Why do you feel obligated and guilty for his actions?"

"Because every time she tells stories of how wonderful Wyatt is, I want to punch something. It's a lie. He wasn't the man any of us thought he was. I'm sorry he's dead, so damn sorry, but I'm glad he didn't live to destroy his family." He stares at me. "How fucked up is that?"

"It's not, not at all. You're grieving your brother, the good and the bad. Barbara probably had some inkling not everything was perfect, women usually do, but when we lose someone, we tend to rewrite history a little bit and focus on all the good things and let the bad fade away."

"So, I should let her go on thinking he was perfect?"

"Absolutely. What point would there be in tarnishing the memory she has of him? It wouldn't make anyone feel better, least of all you."

He nods and rubs his forehead. "You wouldn't want to know?"

I stare at the casserole in the center of the table. Would I want to know if Ryan had cheated on me during our marriage? Yeah, I would, but Ryan is alive for me to confront. Wyatt isn't around to defend himself—not that I can think of a single legitimate defense for cheating.

"No, I really don't think I would. Let her have the wonderful memories. He could have changed his mind. They might have worked it out."

Luke rubs the back of his neck. "You're right, there's no point in dredging it up. I'd like to think Wyatt would have come to his senses."

I cut the casserole and put a slice on each of our plates. "It's going to get cold if we don't eat."

He picks up his fork and takes a piece.

He's not in love with Barbara, but how does he feel about me? I take a nibble of the sweet, cinnamon topped treat.

"About what I said earlier…" I shift in my chair. "That I'm in love with you."

He glances at me and back down at his plate to cut another piece. "I care about you. I like what we have."

"But you don't love me."

"I'm not that type of guy."

"What type is that?"

"The relationship type."

"I see." I lay down my fork and wipe my mouth with my napkin. "Thank you for your honesty."

"That doesn't mean we can't go on as we are, I just don't want you expecting something to happen which won't."

I bite the tip of my tongue to push back the tears building behind my eyes. I align my plate so it's centered on the placemat and fold my napkin and place it next to the plate.

He gave me my answer. It wasn't what I wanted to hear, but that's the risk you take when you ask hard questions.

"Understood." I can feel his gaze on me, but I'm not ready to meet it. "Do you want more casserole?"

"No, thanks though, it's delicious."

I force a smile and stand. "Then I'll wrap it up and put it in the fridge. You can heat up individual pieces for you and your parents when they come."

Luke stands up as I walk around the table into the kitchen and open the fridge. "Olivia, I don't want to hurt you."

"I know you don't. You're not responsible for my feelings."

He's standing in the middle of the kitchen when I find a spot for the casserole dish and turn around. He reaches for me.

I step back butting up against the fridge and put my hands up. "Please don't. I need some time to think." I wrap my arms around my middle and scan the kitchen and family room, the only two rooms I can see and the only ones I've ever been in. "I know I said I'd help you prepare for your parents' visit, but do you mind if I cancel on you?"

"Of course not, but can we talk about this some more? I don't like seeing you upset."

I close my eyes and shake my head. You have no idea how upset I really am.

"Not today. Let's both take the time to think, okay? You have your parents' visit to concentrate on and the holidays."

I walk down the hallway to the front door and put on the coat he gave me.

"Olivia..."

"Please don't say anything right now." The last thing I want or need is to have him give me empty platitudes to make me feel better. I open the door. "Goodbye, Luke. Merry Christmas."

He takes the door from my hand before I can shut it. I meet his gaze and glance away as I turn and walk down his steps. I listen for the telltale clunk of wood rubbing together when a door closes, but it doesn't come. Please don't call out to me, don't say anymore.

When I reach the road it finally comes, the door closes. Tears spill from my eyes. The frigid air chills the salty tears on my face like streams of ice. I trudge up my driveway and walk with my gaze planted on the ground in front of me.

Why doesn't he love me?

He wasn't even open to the possibility of loving me.

I can no longer blame his feelings for Barbara. He doesn't love her. She's not the reason he doesn't love me. I'm the reason he doesn't love me.

What is it about me that men find unlovable?

Am I not attractive enough? Interesting enough?

My front door opens and closes with a soft click. I lean back against the cool surface. My chin trembles and put a fist to my mouth as my throat spasms and a wrenching sob shakes loose. I slide down the door and lay my head on my knees as my shoulders shake.

I can't catch my breath. Tears flow down my face, drenching everything in their path.

I lose track of time.

The sobs lessen. My throat is raw. Pain throbs behind my eyes.

I haven't cried this hard since—never. Not even over my divorce, or when I found out I was pregnant and had to drop out of school. Nothing has hurt this much.

Why did I ever wish to feel this way about someone? The boys and I were just fine on our own and we'll continue to be so once I dig this cleaver out of the center of my chest where my heart is supposed to be.

My leg cramps so I drag myself up off the floor and scrub my palms over my cheeks.

Love sucks.

CHAPTER 37

O li sits on the couch next to me and wraps his arm around my shoulders. "It's the happiest day of the year. Why are you so blue?"

I lean my head against him and watch the boys play with their new dog they named Sparky. It was a heated debate between the two of them when I brought him home on Tuesday whether to keep the name the shelter gave him, Cowboy, or to rename him. The dog seems quite content with his new name and home and owners. He's been a thankful distraction for them the past few days while I wallowed in self-pity.

Dad sits in his recliner dividing his attention between watching the boys and dog play and the television. Mom putters around in the kitchen. She waved me off after I helped her clean up the brunch dishes.

Oli nudges me with his shoulder. "What gives, Sis?"

"It's a long story, not meant for little ears," I whisper to him.

"I think the dog could use a walk. Why don't you two take him outside to play?"

Timmy and Tommy jump up.

"Coats, boots, and gloves, and stay in the yard." They nod in my direction as they herd the dog towards the door and don their gear.

Oli glances down once the door closes behind the trio. "You were saying?"

I look over at Dad.

"You really think he can hear a word we're saying?" He turns to our father. "Hey Dad, what do you think of the Pats trading their star quarterback?"

Dad doesn't stir.

"See, if he heard any of that, he would have had plenty to say. It was the only thing he talked about for most of the summer and fall."

I smile.

"I noticed Ryan isn't in attendance."

"I told you we mutually decided it wouldn't work. We're not in love with each other."

"So this isn't about him?"

I shake my head and sigh. "No."

"School? Work? You said you aced your finals."

"I did and there is something I want to tell you about work. It's a good thing, an exceptionally good thing." I glance around to make sure no one is listening. "Franny is making me a partner in the business. She loved all my proposals. The lawyer is drawing up the paperwork for us to sign."

"That's fantastic!"

"Shh...I don't want to announce it until everything is complete."

"That's fantastic," he whispers.

I shake my head and smile. "It is, isn't it?"

"So, work is going great, it's not school or Ryan. Is something going on with the boys?"

"No, they're good." I pull my knees up on the couch and wrap my arms around them. "You remember my neighbor?"

"The one who's in love with his sister-in-law?"

"Turns out he's not. Problem is he's not in love with me either."

"But you're in love with him? I thought that was over."

"It was, then it wasn't. I went and fell head over heels, but he doesn't feel the same."

"How do you know he doesn't? Wait, let me guess, you asked him."

"Pretty much. Now I've been wallowing in self-pity ever since. He wants to keep things between us the same, basically a friends with benefits sort of arrangement."

"Want me to beat him up?"

I chuckle. "No."

"You sure? I don't mind at all."

"We're not kids anymore—you can't fight my battles for me."

"Sure I can."

"I have to take care of my own messes."

"You always do. You're the most self-sufficient person I know."

"I doubt that, but it's nice to hear."

"It's the truth. So what are you going to do?"

"I don't know. Is it stupid to think he might grow to love me, or am I deluding myself? What would you do if you were in love with someone who didn't love you back?"

"I can't tell you what to do. It's not my heart that's involved. Do you want to walk away or do you want to take a chance he'll wake up and see how amazing you are and fall head over heels in love with you?"

"I'm not a quitter."

"Didn't think so, but the beating him up offer remains if he doesn't wise up."

I laugh and give him a one arm hug. "You're the best brother. I love you and I promise to beat up any woman who you fall for too."

"Never gonna happen, but I appreciate the offer."

I elbow him in the side. "We'll see."

"What would you say if I told you I was thinking of moving back to New Hampshire?"

I sit up straight and stare. "Are you serious? I would love that! But what about your job? Where would you live? Has something happened?"

"Slow down, Miss zero to sixty in three seconds, I said I was thinking about it. I haven't decided yet. Nothing's happened with my job or anything else."

"Then why? Not that I'm complaining."

"I don't know. I'm antsy. Bored with my job and life in Boston. I miss being here with my family. I'm confident I can get a job pretty much anywhere I want."

"Lucky you."

"Hey, when you're good, you're good."

Laughing, I shove his arm. "Well, I would love to have you close by and so would your nephews. Have you mentioned this to Mom or Dad at all?"

"You think I'm crazy? Like you, I'm not saying a word until I reach a decision."

"Okay, mums the word, but just know inside I'm squealing like a little kid."

He chuckles and rubs the top of my head. "Hey, I like the new hairdo by the way."

"Thanks."

"What do you say we join your little monsters outside in the snow?"

I jump up and run to the door to get my coat and boots on. "I say I'm still the reigning snowball champion in this family."

"Ha, you're the only one who has ever called you that." Oli pushes me out of the way to grab his boots and coat.

I hop on one foot trying to gain my balance and fall against the wall. He takes the opportunity to grab the door first. I use my elbow and shoulder to shove him aside and dart out the door.

The boys and Sparky freeze in place when I come running outside.

"Snowball fight!"

They shout with glee and run towards me.

The battle ensues and ends with me covered in snow and the boys declaring themselves the victors. I concede my title to them.

Mom ushers us inside with the lure of hot chocolate and dessert.

Oli and the boys take their mugs into the living room to finish their hot chocolates. Dad naps in his recliner and the dog snoozes in front of the fire.

"It's such a shame Ryan couldn't celebrate with us."

I sip my cocoa and turn around. Mom stands at the sink folding a dishtowel.

"Mom, Ryan and I are divorced."

"He came for Thanksgiving and has been around a lot lately."

If I tell her we even considered getting back together, she'll latch on and never let go. "He'll always be a part of my life because of the boys, but we're not getting back together."

She drops the dishtowel on the counter and takes off her green apron with tiny golden Christmas trees. "He's a good man."

"Yes he is, but I'm not in love with him and he's not in love with me."

She frowns and places her hands on her hips. "What about the neighbor? Are you in love with him?"

I huff out a breath. Of course she knows, she always seems to know everything. I used to think it was a mom trait, but I'm a mom and never seem to know anything.

"Yes, but he's not in love with me either."

Her eyebrows collide over her pale blue eyes. "Why the hell not?"

The shock of my mom swearing startles a chuckle out of me.

"I don't know, Mom. I'm not giving up on him, though."

She nods. "Invite him to dinner. We should get to know him better."

"I'm not sure he's ready for that step."

She slips her arm around my waist. "They never are. Your father made excuse after excuse why he couldn't meet your grandparents. Finally, I resorted to trickery. I told him they were out for the evening when I invited him to dinner and when he arrived, I told him the couple they had plans with canceled."

"I never knew that."

"That's because I never told your father the truth either. He likes to believe everything is his idea and that he was the driving force behind our relationship."

"I had no idea you could be so sneaky."

"You don't know everything about your father and I. Parents should have some secrets from their children."

"On that we can agree." I don't need or want to know everything, nor do I want to my kids to know all my secrets.

Mom laughs and gives me a squeeze. "Your young man needs a push in the right direction. He has feelings for you. I saw that with my own eyes. Give it time."

"Patience has never been a strength of mine."

"Don't I know it."

CHAPTER 38

"*O*livia, there's someone here to see you." Sally stands in the opening between the kitchen and the front of the bakery. "He looks like the picture of the author in the back of that book we read for book club. Ya know, Barbara's brother or brother-in-law or something?"

My hands drop into my lap. Luke is here?

I surge to my feet, then grab the back of the chair when my legs get weak.

"Olivia, do you want to see him?" Franny walks over and puts her hand on my arm. She knows the entire story. I poured my heart out to her after Christmas.

Sally's gaze darts back and forth between us. She steps farther into the kitchen and puts her hands on her hips. "I can tell him you're too busy or that you left."

"No." I shake my head and hold up a hand. "I'll be out in a minute."

Franny rubs my arm. "Why don't you take a few minutes and then I'll send him back so you can speak in private, okay?"

"Thanks, Franny."

She follows Sally back into the front of the bakery while I turn and grab the back of the chair with both hands and take a deep slow breath. No reason to be nervous. Just because I haven't seen him since before Christmas when I told him I was in love with him and he told me he doesn't feel the same, is no reason to feel like I can't breathe or my heart is going to explode.

A throat clears and I turn around. Franny is in the opening with Luke standing behind her. She raises her eyebrows and purses her lips as if to ask one more time if I want to see him.

I bite my lip and give her as much of a reassuring smile as I can. She turns and stares at him for a minute before looking back at me. "I'll be right out front if you need me."

Luke moves to the side to let her pass but doesn't take his gaze off me. My heart flips over. His dark blond hair needs a trim, it's brushing the tops of his eyes. He looks tired. There are dark circles under his eyes.

Is he okay? Did something happen? He didn't have another drinking episode over Wyatt, did he? I take a step forward.

He walks halfway across the kitchen towards me. "I'm sorry for bothering you here at work."

"Is something wrong?"

"No." He runs a hand through his hair and rubs the back of his neck. "Are you avoiding me?" He plants his hands on his hips and shakes his head. "Stupid question."

"I'm not avoiding you."

He stares at me and stuffs his hands in the front pockets of his jeans making his coat bunch at the sides. "I've stopped by your house a few times. You're never home."

"You have?"

He nods.

I wrap my arms around my waist. "I...well, it's been hectic with the holidays and some family drama. My cousin's wedding is off. She found her fiancé in bed with his best man so she was understandably upset and so was her mother—my aunt. It turned into a whole thing. Then, the kids and I went to Boston to help Ryan find an apartment. He got the promotion he was hoping for. My dad fell shoveling snow and broke his hip. So I've been over my parents' house helping Mom take care of him as much as I can. Franny and I have been finalizing all the details with my partnership in the bakery." I shrug. "It's just been busy."

A timer on the oven beeps. I walk over and check on the cakes. The heat from the oven bathes my face. The scent of vanilla fills my nose. I shut the oven off and grab an oven mitt and put the cakes on racks to cool.

Luke stands watching me. I walk back over to the desk and stack the papers I was working on in a neat stack.

"I wasn't avoiding you—not intentionally—maybe a little subconsciously. You could have called." I may have decided I wasn't giving up on him, but I also will not chase after him like some lovesick fool and beg him to love me.

"I started to a dozen times, but what I wanted to say isn't something I wanted to do over the phone."

"Okay, so what do you want to say?"

Luke looks over his shoulder and then around the kitchen. "This isn't exactly what I had in mind. Can I take you to lunch or dinner? Or come over after work?"

I glance at the clock on the wall. It's barely ten o'clock in the morning. There's no way I'm going to be able to wait until lunch or dinner. My mind will have come up with a hundred or so nightmare scenarios by then.

"Look if you just want to dump me, I'd rather you get it over with right here and now." I think I'd rather he did it over voicemail or text. I always thought people who did that were cowards, but being on the receiving end would be better, wouldn't it? Then I could rage over how cowardly he was for doing it over the phone instead of standing here feeling like pieces of my heart are crumbling.

"I'm not dumping you. I thought you had already dumped me."

Frowning, I drop into the chair. "I didn't dump you. I said I needed time. And technically, I couldn't have dumped you because we aren't even in an actual relationship. We're just neighbors who have sex, right?"

"That's not true." Luke comes over and leans against the desk next to me. "You're mad, I get it. I didn't handle our last conversation well."

"I'm not mad." I cross my legs and drum my fingers on my knee. "Okay, I'm a little mad, but mostly hurt and embarrassed."

Luke crouches down so we're at eye level. "I'm sorry."

Tears fill my eyes so I stare up at the ceiling, anywhere but at him.

"Olivia." He puts his hand over mine.

I shake my head and press my lips together.

"I know nothing about being in love but let me tell you what I do know."

Peeking down at the top of his head, I blink back the tears and hold my breath. He rubs his thumb over mine.

"I know I've missed you and the boys like crazy. Wherever we went, to the park, dinner, Christmas Eve, Christmas Day, and every day since, I kept wishing you were there. I know I've told you things I've never told anyone. I've never felt comfortable enough with anyone else to share. I know I was jealous as hell when you told me Ryan wanted to get back together with you. I wanted to punch him the day I saw you with him at the inn. I know being with you has healed me. I'm writing again. My agent thanks you, by the way. I know when anything happens, you're the first person I think of to tell. I know every time I see you, the weight on my shoulders gets lighter. You make me smile and laugh."

The tears I've been trying to hold back spill over.

Luke looks up at me and raises his hand to cup my cheek, wiping tears away with his thumb.

"I know when I imagine my life without you in it, it's a dark and lonely place."

"Well, that's a start."

He chuckles and leans forward to press his lips to mine. I lean my forehead against his and then lean back to sniffle and scrub my cheeks with my hands.

"I need a tissue." I scoot the chair over to grab one out of the box on the corner of the desk.

Luke stands. "So, you're not giving up on me, then?"

I throw the tissues away and stand. "I never was. I just needed time to come up with a game plan to make you fall in love with me."

He pulls me into his arms. His hands rest at the small of my back. "Oh, and what's on this game plan?"

I smooth the lapel of his jacket. "I'm still working on the details."

He lowers his head and kisses me softly. "We could come up with a plan together."

I smile. "Oh? What sort of things would you put on the list?" I clasp my hands together behind his neck.

Luke tilts his head to the side. "Steps one, two, and three involve lots of affection and touching—preferably naked."

"I had a feeling that would be a key requirement."

He closes his eyes and touches his forehead to mine. "Most importantly don't give up on me."

I clasp his cheeks and stare into his eyes. "Never going to happen."

EPILOGUE

*M*illions of lights glow in every direction. Cars fill the streets below—their engines hum, horns honk. Voices from people in the hall and the soft ping of the elevator filter through the hotel door.

"You want to call and check on them again?"

I stare at the reflection in the window of Luke standing behind me in the middle of the room. Smiling, I shake my head. I've called and checked on the boys at least a dozen times since Ryan picked them up yesterday to spend the weekend with him in Boston. It's not the first time he's taken them there, and it won't be the last now that he lives in the city.

It's the first time I've gone away to New York City for a romantic weekend with Luke, though.

He comes up behind me and puts his hands on my upper arms. "They're fine."

"I know." I turn and loop my arms around his neck. "I'm sorry. You've made this Valentine's Day so special with the trip to New York, a scrumptious dinner, and here we are alone in this beautiful hotel room, and I'm worrying about the boys."

My phone vibrates on the table and rings.

"Go, answer it."

I wince. "Sorry, but that's Ryan's ringtone." I step over to the table and pick it up. The boys' faces fill the screen requesting a Facetime call. I press the button and grin as they make funny faces and stick their tongue out. "Hi Mom!"

Ryan's face appears behind them. "Stop worrying and enjoy your Valentine's Day. Luke texted us."

I glance over my shoulder at Luke standing with his hands in his pants pockets. He wore a suit for me and is so handsome he makes my chest hurt. I mouth the words thank you and then look back at my phone.

"Okay, I promise no more calls until tomorrow. I love you both so much!" I send them an air kiss.

"Love you!"

"Thanks, Ryan." I disconnect the call and put my phone down.

Smoothing my red dress over my hips, I turn and smile at Luke. "Now, how should I thank you for such a wonderful Valentine's Day and for being so understanding about my mom worries?"

He grins. "I can think of several ways."

"So can I." I slide my hands over his shoulders. "Have I told you just how good you look in this suit?"

"You might have mentioned it." He spans my waist with his hands. "Have I told you how gorgeous you are in this dress and those heels?"

"You might have mentioned it. But it never hurts to repeat it."

"Beautiful." He kisses my neck. "Delectable." His hands roam over my back. "Sexy as hell." His tongue traces my bottom lip.

Our mouths meld together in heated frolic.

He takes my hand and leads me into the bedroom.

Red rose petals in the shape of a giant heart decorate the bed. A bottle of champagne and glasses sits on the dresser.

"I can't take credit for more than the idea. The hotel staff took care of it while we were at dinner."

"This is definitely a case of it's the thought that counts. Very romantic, Mr. Hollister."

"I'm glad you think so." He takes a deep breath and I turn my head away from the bed to look.

Still holding my hand, he drops to one knee and pulls out a jewelry box. My jaw slackens and my breath freezes in my lungs.

"This was my grandmother's ring. She left it to me. I almost offered it to Wyatt when he said he was going to propose to Barb, but something held me back. Now I know it was you, or the promise of you." He flips open the box to reveal a beautiful ring. The center diamond sparkles as the lights hit it.

My eyes overflow.

"You've shown me what loves is. I love you, Olivia, and nothing would make me happier than to spend the rest of my life with you. Will you marry me?"

I clap a hand over my mouth and frantically nod as words fail me. He slips the ring on my finger, stands, and pulls me into his arms.

He rocks me back and forth while I sniffle into his shoulder.

"I'm really glad you said yes, because Ryan and the boys, Oliver, and your parents have been texting me all night to see if I popped the question yet."

I pull back and stare. "They all know?"

"Well, I had to ask your father's permission, and it wouldn't be right not asking the boys if it was okay if I asked their mom to marry me. Then Oliver cornered me when he was up for a visit a couple of weekends ago demanding to know my intentions and threatening bodily harm if I hurt you, so I had to tell him my plans."

His leg vibrates against my hip and I glance down.

"There goes one of them again. Your family is impatient."

I laugh and dig the phone out of his pocket. It's Oli texting, "What's taking so long? Do you need more pointers?"

I show him the text and giggle. Luke rolls his eyes.

"Are you going to put them out of their misery? I vote for making your brother suffer until morning."

"Let's make a group call and share the happy news. We'll make it brief." I kiss him and stare up into his eyes. "Then you and I can celebrate—just the two of us and I can show you just how happy you've made me."

Luke cups my face in his hands and kisses me. "I'm the luckiest man alive."

THANK YOU FOR READING!

READ REBECCA'S STORY, No Choice At All

READ FRANNY'S STORY, My First My Last My Only.

IF YOU'D LIKE to be among the first to hear about new releases, sales, giveaways, and exclusive content, then sign up for my Newsletter.

ABOUT THE AUTHOR

Denise Carbo writes Contemporary Romance, Paranormal Romance, and Romantic Suspense. She is a voracious reader, loves to travel, is fascinated by the supernatural, and enjoys solving mysteries.

She lives in a small, picturesque New England town with her high school sweetheart and their three amazing sons.

Find out more at https://www.DeniseCarbo.com and sign up for her newsletter to be the first to hear about sales, giveaways, contests, and exclusive content. https://eepurl.com/dt5N7M

ALSO BY DENISE CARBO

My First My Last My Only

No Choice At All

Made in the USA
Middletown, DE
03 November 2022

14101791R00146